Please return/renew this item by the last date shown. Books may also be renewed by phone or internet.

- www.rbwm.gov.uk/home/leisure-and-culture/libraries
- ☎ 01628 796969 (library hours)
- ☎ 0303 123 0035 (24 hours)

Royal Borough of Windsor & Maidenhead

www.rbwm.gov.uk

Praise for *The Coffin Club*

'Slippery as an eel, dark and twisted, *The Coffin Club's* tale of death, deceit and desire is deliciously compelling.'
Sabrina Broadbent, author of *You Don't Have to be Good*

'Original, unsettling and full of secrets, *The Coffin Club* is a compelling debut with a superbly twisted end.'
Sarah Clarke, author of *A Mother Never Lies*

'A riveting, deeply disquieting thriller. Original, seamlessly put together and an experience you will never emotionally recover from.'
Sarah Goodwin, author of *Stranded*

'A dark and gripping debut with sinister undertones from the very first page. I loved it.'
Sophie Flynn, author of *All My Lies*

'A perfect "romantic-noir" – a crime story wrapped up in a love story. The characters draw you in to their world and make you root for them, until a creeping sense of dread makes you cower as you wonder where the fatal blow is going to come from. Well-crafted and chilling!'
S. E. Moorhead, author of *Witness X*

'This is a spine-tingling, unputdownable page-turner and a remarkable debut. I was gripped the whole way through.'
Lucy Martin, author of *Stop at Nothing*

THE
COFFIN
CLUB

JACQUELINE
SUTHERLAND

A Point Blank Book

First published in Great Britain, Australia and the Republic of Ireland by
Point Blank, an imprint of Oneworld Publications, 2022

Copyright © Jacqueline Sutherland 2022

The moral right of Jacqueline Sutherland to be identified as the Author of
this work has been asserted by her in accordance with the Copyright, Designs,
and Patents Act 1988

ISBN 978-0-86154-282-6 (hardback)
ISBN 978-0-86154-283-3 (ebook)

Printed and bound in Great Britain by Clays Ltd, Elcograf S.p.A.

Oneworld Publications
10 Bloomsbury Street
London WC1B 3SR
England

For Euan and my boys – James, Ollie,
Charlie and Harry – with all my love.
Anything is possible.

Graveside. October 2016

Ivy smothers your headstone and I can't see your name for moss. The grave itself is an overgrown tangle of creepers and weeds. How quickly nature takes hold. How cruel to move on so fast. I only knew it was you by the oak tree shading your plot. I remember leaning against its trunk at your service, the only thing that held me upright as they lowered you down. Now it's dropping its leaves quietly, tucking you in for another winter.

I can hardly bear to look, but I need to see you, to touch you, to talk.

Kneeling on the gravel beside you, I tug at a green ivy tendril until it peels from the stone, leaving a skeleton sucker trail, and there you are: Sam Alexander. The lettering knocks me back on my heels, takes me back to another time – not long ago but so far away – when I shared your name, your home, your life.

I trace your name with my finger, wonder just for a split second what you look like beneath the earth before shivering and shaking my head. I've seen your dead face in my dreams ever since the accident. I've relived that exact moment of realisation when you knew you were dying, your eyes locked on mine till the end. I will never be able to erase it. It's imprinted on my soul.

Now though, Sam, I want to think about life. I want to remember the happy times. I start to clear your headstone, one clinging green strand at a time.

I always loved your name; simple and strong, it conjures up so much more than just your face. The soft smell of sandalwood and the taste of Jack Daniels on your mouth. Your eyes squinting shut as you laughed. I can almost feel the gentle heaviness of your hand on my leg when you drove, resting between my thigh and my knee until you had to change gear. A million moments, a thousand memories flood in and wipe away time. My breath catches in my throat. So much has happened since I last saw you, but it finally feels like things are coming good. That's the main reason I had to come back. To tell you that the part you played in my life made all the difference. It's all down to you.

It was all so much simpler at the beginning, wasn't it? Our first dates seemed endless, a summer of country pub gardens and rooftop restaurants that blended into a winter of skiing and log fires. We moved seamlessly into an expensive engagement party in a swanky bar, surrounded by lots of people I barely knew, and then, of course, a white wedding. Your dad clapping you on the back and welcoming me to the family, champagne flute in the air.

I remember the rub of your thumb that first summer, stroking the freckles on my forearm. Your palm in the small of my back as you steered me round parties, so familiar to you, a minefield to me. Making me think everything was all right, that you would be the one to give me my happy ending.

You were unlike anyone I'd ever met. Moving in circles that I'd only waitressed in. Driving convertibles and wearing watches on your wrist that would pay off my loans on the spot. And you loved me. The way you watched me as I spoke, the tilt of your head when I said your name. The look that scorched me across a room and made me want to go straight back to bed. Or a smile of pride, like I was something to look up to, a role model of a wife.

The headstone is almost clear now, a small twisted pile of ivy beside me. I sniff noisily, clear my throat. I wonder if you'd still look at me the same way now, or even recognise me. I rub my fingers down my scar, feel the pits and pulls of my face stitched together, eyebrow to jaw. A permanent reminder of the accident. An everlasting mark of loss. An end to Sam and Kat Alexander.

That's the thing I came to tell you, Sam, that I don't have your name any more. I'm officially no longer your wife. I am, in fact, someone else's. And I am at last a mother, and I so hope you'll be pleased for me. Knowing how I longed for a child. Knowing how we both did.

But let me start at the beginning, when I moved to Lower Doyle after your funeral, looking for a new start. I bought The Nook, and met Ginny. But I hadn't yet heard of the New Horizons Club, where it really all began when I met Nico, my new husband. The club that promised "a second chance to find love". Little did I know what lay ahead.

But at least knowing what *you* know about me, Sam, I can tell you the truth. I can tell you the whole story.

It started with a deer.

I'd thought about killing myself a few times since your funeral, but the day I hit the deer I decided that was it. My turn to die.

Before, I'd just been mulling it over, tasting the idea on my tongue before swallowing it again, not really allowing myself to think about how or when. Pills or gun. Just conscious of the feeling of not wanting to go on.

But that day – the deer day – was different. An ache in my chest woke me up as normal and I already had a sore, wet face on the pillow. The house yawned around me, tap dripping somewhere, crows cawing across the fields. Loneliness sat on me with a weight that made my breath shallow. None of that was unusual. But when I looked at my mobile phone and saw it was 30 September, the last day of another month, I suddenly realised I didn't want to do another winter on my own. Not even a week. Not without you. In fact, I didn't want to do another day. And as that thought emerged, cleared itself from the fug in my head, it became a decision. For the first time in over a year, I got out of bed with a purpose.

The armchair in the corner was smothered with clothes and I rummaged, pulling on a jumper, covering it with a cardigan, hoisted up baggy old joggers over the pyjamas I'd worn for the past few days. Who cared? I hadn't seen a soul since the supermarket delivery guy, whose only comment had been about how much wine I'd ordered as it clinked in the crate. I felt like banging him on the head with a bottle but you know me, I'm not a violent person, and satisfied myself with flipping him the finger as he drove away.

I paused at the bedroom doorway, suddenly struck by the state of my room. The piles of clothes jumble-sale like, the floor decorated with knickers, socks, dirty plates and a couple of books, spines open but face-down, forgotten. The smashed mirror. The remains of days. The debris of weeks. Should I tidy it up before I went? Otherwise, who would be the first on the scene? My eyes stung with the realisation that it would be a cleaning team – hired by a probate company – because I had nobody left without you. No family alive and hadn't seen any so-called friends since the "episode". Couldn't blame them really, I guess. As a nod towards my old self, I smoothed the duvet over the bed and plumped my pillow. I pulled the door shut behind me. Done.

The stairs still creaked on the landing as they had when the estate agent showed me around the year before. He'd extolled the virtues of older properties, and pointed out the high skirting boards, the deep coving, anything rather than look directly at me. I'd followed, numb and nodding. He must have been relieved that the outside of the cottage hadn't put me off. The rambling rose that smothered the front wall, long ago flowered and never deadheaded. A grey slate roof, missing a few tiles, almost merged with the bleak winter sky, apart from the round turret bedroom with blank windows. The previous owner, recently deceased – not in the house, thank God – hadn't had much of an eye for interior design. The Nook was "a doer-upper", the guy said, flicking his pink tie between finger and thumb, "with amazing potential". All it needed was a bit of TLC, he said – and a wad of cash, I thought. But that was one thing I had in spades. I silently followed him until we reached the turret window and then, all of a sudden, my mind was made up. The view was perfect. I could see right through the valley. Fields of furrows. A border of woodland. Open space, spread out before me like a blank canvas. It gave me the same sense of hope that a new calendar used to evoke every New Year's Day.

I bought the house, grasped the chance of a new start in unfamiliar surroundings with strangers, thinking it would help me to deal with your death. I had a rosy notion of log fires and country pubs, friendly locals and mugs of tea. In reality it had been overflowing gutters, and damp green smears appearing down the outside walls. The blackest nights came by four o'clock in the afternoon, no streetlights to hold them off. No fairy-lit restaurants to brighten the sky. The harshest winter, snow blocking the track to the lane for a week, breath pluming inside the house even with the heating on. It drove me to bed with an extra duvet after lunch, originally intending to read. But I couldn't concentrate long enough on anything. My thoughts would always drift off somewhere. I'd come to, in a random chair, with a cold cup of tea in my hands, blankets pooled around my feet. Eventually it became so bad that I didn't really get out of bed much at all.

I didn't realise it was Christmas until a few cards turned up. Only four, actually. One from the estate agents that had sold me the house, wishing me health and happiness in my new home. One from the local gardening service, with a handwritten message – 'We can take care of your holly and your ivy' – signed by Bob. Whoever he was. And two for the previous owner. The picture on the front, a striped Christmas stocking hanging at the end of the bed, reminded me of our last Christmas together. We'd just started talking about babies again, and I'd wondered how many stockings we might need in the future. As it turns out, none. I'd put the cards in the bin, then felt guilty, took them out and put them in the recycling. Since then, I'd not had a single communication that wasn't a bill, or a junk flyer. In over nine months.

The stone kitchen floor was cold through my bedsocks and I pulled on a pair of wellingtons that had stood by the back door since I last went out. I couldn't recall exactly when that was, but I remembered being in the garden one night. The stars had been so bright and numerous I'd found myself underneath them, feeling myself even smaller, wondering if you were out there somewhere. And if you were, what would you say to me? Ridiculous. I must have been drunk. Judging by the number of bottles on the enamel draining board, I'd been getting through quite a bit.

Maybe that's how I should do it – kill myself, that is – an overdose? I checked the cupboard. Two bottles of wine. Would that be enough? But when I checked the medicine cabinet there was only a pack of Rennie in it and two Nurofen left in a discarded foil. I'd never heard of anyone killing themselves by indigestion remedy, so I had to find another way.

I had no gun. No rope. No razor blades. My legs were as hairy as yours used to be. So I just picked up my car keys and went out. Didn't bother to lock the front door, might as well make it easy for the people who would have to come in.

The new Audi smelled of leather upholstery as I slid into the driving seat. It started first time, as though it had been waiting for me. Brand new but unloved in the garage; I'd bought it with the insurance from the write-off and could hardly bring myself to look at it. Now, I reversed into the drive and pulled out into the track that led to the lane. It was drizzling, again, and the road shone. I had no real plan in my head. Just a buzzing feeling of energy, that I was finally doing something to end this constant nothingness. Overhanging trees dripped and swayed. There was still mist on the fields. My foot pressed harder on the pedal while my hands felt like they hardly touched the wheel. There were a few miles of curves ahead, countryside bends with high banks draped in wet bracken and fallen branches. I sped through them, taking them generally too fast but already thinking ahead to the long straight at Deppenhall that ended in a tight S-bend and a stone bank. Warning signs lined it, a known danger point, and perfect for today. As I took a right and approached the long stretch, I put my foot down hard and kept it there. The car skidded round the final corner, kicking out slightly at the back, and then the acceleration picked up with a steady momentum. I let my fingers slacken on the steering, eyes fixed on the bank directly in front of me, just a few hundred yards away. No thought in my head. Nothing. Just a breathless feeling of something being in reach. Almost touchable. An end.

My foot pressed to the floor.

And then the deer leapt from the side. A metre from the ground, the white of its eye visible as it crashed into my bonnet on the passenger side with a noise of crunching metal and cracking bones I'd heard before. It ricocheted into the windscreen and smashed it straight through before rebounding off to the verge. In my rear-view mirror I saw its body bounce, twist and break, hit the floor. I slammed my foot on the brake automatically, skidded to a halt before I even realised what I was doing. Leaving the car door wide open, I ran back to the animal lying half on the road, half on the grass, chest heaving, eyes rolled back in pain. God, it was in agony. Grunting came from its narrow, hairy lips. Holding my own face in my hands, I looked up and down the road, for help, for advice, for anyone, but it was empty and quiet. There was nothing except for the tortured breath of the deer and the hum of my engine. I had to get help. Maybe I could take it to the vets? I looked at my watch. Still not even 8a.m., so they wouldn't be open yet and this poor thing didn't have much time. I slapped my thighs in frustration, feeling the scream build in my throat. The pain was white in the animal's eyes and every time I looked at it, I saw your face in the wreckage of our car. Your twisted body, the blood that leaked from your ear and the corner of your mouth. The confusion in your eyes as you tried to make sense of what had happened. I knew then. I had to save the deer.

I recalled a hand-painted sign, about a mile back along the lane, 'Ginny's Animal Sanctuary'. It had a picture of a hedgehog on it. Maybe someone there could help. They'd know about animals.

I sprinted to the car and reversed, right up to the deer. I lifted it from behind, grabbing it under its front legs, and it kicked frantically at the back as I lugged it to the car and loaded it into the boot. It wasn't so big. Just a baby really.

I jumped back in the car. My hands slipped on the wheel and I wiped them bloody on my thighs before turning the Audi round and speeding off. My breath was shuddering noisily as I tried to remember where I'd seen the sign. But then there it was. Nailed to a wooden crossbar gate, already open to a track. I took the turning and drove too fast down a potholed driveway. We bumped to a stop in front of a run-down house surrounded by a vague assortment of barns and outhouses. I breathed out in relief as I saw lights in the kitchen window, somebody moving inside. I banged the horn a few times and jumped out of the car.

By the time the farmhouse door opened, I had the boot open and had managed to drag the animal back onto the gravel, where it writhed blindly. I felt something inside me twisting with realisation. The animal was beyond saving. It was dying in front of my eyes. It felt as though I were breathing through a wet towel.

"For fuck's sake!" A woman marched towards me, broad-shouldered, booted, wearing some kind of army surplus coat. She dropped to her knees on the wet gravel beside the deer.

"Can you help?" I said and my voice sounded rough, hoarse, I hadn't spoken for so many days.

"Did you hit it?" she asked, swinging to look at my car, the crumpled bonnet, the smashed glass. I nodded and felt my eyes burn hot. God, it was my fault. Again.

"You should have finished it off," she said, shaking her head. "Just run over it again." I stepped back, horrified.

"I couldn't do that," I said, and it came out on a shudder.

"Kindest thing sometimes," she said, standing up. "Cruel to let it suffer."

She straightened her back, took a deep breath and disappeared back into the farmhouse. A rising horror was making me shake. My hands fluttered beside me pointlessly, nothing to do, no comfort to give. I dropped to my knees where the woman had been and put my hand on the deer's dappled flank, as though to ease the breath that heaved it up and down. The tufted hair was coarser than I'd imagined, the skin warmer, the fear tangible. Crows' wings of panic flapped at the corner of my vision, closing in. The animal made a wheezing sound and blood frothed between its teeth. Then, just for a second, its eye widened. A back leg suddenly stretched, shaking against the stone, and as it relaxed again its heart stopped beneath my hand. A last breath left its body with a long sigh.

The woman's boots crunched towards me again.

"I hate to have to do this," she said and waved a small black handgun vaguely in my direction.

I managed to stand upright long enough for the woman to shake her head at the corpse, realising it had already gone, and then at me, gun hanging by her side.

Then everything went black.

So, the deer was dead and I was not. I came round with the woman's boot nudging my hip.

"Come on, then. Can't be lying around," she was saying as I opened my eyes, facing directly the unseeing open eyes of the animal on the ground beside me. She hoisted me under the elbow to help me to sit up. I wiped my mouth on the back of my hand, cleared my throat. What an idiot.

"Let's be having you," she said and tugged me to standing, where I wondered if my legs would hold me.

"Must have got separated from her mum," she said, nodding down at the fawn. And to top my embarrassment, I started noisy gulping sobs that took us both by surprise.

Five minutes later, between shuddering breaths, I sipped tea from a china mug with a chipped rim. I sat at her wooden kitchen table, while she mainly ignored me and set about "getting things ready". Hanging her handgun on a hook on the wall, she busied herself in cupboards that were full to overflowing, making mixes, adding milk to concoctions, all without taking her coat off. There were at least three cats in the room, two tortoiseshells curled on cushions on the window seat, a ginger one leaning on the Aga with its eyes squinted almost shut. A black Labrador sashayed in and out a few times while I drank my tea, prodding me with a cold nose, looking for attention. A radio played somewhere in another room and the house smelled warm and safe, like hay. The tea was the best I'd drunk in a long, long time.

"Just stay here a moment," the woman said, and fixed me with a look. When she went outside and pulled the door shut behind her, I knew she was off to deal with the deer and I was glad to stay inside, sipping, breathing, sipping again. I was just trying to rinse the ingrained tea stains out of my cup when she came back.

"I'm sorry," I said. "I should go." But I didn't move from the sink.

"Where were you going before? When you hit it?" She nodded towards the drive. I put the chipped mug carefully on the plate rack, keeping my back to her.

"To kill myself," I said. The dog scratched in the corner and its collar jangled. The radio presenter introduced the next record and the woman behind me sniffed in consideration.

"You could have picked a better day for it," she finally said and I turned to face her. "The weather's filthy." She glanced at the window and flicked a half-smile. My mouth twitched and I had a stupid urge to laugh. I couldn't read her expression but she held my look.

Her fox-red hair was shot through generously with silver. It was caught up in some kind of loose bun, but curls and twists hung round her face. Freckled and pale, she was broad-cheeked and voluptuous, with deep laugh lines around her eyes. She reminded me of Charlie Dimmock from the TV, garden-lovely, capable and strong.

"Seems like it was meant to be," she said, as if making up her mind. "I need some help this morning. Got a new resident." She shoved a box towards me, full of pipettes, plastic tubs and cloths. "Nothing better to do, have you?" she said and again I coughed rather than laugh and shook my head. Maybe I was hysterical.

"Got a hedgehog needs a dressing changed, easier with two pairs of hands."

When she opened the kitchen door I just followed her, let her lead the way across the courtyard outside to the closest barn, which was separated into stables inside. But it didn't hold horses. In each stall there was a different animal. An Alsatian dog padded about.

"That's Cleo. She's mine," the woman said. "Just got lucky, didn't you girl," she went on, scratching the dog's head. "Had a visit from the local stud dog. Litter due in a few weeks." I noticed the slightly rounded underbelly, felt the immediate tug in my own, shut my eyes and moved on.

The second stall had been fenced off and had a wire lid on it, making it essentially a small crate. A cat crouched at the back, making a low growling noise.

"She's feral," the woman said. "I call her Madcap. She's got a torn cruciate ligament, so she just needs to be kept in for four to six weeks to let it heal. Much to her disgust." On cue, the cat spat towards us and bristled its back into a perfect arch.

"Ah, fuck off yourself, I'm only trying to help," the woman said, with a little chuckle.

The third stall was crammed with a terrace of hutches, rabbits twitching noses at me through the cages.

"Five rabbits currently," the woman said. "Dog attacks, one rat-trap victim, one a car clip."

She carried on to the back wall, which was lined haphazardly with cages and boxes on top of each other. No two containers were the same, and the different sizes and shapes made it look like a crazy-paving block of flats.

"Hedgehogs," she said. "Trying to get them sorted in time for them to hibernate."

I drifted towards the cages, peered in. A spiky ball was curled at the back, expanding and contracting with each breath, oblivious to us.

"When's that?" I said, voice still gruff.

"Middle of November."

She moved next to me, checking in each of the cages as she spoke.

"Here," she said, passing me a flask out of her box. "Top up the water for those two." She nodded at the end cages, balanced one on top of the other. She opened another cage and forked cat food into the small, plastic feeding bowl, then closed the catch and started on the next one.

I opened my cage quietly so as not to frighten the hedge-hog, but it didn't startle. In fact I had to gently shove the snoring creature away from the water bowl to pour a few glugs from my bottle.

The second hog was bigger, rounded, but again didn't mind me helping. I wished they were soft enough to stroke.

The woman nudged me out of the way with an elbow and forked food into their bowls, scraping out the bottom of the Valu cat-food tin, which smelled terrible.

"Right, on to Al Pacino," she said, opening the last of the shanty hutches and lifting out a small hedgehog who balled immediately between her gloved hands. He had a dressing down one whole side of his body, the white bandage looking like it had seen better days.

"Strimmer," she explained. "Very close call. He's been stitched back together but he'll have a good scar. Especially on his face."

"Aha." I said, deadpan. "Al Pacino. *Scarface.*"

The woman shot a look at my own stitched-together face to check whether I found it funny or not, or to work out what to say next. For one second she looked self-conscious, but then she just changed the subject entirely. Like everyone always does.

"You hold him. I'll change the dressings."

I put my hands towards her but she snorted. "There's gloves in the box."

It only took a few minutes. I held him gently but firmly, as instructed. She chattered – to the hoglet – the whole time about how well he was doing. How he could soon go back to the garden and woo the women with his rugged good looks. Then he was popped, a bit shell-shocked but clean and well, back in his cage.

"Thanks," she said.

I straightened. My job was apparently done. Did I have to go? My stomach tugged at the thought of having to go back to The Nook and be on my own. Nothing to do but drift between rooms, or bed and chair, and alternate between drinking tea and wine. Although I didn't want that, I didn't think I wanted to kill myself any more either. I pressed my lips together, waited. She was watching me.

"Field crew next," she said, walking towards the barn door, and I let my breath out slowly.

The next hour was like free therapy. An old polo pony that had been abandoned stood stoic near the hay bag, waiting silently. It had the softest muzzle – but the hardest kick, she warned as she steered me away from its back end. Three sheep that had been mauled by dogs baa-ed as she came near. A goat with eyes that freaked me out, ghost-like, off-centre, jumped up on a tree stump to bleat a welcome. And I followed her, doing as she instructed and watching her work. I filled food bowls, sluiced out water buckets, forked up dung and threw it in a wheelbarrow. And I talked. Falteringly at first, but then with a torrent of words. She didn't ask me anything, not even about what I looked like. And I did look a sight. All she wondered was why I'd chosen today to kill myself. So I told her about the yawning chasm of winter ahead and how I couldn't see my way through it. How I was so lonely I wanted someone to talk to. But how I was so depressed I had nothing to say.

Finally, I told her about you. How much I missed you, every hour of every day, and the future we could have had. How when you died, all my dreams did too, of being a wife and a mother, and I didn't speak for a week. How you'd always looked after me, emotionally, financially, everything, so that now I felt like I had no walls around me. Nothing to hold me together. I told her how I'd lost everything I wanted and had loads of what I didn't need.

She listened as she stroked, cleaned out, dosed and fed. It meant she was hardly looking at me and I could say anything, as though she was actually deaf. I talked until my voice was clear and then until it sounded hoarse again. By the time we reached the front gate and she propped up a sign saying 'Open, Visitors Welcome', I'd told her everything, almost.

"Sounds like a shitstorm," she said, lifting the lid on a box marked 'Donations' and picking out a few coins. She shook them in her palm.

"One pound twenty-three." She shrugged. "And they say Britain is a nation of animal lovers." There were also a few tins of cat food and a small bag of dog biscuits, which she put in her box.

"Right," she said as if to go, and my guts hollowed out.

My legs ached from walking around the fields, my joggers were wet and my fingernails were black, but for the first time in a long time I felt something. Not happy. Not hopeful. But just something other than nothing. I didn't want it to end.

The woman sniffed and wiped her nose with the back of her hand. A good amount of her hair was now down and her cheeks were pink. She looked like a windy walk.

"I'm Ginny," she said and I nodded.

"Kat," I said and tried a smile, but it slipped off. I wasn't used to people looking at me.

"Why don't you come back tomorrow?" she said.

And so it began.

The phone shrilled through the house in the navy haze of the early hours and had me sitting up before I was awake. A night-time phone call meant trouble and my blood was banging as I answered. It was Ginny and she needed me. Cleo was trying to whelp the pups and things were not going to plan. I pulled on my jeans and jumper, these days folded neatly on the chair from the night before. Grabbing my coat and car keys from the hook, I was out of the house in two minutes flat.

Hollow Farm had become a sanctuary for me, as well as the animals, over the past couple of months. I'd arrive early for the first feeding round and then stay and "make myself useful", as Ginny said, for the rest of the day. I got used to my part in the routines, cleaning out, feeding, watering, while Ginny mended fences, made cages, created another ramshackle home for a new guest. The animals came in from everywhere, all wild, injured, lost or malnourished. In the afternoons I kept an eye on Cleo, who got bigger every day. I gasped the first time I felt a kick from inside her, more of a wriggle, as the pups moved around. It was the highlight of my day to sit with her and lay my hand on her tummy as she slept. Feeling the life inside her as it grew stronger and more active made my eyes water. I wouldn't let her, or Ginny, down now.

"Over here," Ginny said when I ran into the barn. She was kneeling next to Cleo's birthing box. We'd made it a week ago and Cleo had slept in it the last few nights, preparing her space. It was warm, insulated from the cold barn floor with newspapers, and padded with folded blankets and towels. But Cleo looked anything but comfortable now. She was anxious, moving side to side, tail between her legs. Beside her lay three mewling, writhing puppies, cleaned and healthy, but she was distracted, awaiting something else. Even as I watched, her stomach moved inside, alien, alive. More pups to come.

"Nothing's coming down even though she's contracting," Ginny said.

"Have you tried the vet?" I asked as I knelt beside her, knowing that someone called Jim helped voluntarily when he could.

"Out on calls," she said, pushing her hair off her face.

Cleo began to pant heavily.

"Fuck," Ginny said. "Something's definitely wrong. It's been more than two hours since the last pup." She eased her iPhone out of her back pocket and wiped her hands on her thighs.

"How often should they come?" I asked.

"Quicker than this," she said, pressing the home key so that the screen lit up.

Cleo whined and started to pant again. Her paws looked giant and dangerous next to the puppies on the floor. I put out a hand automatically, felt the hot damp skin of one of the newborns and pushed it back against the side of the box, out of harm's way. Then I did the same for the other two, amazed at the feel of their coats, sleek as seals. Ginny was tapping at her phone, scrolling down a list of videos, before clicking on one and then tilting the phone towards me so I could see too.

"Think she's got one stuck," she said. Sure enough, Cleo chose that moment to turn in the bed and we could see a pair of tiny legs in a sac extended out of her birth canal, which was distended but still. I cringed.

The video took a couple of minutes to watch, minutes I wasn't sure Cleo – or the pup – had. Afterwards, Ginny tossed the phone onto a bale of straw and reached into the bucket in the corner, washing her hands and liberally soaping them up.

"Hold her collar," she said, "so I can get to her back end." I stood and reached for Cleo, but she growled and backed away. Ginny and I flashed a look at each other. The dog was normally so gentle, despite her size. I put a hand out towards her again, palm up. She raised her hackles just once, but that was enough for me. I shook my head.

"I'll hold her. You'll have to do it," Ginny said, and nodded towards the bucket of water. I was halfway through washing my hands before I even wondered what the hell I was doing. I'd just watched a video on puppy birth but that didn't make me a vet.

Ginny didn't hesitate, though. She approached Cleo as normal and Cleo accepted her, licking her fingers and allow-ing her to take a hold of her collar. I took a deep breath and went to the other end. The little legs hanging down were impossibly small. And still. That was what finally spurred me into action. If I didn't do anything the pup might die. And so might Cleo. I'd had enough of death to last me a lifetime.

I tried to catch the legs in my hand. They slipped through the first time, slick with amniotic fluid and blood. The second time I got a grip, as firmly as I could without hurting those tiny bones. Cleo whined and tried to pull away from me but Ginny held her, whispering to her low and loving.

I pulled once and my stomach lurched. Nothing happened.

"Pull slightly outwards – and down," Ginny instructed, repeating the words from the film.

I tried again, equally horrified and amazed as the puppy started to move down. Cleo panted, mouth wide. The tiny body, encased in its sac, began to appear, inch by inch. The head slipped out last, eyes stuck shut. I held it bloody in my hands. Warm, wet, alive. Its cord hung behind it, afterbirth still attached. I couldn't believe I was actually holding that stuff.

Ginny took over. Leaving Cleo with a "good girl" and reaching for the puppy, she cleared its mouth and nose with rough hands and then rubbed it briskly. It flicked side to side like a rag doll. Ginny scrubbed at it again and its head rolled. Cleo whined, a desperate sound, and I felt like echoing her. This couldn't be it.

I pushed myself to my feet and took the body from Ginny's hands. I laid it belly-up in my own palm, as in the video, and secured its head between my thumb and forefinger. Holding it in position with my other hand, I lifted the pup to head height and then swung my hands down between my knees. I did it three times, with real momentum, before I let myself look.

This time it opened its mouth and took a breath and I felt like crying. I brought it to my chest and held it to me. My heart was pounding. We'd done it. She was alive.

A moment later Cleo was roughly licking her newborn, head to tail, getting its blood pumping, its pulse beating, then tucking it in with the rest of the litter. Until another pup came, this time without complication, and another. And finally an eighth, just before dawn.

"Thank God for Google," Ginny said, leaning back against the stable partition, legs out in front of her on the floor. "Has the answer to everything."

"Almost everything," I thought as I moved to lean next to her, watching the new mother tend to her babies. My eyes burned. It was beautiful.

Ginny pulled a hip flask out of her jacket pocket and took a swig before passing it over. Whisky. Which I normally hated, but that night it was perfect, earthy and strong.

We'd never had a drink together before. It had been tea until then. Ginny with her three sugars and me with none.

The puppies had found their mother's teats. They suckled ferociously, taking their first milk. Cleo lay patiently. She had just struggled for hours, had nearly died herself, yet she was still content to feed. I felt the old tug deep inside me, resurrecting itself after all those months. The pull of babies. One of my own.

"So amazing," I said and Ginny passed me the whisky again.

"Nature at its best," she said.

"Have you got kids?" I asked, conscious it was more personal than our normal chats. But she'd once referred to someone as her "old man", another time as "Fuckface", so I thought she'd been married sometime before, although he certainly wasn't around now. And she was old enough to have had some kids early and for them to have already left home.

"I prefer animals," she said with a lopsided smile. "You can rely on them."

The puppies were sleeping now. Cleo checked them with her nose, nudging, licking. It made my arms ache with wanting to hold one.

"Literally," I said, "you've never had the urge?" I was genuinely interested.

She shook her head and swigged.

"Nope. Never had what you might call a good 'family example'. My dad was nothing more than a one-night stand and my mum couldn't cope."

"That's hard," I said. "I was lucky with my mum. She was the best. But she died when I was seven."

"Mine didn't die. She just left me at social services when I was four."

I gulped. I knew without a shadow of a doubt that my mum would only ever have left me through death. "Christ. How do you feel about that?"

She swigged again. Longer this time.

"Just wish she'd done it when I was younger. Before I could remember it."

The horror of that took my words away for a moment. The idea of it. "It certainly gave me some reasons to hate myself when I got older." She pushed her sleeve up and showed me the soft blue white of her inner forearm. It was a criss-cross of old scars, wrist to elbow. Something inside me swelled. Ginny had scars too, just not quite as visible as mine. I reached a hand over and pressed it on her arm before taking the flask, swallowing a big shot and handing it back.

"Do you get lonely?" I said eventually. "Out here on your own?"

She shrugged and glanced at the stalls.

"Sometimes. I mean, they're not the best conversationalists."

"You're welcome to come round to me any time," I said, suddenly. We'd never met anywhere apart from the sanctuary, but I wanted to give her what she was giving me. Company. Friendship. Purpose.

"Thanks," she said with a smile, saluting the hip flask in my direction. She swigged and passed it over. The whisky scorched right to my gut. "Anyway, so no kids for me. You?"

So many things I could say. Yes I have the urge. Yes, I've felt it for years. Yes, I wanted a baby with you so badly it hurt. So badly that it changed my life, and yours. But all I could do was answer with the truth. One of my blackest truths. One of my secrets.

"I can't have children," I said. "Ever."

2010

*T*he early days of baby-making were so exciting. We were just married, so confident – so fucking idiotic looking back at it now. You and I with big shit-eating, hopeful smiles on our faces every time we had sex.

It was easy to convince you we should try for a baby right away. I didn't even have to twist your arm. Lots of happy, giggly love-making, followed by spooning and "what if that's it?" conversations. So when I got my period as usual after that first month of "trying", it was a bit of a bloody shock. Literally.

I couldn't quite believe that it hadn't worked. We agreed that it would have been "really unusual" for it to happen straight away, but secretly I was pretty confused. I wanted this to happen so much, my body must know that, right? What the hell was it playing at? I was slim, late twenties, fit (ish). I should be at my peak baby-making game, shouldn't I?

Second and third months had me turning to Google. My iPhone was permanently searching "how to get pregnant" or "top tips to conceive". I read forum threads, doctors' columns, NHS advice. I trawled through women's personal stories to find the one tip that might make the difference for us. I started counting the days of my cycle and making sure we had lots of "good" sex around days twelve to fourteen. And by "good" sex, I didn't mean the type that left me pink-cheeked and exhausted. I meant the type where you hadn't ejaculated for forty-eight hours before and so there was a good supply *of quality sperm, as advised on a mums' forum. I stopped spooning afterwards too. Instead, I'd turn and put my legs up the wall, trying to give everything the best chance of going in the right direction. You thought that was pretty funny, but I just laughed along. I knew what I was doing.*

Month four, I started taking my temperature every morning, keeping a little pencil and chart on the bedside table. "Basal body-temperature monitoring", which would help me spot when I was ovulating, so that I could time our sex more precisely. I had to stay really still in bed on waking, a conception column told me, and take my temperature before I did anything else. No running to the loo for a morning wee. No cuddles with my husband, and definitely no taking care of your morning glory, much to your disappointment. No activity whatsoever before taking the temperature and writing it down. I pored over the charts for a tiny dip that meant I was about to ovulate, or a rise that meant that I had already ovulated. Sometimes I missed the dip – it could be less than one degree sometimes – and only knew when ovulation had already happened. Then I'd be kicking myself, as the egg only lasts about twenty-four hours and it was a race to get sperm to it quick enough. One time, you were away with the boys and I knew the window would be closed by the time you got back. I actually considered taking the train to Manchester for a late-night booty call. I should say late-night "baby call". But when I rang you to suggest it, you'd already been out with your friends and had sunk far too many beers to have any quality product left for me, so I didn't bother. I went to bed and cried myself to sleep instead.

Anyway, whatever I did, none of it seemed to work. My periods just kept coming. Regular as clockwork. I went to my GP.

"You're young, you're healthy," she said. "Give it time. We normally allow a year before we do any investigations at all."

"*Good things come to those who wait,*" I said, remembering my mum's advice.

"*Exactly,*" the GP said, with the smile of a woman who popped kids out without a problem, judging by the framed photo on her desk. I wanted to slam the door on the way out, but clicked it quietly shut.

I went back to Google. I cut out alcohol almost completely. I decided I should get fitter, but then agonised over which form of exercise I should take up. Something that wouldn't harm the baby if I was, actually, already pregnant. I eventually decided on swimming but then found that pools were like magnets for pregnant women. Rounded bumps of various sizes straining against swimming costumes or even sometimes spilling out of the gap between tankini top and bottom. I couldn't take my eyes off them and, as a result, hated my flat stomach. I wanted it to fill my hands, push out, beat with a heart. But it didn't.

You were much more chilled about it than me. But you didn't have the same need. You'd say things like "*Just means we get to have more fun trying,*" which made me smile in the beginning, but after about eight months it just set my teeth on edge. I didn't want to keep trying. I wanted a baby. Without you knowing, I ran your baths slightly cooler, for healthier semen, and made you snack packs with Brazil nuts. I bought you some nice loose-fitting underwear in cotton, to stop your own nuts boiling. If you suspected, you never said a thing.

At any time of any month, I could have told you when our baby would be due if I got pregnant NOW. I persuaded myself that a spring baby was best, or a summer baby would be easier, or that an autumn baby would be oldest in the school year and therefore have an academic advantage for life.

I planned lives for us with a son – football on Saturday morning, or rugby on a Sunday. George, or William potentially, would be *sporty. The alternative life with a daughter, May or Charlotte, would be similar but different. Lacrosse or netball maybe. But still home for hot chocolate and crumpets. A Disney film later on. Maybe, a glass of wine for you and me while she/he was absorbed in* Aladdin. *I could see it all.*

I just couldn't get it to actually happen. My year of "trying without investigation" was just about up and I booked another GP slot. The system was slow, appointments seemed to take forever to book and arrive, and my period always came.

But then October came and I started to feel different, slightly bloated in my belly, wanting to wee a lot. I hardly dared hope. All month I touched wood, saluted magpies and spat if I saw a black cat, which was quite often as we had one next door. I googled all my symptoms and they all said, yes, they could be early signs of pregnancy. Or they might be something else entirely. I read about the other early symptoms and tested myself rigorously against them. Did I have sore breasts? I held them. Not really. Squeezed them. Maybe a touch tender? Did I have a metallic taste in my mouth like I'd sucked a two-pence piece? Hmm, the more I thought about it, I convinced myself maybe it wasn't last night's curry. I even bought a pregnancy test, after researching the best brands, to be ready for the day I was due my period. I hid it in my knicker drawer to surprise you with.

But my period beat me to it. The blood came, heavy, clot-like this time and with quite a lot of pain. I curled on the bed and I let go, cried and ranted and threw things, but none of it made me feel any better. I hated my body, I hated myself. I was a failure. You held me, made me tea, wiped my cheeks. You were nothing but kind and gentle and loving. And useless.

Unfortunately, the pain didn't go, even when my period had stopped. Stupidly, I still didn't think anything was wrong. It was the smug GP, the one with the clutch of blond kids at home, who said she wanted to do some further investigations — a scan and some internals — to understand what might be happening. The hospital appointments were made, and attended. New tests were ordered, and conducted. All the while, we carried on with our baby-making efforts. Legs up the wall. Lots of warming foods. Chinese herbs and a spot of acupuncture. For fuck's sake.

It was all for nothing.

The tests came back and you and I sat side by side in the GP's office. I noticed she'd turned her family photograph slightly away and was glad I didn't have to see the chubby smiles, the missing teeth.

"Seems like we do have a problem," she said and I felt you shift in your seat.

"Fibroids," she went on. For some reason I imagined fleshy aster-oids inside me.

"They're large, grapefruit-sized, two of them." I put my hand against my stomach, stupefied. Why couldn't I feel something that big in there? What else could be in there without me knowing it?

"The biopsy we've done shows that they are not cancerous."

I breathed out. Not cancerous. Not cancerous.

"However, any benign growths of this size give us serious concern that the next growth could be malignant. We need to remove them as soon as possible." She was still talking. "The location of the fibroids mean it is a major procedure." She was already scanning a portal, looking at a calendar. You reached over for my hand, held it in your own. We still didn't understand. Then she said it. The words that changed my life completely.

"It means we have to remove your womb," she said, and her eyes found mine. "It will be a full hysterectomy."

Ginny was a godsend, truth be told. The sanctuary filled my days, and knackered me out for the evenings. I can't say I was loving life, but I was living it again.

I walked the short-cut across the valley now in the mornings, crunching frost under my boots. I'd feed, clean, water until noon. In the quiet of the afternoons I stayed and answered the phone to any enquiries, painted new and better signs for the gate. Ginny would be off checking the beehives she kept on neighbouring properties and nearby farms, her "honey homes". The variety of locations gave her a range of different honey as the bees collected pollens from different plants. The thicker honey came from the rape fields, the scented from the lavender farm. She kept the landowners sweet with a personal supply of jars in return for a corner of their fields. If she wasn't out and about, she'd spend the afternoons in her pottery, a small brick-built studio next to the barn, which she said was her "bread and butter".

"The sanctuary doesn't run on fresh air." She shrugged. "Or dog shit, for that matter," she said one day as she pulled a dog-poo bag, tied and full, from the donations box at the gate.

She'd stay for hours at her potter's wheel, hunched and absorbed, creating mugs and plates, jugs and fruit bowls ready for firing and glazing. Every batch was delivered to Barnham for sale in the craft shop. She also sold honey and beeswax beauty products through the farm shop. "Every little helps," she would say, with a false smile, like a Tesco advert.

I walked back to The Nook in the late afternoons, cheeks red as apples, and spent the rest of the evening painting walls, stripping wallpaper, sanding floors. I worked up an appetite, so I stocked the cupboards again: soups, broths, beans and bread. Something quick to heat and eat, sat in front of the TV, fire burning brightly in the grate. When I was tired, I went to bed and slept like someone who'd been physical all day in the fresh air. The simple routines were holding me together. I did laundry and had a selection of clean clothes to put on. I no longer wore my PJs as a base layer. Although, considering how much effort Ginny put into her own appearance, I really needn't have bothered. She rocked her army surplus chic and quite often wore straw in her hair.

I felt like I was on a recovery programme. As long as Ginny was happy to have me, I was happy to be there. The sanctuary gave me a reason to get up in the morning.

And then Ginny gave me another one.

It was a Thursday when the pups turned six weeks old. Five dogs, three bitches, black and tan bundles of fluff. Cleo had almost tired of their demands and needed regular breaks from them now. I played with them in the afternoons so that she could rest, and the look in her eye when I arrived always said, "Thank fuck for that." They were boisterous, bouncy and hilarious. Their feet were huge and they bounded and bundled and fell. You couldn't help but laugh at them.

I didn't know the plan for them, but I'd assumed that when the time came, we'd advertise them at the farm shop. I'd seen Ginny scanning the noticeboard there to "check out the competition". So when the police van pulled into the drive and a man and woman got out in uniform, panic grabbed my chest with a fist and squeezed. It was like déjà vu. I could hear my own breath as they shut the van doors and straightened their jackets.

I only realised they were the Dog Handling Unit when they approached and leaned on the stall gate with Ginny. Still, my heart raced and I stayed inside with the pups, wanting to pull them to me, keep them safe. I let my hair fall over my face. Cleo was in the stall next door but let out a low warning growl that I'd not heard before. I knew how she felt.

"It's okay, Mum," the policeman said to Cleo, extending his hand, "we're not going to hurt them." Cleo sniffed cautiously and then licked, tail wagging.

"Eight," he said, nodding at the pups.

"Inoculated and wormed, good human contact," Ginny said, nodding towards me. There was a tone in her voice that I hadn't heard before; she was eager to please. Normally she didn't seem to give a monkey's what anyone thought, but she was looking at this guy like he was important.

"Right, let's have a look at them individually, then."

Ginny pointed and I picked up the nearest, Ricky, and passed him over the gate, avoiding eye contact. We'd named them all according to size, shape and character. Ricky (Hatton) was a scrapper. Barbra (Streisand) howled a lot. Dirk (Diggler) humped everything that moved. And some things that didn't.

The dog handlers lifted Ricky's jowls and inspected his teeth and gums. They extended his legs, front and back, to check his hips. Smoothed their hands down his spine and looked inside his ears. Ricky wagged and wiggled and tried to chew the handlers' gloves with his needle teeth.

"Good size," the man said to me, as though I was something to do with it. I passed him the next one, face averted, saying, "This is Oliver. He's always hungry," which made the man chuckle. Soon, he'd checked them all and passed the last, Bolt, back to me.

"Let me guess, he's the fastest?" he said with a smile. I felt some sort of stupid heat on my neck and knew I was blushing. I turned away to the pups.

"It's a good litter," he said to Ginny, and her shoulders dropped an inch. His approval obviously meant a lot. He turned to me and caught me looking at him, full face. He started, blushed and dropped his eyes. It was not a good reaction.

The woman, oblivious, got her iPhone out and started scrolling the calendar, and he joined her, eyes glued over her shoulder to the phone.

"So they'll be eight weeks on the tenth of January…" The woman pursed her lips, considering something. "Foster parents aren't available until March…" She shook her head and then scrolled again.

Cleo let out a whine and put her front feet on the gate. Obviously she'd been separated from the pups for too long. Ginny took the hint and opened it, letting her back in to her pups. They threw themselves at her, hungry, and I was forgotten.

The dog handlers were talking among themselves and Ginny jangled her keys in her pocket, waiting. When they turned to her again, she stopped and stood still.

"They'll be great dogs for the force. We'd be happy to take them," he said. "£800 each." Bloody hell. I nearly coughed. Ginny breathed out slowly.

"But we can pay you a keeper's fee on top if you hold them until March, when the foster homes are available."

Ginny's eyes flashed wider and then she sniffed and shrugged, as though considering.

"We'd pay the normal £100 per week for the feed and bedding, and if you train basic commands – sit and stay – we'll pay an increment."

Cleo came to sit beside me, nudged me with her nose. I rubbed the top of her head, wondered if she knew what we were talking about. Ginny shook hands with the man and the woman pulled out some paperwork for her to sign.

"We'll take all of them," the man said, turning to look over the gate again, almost at me, but not quite. "Except that one." He pointed at the smallest bitch, named Roo because one day she might actually grow into her ears. They twitched tall and pointed on the side of her head like a kangaroo and her pet name had come because of them. "She's the runt." I felt for the puppy so hard that I could have cried. I scratched her gently, and she licked my hand.

As Ginny showed them out, the guy waved in my direction. He didn't make eye contact, though, so my wave back was wasted.

"Eight hundred pounds each!" I said as the van pulled out. "That'll keep you going for a while."

She snorted.

"Half of it's already gone," she said. "But you're right. It is great. For the pups too." She climbed over the gate and joined me, ruffling the heads of the pups, one by one, as if to say "thank you".

"That bloke fancied you," she said.

"Get out of it," I said with a pang of guilt, an image of you in my head. You were still my husband after all. It's not like

I got a divorce when you died. I tried not to think about the way I'd blushed. It was like cheating on you.

Ginny just laughed. "You ought to get back out there."

I shook my head, but there was a little disloyal thought at the back of my mind. I *was* lonely. And The Nook was very quiet in the evenings. It would be nice to have someone, wouldn't it? Or would it just make everything feel more pointless?

"Why not?" she said. "Sam wouldn't want you to be on your own. He'd want you to be happy." The way she casually threw your name into the conversation made me blink. I wasn't so sure she was right, and anyway, nobody was mentioning the elephant in the room.

"No one's going to want *me* though, are they?"

I lifted my chin and turned to face her. I tucked my hair behind my ear instead of letting it swing. It was the first time I'd acknowledged to her the scar on my face, the jag that ripped from eyebrow to jawline. A year after the car accident, it was still vivid red. It had taken sixty-two stitches to hold my flapping cheek together. Look at me from the left? You'd think I was normal. But from the right? Well, let's just say nobody would ever sit on that side out of choice. The skin pulled in on my cheek and up. I was lopsided, red and shiny. My eyelashes didn't grow in the middle of that eyelid, so the eye wept intermittently as though permanently crying for my lost face. It could have been so different if I'd just kept my seatbelt on. You wouldn't have hit a tree. I wouldn't have gone through the windscreen. My face wouldn't make people stare and you'd still be here. My eyes got hot and I blinked. Ginny held my gaze and then shrugged.

"It's not as bad as you think," she tried.

"Did you see his face when he saw it?" I snorted, but felt the threat of tears again. "If he had been flirting, he sure as hell stopped then." She shook her head but didn't say anything.

"What about you?" I shot back, attack being the best form of defence. "You've been on your own for how long?"

"Ten years" – she shrugged – "since he accused me of caring more for the animals than for him." She smiled. "He was probably right. Especially after I caught him shagging my best mate."

"You didn't?" I gasped.

"Right in my own bed." She spat on the ground beside her. "Since then it's just been me and the animals."

We settled back against the stable wall, watching the pups play.

"What about Roo?" I said to change the conversation and the pup cocked her head at me at the sound of her name.

"I've got just the answer to her problem," she said. "And the answer to one of yours too, actually." She scooped her up and squeezed her. "You want a baby." She passed me the armful of hot fur. "And now you've got one."

It was my birthday in March that made me do it in the end – put myself back out there, on the market. Well, that and three bottles of wine.

Ginny turned up unannounced with cheap Chardonnay and a beeswax candle, handmade and labelled with my name. It smelled divine, lavender with lemon, and I was really touched. Nobody had bought me a gift for over a year, let alone made me one. It reminded me of when you used to make me a breakfast tray and write a little nameplate to go on it.

It was not the first time Ginny and I had met in the evening. Since we'd whelped the pups, we were closer. We'd tried the pub a couple of times, but there were always ancient locals propping up the bar or young farmers hee-hawing in the garden over a pint of cider or a traditional bitter. Where the normal people drank, I had no idea.

"Nice in here," she said as I led her through the kitchen and TV room, which made me see it with fresh eyes. The patchwork throws, a burnt-orange rug, the magazines and cushions. A vase of cut daffodils on the windowsill. It looked more like a house now and something good swelled in my chest. It was mine. "Looks like something out of a magazine," Ginny said and plonked herself down like she was on a mission.

The first bottle didn't even touch the sides. I seemed to be very thirsty and my glass was always full. Ginny was on good form and my scar stretched more and more into a smile.

"Business looks like it's going well," she said, nodding at the other dog in the garden, a King Charles spaniel, a boarder, staying with me for a week. For the last month, I'd often had at least one extra dog staying overnight, and walked between four and six others during the day. It wasn't big money, but I wasn't in it for that.

Ginny had lit the fuse, after I'd been helping out at the sanctuary for a few months.

"Don't you need to think about getting a proper job?" she'd asked.

That stopped me in my tracks. Although I didn't need one, thanks to you, and would never need one again, I agreed it might be a good idea. To give structure to my day, some outside contact, and other things that healthy, well-adjusted people did who didn't feel like killing themselves any more. So I started my dog-walking service with a white postcard stuck up on the farm-shop wall, a pair of walking boots and low expectations. But the phone started ringing and word started spreading and soon I had regulars and occasionals. Sometimes I walked three or four times a day, but I always still found time for the sanctuary first thing to do the rounds.

It wasn't until the end of bottle two that I realised I hadn't eaten any dinner. We took the party to the kitchen, much to the delight of Roo, who fell out of her bed and proceeded to tear up an old newspaper on the floor. I loaded bowls with crisps and peanuts to snack on, but by then, the damage was done. I was more than half-cut and Ginny was already opening a third bottle.

"Look how far you've come!" she was saying, waving her arms around. "Business. House. You're a new woman."

I grinned, glugged a mouthful of Pinot Grigio and dropped a peanut down my front.

She leaned forward conspiratorially. "So now's the time for the next step – a man!"

I spluttered, and she clapped me on the back. "To tell the truth, I don't know how you've gone this long without getting laid."

"Oh my God. You've got no filter!" I said and she snorted.

"Filters are for oil changes." She shrugged. "Seriously though, aren't you missing it?"

I laughed, blushed.

"If not the sex, then the 'companionship'." She did bunny ears with her fingers around the words like it was the most ridiculous thing ever.

"But…" I pointed with both hands at my face. There was no way anyone was going to go for that. I looked like a horror movie.

She grabbed my hands and held them to the table. "But nothing," she said, authoritatively. "Let's have a look, shall we?" She flipped her phone out and pulled her chair closer, budging into mine. "Welcome to the world of online dating."

"I don't even know how it works," I said and she snorted. "I don't!" I said again. "'Online' wasn't a thing when I was last single, or if it was, I ignored it…"

I flashed back to when I met you. I was waitressing an event you were attending. The flash of your eyes, a connection I felt immediately in my stomach and my pants. Me knowing immediately that you could be the one. How were you supposed to get that feeling through the phone?

"Well, it's the norm now, so let's get started."

She showed me a profile page – a picture of her and Cleo. There was a short write-up underneath,

"Ginny. Early fifties. Not looking for love."

My eyes widened until my scar pulled. Talk about blunt.

"It's simple once you're set up, makes meeting people so easy," she was saying. "You just set the boundary ages of people you'd be interested in meeting." She pointed to hers, which said twenty-five to sixty, so she seemed to be keen not to restrict her options. "Then you set your geographical catchment area." This was more defined, a ten-mile radius – "Who wants to drive further than that?" she said. "Then you see who fits."

She clicked to her results and showed me Doug, 45. I started reading.

Looking to meet an interesting lady. Rolling the dice. What would you prefer? Coffee and a chat? Lunch with a glass of something? Dinner with a bottle? You decide…

Ginny swiped left.

"That means I'm not interested. I don't want to be an *interesting lady*. I want to be a one-night wonder." She laughed and glugged some more wine. She flicked to the next one. He was bare-chested and stubble-chinned.

Marcus, 47. I'm good. Trust me. Or try me.

"That's more like it. I could do him some damage." Ginny giggled and swiped right. Seeing me shake my head, she laughed out loud. "Let's try somewhere else. There are dating apps for all sorts of interests. Let's look at one for people who live in or love the countryside…"

She scrolled and clicked, and then showed me the phone screen. Latest members – Liam, 34. "Look!" she said. "He's holding a lamb, you could tell him all about the animal sanctuary!"

She swiped frantically again.

"Or Ben, forty. He looks nice. And he has a dog. Just like you. Is that too old? Forty? What do you think?"

She was swiping again, flicking repeatedly, chuckling to herself. I swilled my wine glass empty and refilled.

"It's always better if you've got something in common." She was frowning, thinking so hard it showed. "Then you've got things to talk about. Similar backgrounds, or hobbies. Then you can meet someone who likes what you like. Wants what you want."

Leaning back in my chair, I waved a hand at her, to get her off my case. But as I sipped and closed my eyes, I knew the seed had been sown. Roo appeared by my side and leaned against me, but something was still missing.

A few days later, a flyer arrived in my post, bundled in with the junk mail. Luckily it was top of the pile or it might have ended up straight in the bin. As it was, it caught my eye and I paused halfway across the kitchen, reading.

It advertised a club for widows and widowers, called New Horizons, which promised a "second chance at love". 'They'd want you to be happy' was emblazoned across the banner in curly, red writing. The pictures were of smiling faces, a group outing, a list of dates and some contact numbers. It was enough to make me chew my lip, hopeful but terrified that it might be a good idea to join. I folded it in half once and tucked it in my jeans pocket until I got to the sanctuary.

"Bugger me backwards," Ginny said, when I passed it over in the barn. "Look at that for a direct hit." She took off the gardening gloves she'd been wearing to clean out a cage and smoothed out the creases of the paper. "Now that's what I meant about having some common ground to start with."

"I'm just not sure about it," I said, looking at it again over her shoulder.

"Why not?"

"I don't want to go hang out with loads of depressed people, all of them with a dead husband or wife."

"How do you know they're depressed?" Ginny challenged.

"Because I was," I said, and knew what she'd say then before she said it.

"Exactly, *was*. Not any more. Time to move on."

Ginny was tapping on her phone, peering at the flyer and then her screen, looking up the website.

"They meet quite regularly… outings… theatre trip, pub night… do things as a group."

I chewed my nail. There were lots of photos of people having fun, laughing out loud. Not what you'd expect from a group of people whose partners had all died. It didn't look like anyone was crying or throwing themselves on the ground. I shifted a bit.

"Monthly pub quiz nights…" I read aloud. I used to love a pub quiz. You always used to say I was good at them because my head was full of trivia. "Useless knowledge," you used to call it. "Until it wins us the bottle of wine," I'd always reply, holding it by the neck and grinning. God, it seemed a long time ago.

"Looks like you need to apply for national membership and then they invite you to stuff in your local area." Ginny was well into this but I still wasn't sure. It wasn't just my face that was holding me back. It was the thought of meeting someone new. Someone who didn't know me like you did. All my good and bad. And still loved me.

"I don't think so…" I shook my head, sat back.

"Let's just have a look at some of the members." She wasn't giving up. She clicked on the image of a man, round-faced and bald, the hint of a football shirt showing at his neck.

"Not exactly my type," I said with a sigh.

"Never judge a book by its cover," she said and for one moment I thought she was referring to my face, but then she said, "You never know what he's got in his pants," and I laughed.

She clicked on another one, a woman.

"Just to see what your competition might be like…" The woman was in her late thirties or early forties, short hair, bookish. "You'll walk it," she said with a mean giggle and tried another.

"This one's got kids…" she said, almost to herself, plonking herself down on a bale of straw.

She clicked another.

"And this one too."

I leaned in to see. The picture was a man with a couple of children, a boy and a girl, maybe five and eight. They beamed in front of him, gap-toothed and knobbly-kneed. He had his arms round them both, holding them against his chest. It looked like a theme park day out – sunshine and fair rides and hot dogs. The only thing missing was a mum.

"You get a ready-made family with that one," Ginny said, clicking on to the next.

I sat beside her on the bale, twiddled a strand of straw between my fingers as I considered my options. Here I was, alone every night, talking to the dog. No nearer to having someone to love than I had been last year. What did I have to lose? Nothing. I looked again, bit my lip. The little girl in the photo had freckles, a smattering across her nose. What could I gain? Everything.

"How do I join?" I said.

2011

*T*he hysterectomy didn't just take my womb with it. It took our future. My every hope and dream was in a hospital incinerator. So I thought.

You were much more concerned with the present, looking after me on a day-to-day basis. Helping me to the loo when I came home from hospital. Lowering me into the bath when the stitches were out. Not letting me lift the shopping out of the back of the car.

"Take a bit of time to yourselves," the consultant said, and I remember thinking: what other kind of time is there now? We'd never be more than just us. A forever of "you and me". No "baby makes three". But then she said the words that gave me hope.

"The eggs we retrieved are viable, so when you're ready we could look at other options – if you're still keen to try for a baby." Something lit inside me again. The yearning was back.

"How?" I said, sitting forward in my chair.

"Surrogacy would work in your case," she said. "We fertilise one of your eggs with Sam's sperm and then implant it into a surrogate to grow the baby. It's a fairly standard procedure now." If she'd had a contract on the desk, I'd have signed on the dotted line then and there.

You were more sceptical. It took a bit of persuading, truth be told. For weeks, every time we talked about it, you kept bringing up all the downsides.

"What if it doesn't fertilise? It didn't fertilise inside you so why should it fertilise in a Petri dish?"

Or, "What if it doesn't implant in this other womb? It might know it's not its mother and not want to stay?"

And, "What if she wants to keep it when it's born?"

"We've got nothing to lose," I reasoned.

"What about the legal rights of the mother? She'd be its birth parent. We'd have to adopt it at birth." Your list of negatives made me grind my teeth.

"We've got everything to gain," I cajoled.

Eventually you agreed.

"I suppose it IS still our baby," you said with a shrug, "technically speaking."

It was all I needed. It was a green light. I spent months looking for the right surrogate, meeting people at surrogacy events, screening potential baby growers. I thought several of them would have been perfectly adequate, but you seemed to be writing people off for no good reason.

"She lives in Sheffield, it's too far away." Or, "she already has three children, her body might be worn out." "Has a dodgy boyfriend." "Eats with her mouth open."

I knew you just wanted the best, but it made me hold a towel over my mouth in the bathroom to scream.

Finally we met Susan. She was dimpled, curly-haired, smiley. Lived half an hour away. Knew how to finish a mouthful before answering a question. She was perfect. And you said yes. We signed contracts, agreed expenses up to £15,000, although I'd have paid ten times that if she'd asked. I worked out the dates from our hospital appointments. If everything went to plan, I'd be a mum by Christmas. The most amazing Christmas present ever. At last, things were looking up.

The call came at five to eleven on the Thursday morning before our first appointment. It was a perfectly acceptable time for a call and I picked up the phone, cup of tea on the side, radio playing in the background. No cause for alarm at that point.

"Mrs Alexander," my consultant said. "We have some bad news."

My instant reaction was to think Susan had dropped out. That we'd need to find another womb. The idea made me flash hot with the fucking irritation that my Christmas dream was not going to come true. Who knew how long it would take to find another womb and woman that would meet all your requirements.

But it was worse than that.

"Mrs Alexander." Her voice was grave, softly spoken. "We had an incident in the fertility centre last night. The temperatures started to rise in the liquid nitrogen storage tank where the eggs and embryos are stored."

I clamped the phone to my ear.

"The centre was unstaffed at the time."

I noticed my knuckles gripping the counter were white.

"The remote alarm system was off."

I could only stand there and wait for her to say it.

"Mrs Alexander, I'm sorry to say that your eggs were destroyed."

The first meeting of the New Horizons Club was a bit of an eye-opener, to say the least. So many stories. So many ways to die. Turns out, a car crash is really not that exciting in the grand scheme of deaths.

The members had an assortment of experiences – a suicide by hanging, a murder, a drowning, a hit and run, a work accident where someone got crushed to death by a reversing forklift truck. Someone even choked on a grape at a birthday party. I mean, Jesus! Naturally there were a few cancers and a heart attack, but they were almost as unremarkable as our car crash.

My scar also seemed fairly run-of-the-mill. It got a mention at most.

"Get that in the accident, did you?" seemed to be a common question.

"That's some badge of survival," one man said approvingly, which made me reconsider everything. I'd never seen it like that before. I'd always worn it as a mark of your death rather than of my ongoing life. The thought made me stand a bit straighter and tuck my hair back behind my ear.

The group were a range of ages. I was probably smack bang in the middle. There was a bald man who looked like my old art teacher. A girl in her early twenties, widowed when her boyfriend drowned while surfing drunk. He'd left her with a six-month-old baby, who was now almost two. I couldn't help but think she was one of the lucky ones. At least she'd got the baby. I couldn't keep track of all the names; there was quite a crowd. We had the back room of the Sovereigns to ourselves, the first and third Thursday of every month, but restocked ourselves from the front bar. I'd driven in, so was nursing a glass of dry white wine a lot longer than it normally would have lasted and wishing I could have another.

Most people knew each other. There was only me and one other new to the group that month, so we drew quite a lot of attention. Nobody sat down, which I was glad about. Pity the poor person that got stuck on my right. But there always seemed to be a little circle around me, chatting. Everyone was warm and welcoming and I was enjoying myself more than I'd thought I would.

"We're a bit of a group support, really," one woman said, conspiratorially. "It's not all about romance. More about having someone to talk to." She pulled her cardigan around her shoulders like a hug.

Others seemed more like they were speed dating.

"Like football?" one of the men asked me when he arrived at my shoulder.

"Prefer rugby," I said and had to suppress a chuckle as he excused himself to "get another drink" within five minutes.

When my glass was finally empty, I debated having another. But the idea of driving the small lanes home, the possibility of an animal jumping out of the banks, was too much of a worry. The image of the deer was still too fresh, the crushed side panel of my bonnet, the smashed windscreen. Even though the paintwork and metal was now perfect again, I'd always know it had happened. The car bore its scars secretly. Mine were a bit more visible.

I wondered if it was time to slip away. I'd promised Ginny I'd go for a drink and I'd kept my word. They were a nice enough bunch, but the socialising was exhausting after so many months of hibernation. I'd spent an hour choosing what to wear, ending up in a shirt and jeans. I wore a slick of lipstick and a dash of mascara. I'd calmed the red of my scar with some foundation. It was more effort than I'd made for so long that by the time I'd pulled into the car park outside, I felt like it was too much. Maybe it was just too soon for this. However much I wanted it.

I managed to get as far as the bar, and pop my empty glass on it, before the man stopped me.

"Going already?" he said from his stool. I knew we'd been introduced but I couldn't remember his name. Olive-skinned, smile-lined but tired-looking. Obviously good-looking enough to make me glance away.

"Caught in the act," I said.

"Too much for you?" The rolled r's of a Spanish accent, softly spoken.

I nodded, almost relieved to admit it.

"One with me before you go?" He nodded at the empty stool beside him.

"I'm driving," I said with a shake of my head, already wanting to be at home but not wanting to be rude. Roo would be waiting to go out for a wee. My bed had fresh covers on it. The house would be cosy. And quiet.

"It's your first time?" he said. I nodded.

"Me too," he said.

I tried to remember his death story. Was his wife the choking? No, I remembered, she'd drowned. Fell off the back of a speedboat. God, you couldn't write this stuff.

"I'm making the most of the night off," he said. "I don't get many." He raised his glass of red wine towards me in a salute. His eyes were like those of a blackbird, dark and bright.

I could smell the lemon of his aftershave. The bartender collected my glass and took it away for washing.

"Babysitters are expensive here." He refilled his glass from the bottle in front of him, a Rioja, one up from the house red by the looks of the label.

"You have children?" I said.

"Just one. Magdalena. She's five." He picked up his mobile phone from the beer mat and there she was as a screen saver. Dark-haired, dark-eyed, just like her father. Holding a wriggling puppy and laughing in delight. I could almost hear her.

"You've got a dog?" I asked, sticking to what I knew.

"She wishes." He chuckled, low like a cello. "It was a friend's." He put the phone back on the bar. Turning to me full face, he put his head to one side, strangely foreign. Something inside me moved and I swallowed. Licked my lips to wet them.

"Sure you won't stay?" he asked again.

I let go of you in that exact moment, Sam. It was that microsecond that I moved away from hurt and regret and towards something that felt like hope. I'd thought my whole life would be spent with you and our children, but you weren't there. And he was. With a little girl who liked puppies.

"Maybe just a Coke?" I said.

I pulled the stool out bedside him. Poor Roo would have to wait.

I'd stayed for more than just one drink and when I got home Roo had chewed up the rug. But that couldn't take the smile off my face for the next few days. I tried to distract myself from thinking too much about him – Nico – but I couldn't help but sound out his name on my lips, to see how it felt, and it made me smile every time. I kept busy by helping Ginny with deliveries on the Tuesday. Business did not look to be booming. In fact, her pottery shelf at the craft shop still looked remarkably full seeing as we'd not restocked for a fortnight. She sighed beside me and then got to work on the merchandise to make the best of the display. As she repositioned plates, and stacked cups on their matching saucers, I noticed her nails were black with grime. Sometimes she was not the best advert for herself.

"Ah, Ginny." The smock-wearing owner appeared. "Glad you're here." She didn't look it, glancing up and down with a frown. I hoped Ginny would keep her hands out of sight. Customers bustled behind us, but did not seem to pay much attention to the handmade crockery.

"Look, we might need to rethink stocking the pottery," the owner said. "Haven't sold anything for what seems like weeks," she went on, rolling her eyes. "It's not the beauty that's in question" – she waved her hand expansively at the crockery, the vivid blues and greens of the glazing, the hand-painted details – "it's the fact it's not dishwasher-proof. It's putting a LOT of people off."

Ginny visibly bit her lip to stop herself saying something. Then tried a smile, which I could see was fake.

"Could we leave it through the summer holidays? We normally do good sales to the tourists."

The woman looked doubtful, as though she had already promised the shelf to another supplier.

"It's only a few more months. Then we could review in the autumn." Ginny sounded more determined, but there was an underlying desperation in her voice.

"That sounds reasonable. Just wanted to give you fair warning," the woman said and turned away, leaving us in no doubt that come September, Ginny's shelf was gone.

"Fuck's sake," Ginny growled. "I know exactly who's put off by the fact it's not dishwasher-safe. All those Barbour-wearing twats that roar around in Range Rovers thinking they own the village. They only turn up every few weeks to light the fire in their second home, and 'get away from it all' for the weekend. Shame they don't want to get away from their fucking dishwashers." She pulled a red pen from her pocket and starting marking prices down on the shelf, a few pounds off this, a pound off that.

"Let's see if this will help shift some," she ground out, pen nearly going through the card.

My phone pinged and I pulled it from my pocket. A Whatsapp message, from Nico.

"Are you going to Coffin Club on Thursday?"

I felt my mouth twitch. Coffin Club. It was what we'd been calling the New Horizons Club the other night at the bar. A private joke, just between us. It had been him that said it. How he was having much more fun than he'd expected to at a "Coffin Club" – I was a bit shocked at first but had to admit it was funny. Now, seeing his name, my mouth went dry and I had to swallow twice to wet it.

"They've got the money to pay full price too, fucking cheapskates…" Ginny was raging next to me. Eight words and a question mark, that was all. But it was enough to start a buzz in my belly.

"You listening?" Ginny asked, swinging towards me, then raising her eyebrows when she saw me on my phone.

"Message from one of the guys at New Horizons," I said, feeling a blush hit my face.

She rubbed her hands together in glee, previous mood forgotten.

"Someone sliding into your DMs?" she asked.

"Nico," I replied and showed her the message.

"Nice?" she said, and then laughed. "Nice Nico?"

Was that the way I'd describe him? His eyes, chocolate and gold. A quick smile. The way he'd looked at me full-on whenever I said anything, as though my face was the same on both sides. I could feel the flush spreading down my neck.

"More than nice, actually."

"Message him back then!" Ginny nudged me.

My finger hovered, brain suddenly blank.

"Yep, see you there?" I typed.

"What about 'looking forward to it?'" Ginny urged, reading over my shoulder, but I shook my head and pressed send. Didn't want to sound too keen.

It tinged back almost immediately.

"Great. Looking forward to it. N."

"Told you," said Ginny, smug.

I realised it was only Tuesday. Thursday suddenly seemed a long time away.

The next meeting of New Horizons was much more fun. Maybe it was because I recognised a few faces around the bar and they all waved a hello or raised a glass towards me when I arrived. Maybe it was because I had booked a cab to take me home this time, so I was planning on having a few drinks. Maybe it was because I was wearing something new, felt more confident in myself. Probably it was all those things, but mostly, it was that Nico smiled as I opened the door, as though he had been waiting for me.

I pointed to the bar across the pub in a question and he shook his head. Raising his bottle of Rioja, he then lifted two glasses with a nod back in my direction. Looked like we were sharing. A butterfly took flight in my stomach.

A shy man whose wife had died suddenly of a heart attack went home about nine, mumbling about an early start. A youngish woman who had tragically lost her husband to bowel cancer went to relieve the babysitter at ten, checking her watch five times as she left. Several others disappeared in between and yet I was still standing next to Nico and we'd ordered another bottle. His accent curled around words, making me listen in, lean closer sometimes to ensure I understood, and when I did, he smelled of fresh laundry and lemons. He told me how he worked as a carer at the nursing home, "because there is not much call for a speedboat driver this far from the sea." He told me funny stories about the people that he looked after, and about his daughter and her funny mannerisms. Her inability to say breeze block – it came out as bleezebrock. The way that she talked in her sleep.

The bar thinned out and the group eventually shrank to six of us. We circled our stools around a high table crammed with empties. The drink was certainly flowing. When Nico and I edged into the gang his knee was pressed against mine under the table, burning through my jeans.

"Let's play a game," Fiona said. "Never Have I Ever?"

There were a few murmurs of agreement immediately and a buzz of excitement.

"It's a drinking game," she explained to Stephen, who was older, tended to slick his hair back and wear chinos, and hadn't heard of it. "We each take turns to ask a question. If you have done the thing in question, you have to take a sip." He was looking confused already, but she pushed on. "You'll get the hang of it," she said. "Right, never have I ever… broken a bone."

"My arm," said Kerry, raising her glass and taking a sip of her wine.

"My ankle," said Alex, swilling his bitter.

"My cheek," I said, sipping my wine without raising my eyes.

"Got it?" Fiona checked. "Okay. Kerry, your turn."

Everyone was up for it, elbows leaning into the table, and every now and then there was the rub of Nico's shoulder on mine. Kerry went next: "Never have I ever… done a bungee jump!" she said. She had, in fact, done a bungee jump herself; but obviously just wanted to have a drink as she slurped a mouthful of wine. A few others drank with her and exchanged a few words about where they'd done theirs: New Zealand or Brighton. Nico and I held our glasses still, waiting.

"Never have I ever... eaten cat food or dog food," Stephen said, to everyone's disgust, and then hysterics when Kerry drank again, with a wry shrug. "It was a dare, what can I say?" She laughed, cheeks pink.

"Never have I ever... farted and not owned up!" said Alex and then snorted and banged his glass noisily against every single one of ours as we lifted our glasses in a mass cheers.

"Never have I ever... been jilted at the altar?" said Fiona and everyone looked at each other, curious. Nobody lifted their glass and everyone jeered Fiona, who then had to take a drink herself.

As people got more drunk, the questions started to get more interesting. I drank to admit I'd "gone commando", which made Nico raise his eyebrows at me with a chuckle when someone translated for his benefit that it meant going without underwear. He drank to "checking his phone for messages every ten minutes" and I wondered with a thrill if he was hoping to hear from me. We both drank to "playing strip poker", and Nico nearly spat his beer out when Stephen drank to "having worn women's clothes".

It was all going so well, until it was Nico's turn.

"Never have I ever... been in handcuffs!" he said.

My breath stopped in my throat. I could feel the cold bite of the metal around my wrists. Stephen lifted his glass. A little noise of surprise rippled the group.

"Dispute with a neighbour, can you believe it?" he said, indignantly. "She said I was being threatening! I still say I was just stating my case. She should have kept the hedge cut."

There was a little embarrassed silence as he guffawed into his drink. Everyone else glanced around the table and my hand shook as I lifted my glass, unable to help myself. Nico tilted his head to the side, still smiling.

I opened my mouth but it was empty, remembering how hollow I'd felt that day as the policeman radioed ahead to announce I was restrained and on my way. I sat with my handcuffed hands in my lap, numb, as the car crawled past concrete towers that blended into a grey winter sky. I felt nothing. Inside or out.

"What did *you* do?" Kerry said in surprise, leaning across the table. Everyone was looking.

What did I do? I lost myself completely, that's what I did.

"Were you a young rebel?" asked Stephen. I shook my head just once, knowing I was making it worse. I should just make something up, something funny to make everyone laugh, but my mind was black, dead, like it had been that day.

"Drunk and disorderly?" Kerry slurred and I swallowed around a stone in my throat.

"What was it then?" Nico asked, touching my hand on the table. Everyone was looking, almost frowning now, waiting for the big reveal. "Did you steal something, Kat?"

His eyes were the darkest brown, with tiny flecks of yellow.

"Yes," I said and it juddered out of me as I said it, just to him. "Yes."

A wave of relief around the group turned into laughter and I raised my glass and sipped, wetting my throat. Everyone said things like "you're a dark horse" and "everyone nicks *something* as a kid."

The moment passed and the next question was asked, and I smiled and drank along with everyone else. But I wondered what they'd say, especially what Nico would say, if they knew the whole story.

That it wasn't some make-up that I pocketed as a teenager. It wasn't a shampoo set from a hotel that I'd just popped in my bag. Nothing so inconsequential.

I'd stolen a baby.

2012

I grieved every one of those eight little babies that could have been. The media referred to them as "eggs", like commodities you buy by the dozen. But they were my children, each and every one of them. All the compensation the facility gave me meant nothing at all.

Days became weeks and turned into months, no longer marked with a period. No more opportunities or monthly mournings. My scar healed but the gap inside just got bigger, darker, until it was black and I was hollow. The doctor signed me off work for another three months, stating depression.

You bounced back after the initial shock, and tried to bring me with you. You'd put your arms round me and murmur into my hair, muffled words of love. How we still had each other. How you'd never leave me. How we had the rest of our lives together. I tried not to think of it as a sentence. Something that I would have to endure. I loved you, somewhere. I knew it, but I couldn't feel it.

I broached the subject of adoption and you promised to think about it. I mentioned using donor eggs, and you twisted your lip under your teeth. There are other ways, I cajoled. But you looked away, you sighed, you shook your head.

"It wouldn't be ours," you said. "I can't help how I feel."

You changed the subject. You stayed out more. You moved on.

You started playing squash, like you needed a hobby. Came home flushed and happy. Alive-looking. I shrank smaller in my dead little world. They said exercise is good for mental health, so I'd walk round *the block every day, robot-like, automated. I'd cook dinner. I'd try to watch television, but every channel had a baby. Every film had a cute kid. Every book I picked up was about a family. One day you came home and I'd smashed the TV screen right through. I heard your sigh of exasperation before you managed to swallow it.*

The "episode", as it came to be known, happened really naturally one day when I was out for a walk. I'd taken to long walks in the afternoon, trying to put off the moment when you would come home for the evening and want to play "happy families". The pound of my feet on the pavement helped to ease the banging in my head. I was passing the children's nursery on the high street and I paused on the pavement to let a hassled-looking mum out of the gates with a sickly toddler on her hip. I just meant to give her the right of way, so that she could get the poorly child home more quickly, but she held the gate for me as she came through.

"Must be something going round," she said, thinking I was there to pick someone up.

I didn't even think about it. Not for a second did I consider what I was about to do. I slipped inside the railings, caught the security front door just before it clicked shut and, just like that, I was in the entrance hall of the nursery.

Brightly coloured paintings were pinned to the noticeboard. Children were singing and clapping along to a recording down the corridor to my left. So I turned away, headed for the quiet. Down the corridor. Looked for the dark.

The first room I came to that had its door pulled to, but not shut, had exactly what I was looking for. The babies, sleeping in their line of cots. The lighting was subdued and the only sound was the rasp of the baby monitor on the shelf above the changing station. I checked the first cot: a boy, red-cheeked in his sleep. The second, another boy, was smaller, younger, with a bald head. He sucked in his sleep, looking for food.

It was the girl I picked up, so gently that she didn't wake. She was maybe three months old, swaddled in a white cotton blanket. She smelled like milk and hot-water bottles and her eyelashes lay dark and long on her cheeks. She fitted in my arms so perfectly that I had no doubt: she must be mine.

They heard me singing a lullaby on the baby monitor, apparently. It was a young nursery assistant who came to investigate, and she raised the alarm with a code word that triggered the police being called immediately.

I didn't hurt the baby. Well, I didn't mean to. But they tried to pull her out of my arms and I held on just a little too tightly, until she suddenly wailed, her little mouth a perfect red wet o. Then I gave her up, horrified. My little girl. Crying.

'I'm sorry, baby, I'm sorry,' I said.

The other babies were removed by staff with soft-soled shoes that squeaked on the lino as they crept out with their blanketed packages. Most babies stayed asleep, but one woke and watched me with big, unblinking eyes. I tried to smile so she wouldn't be afraid, but my lips weren't working. They felt slack, numb.

Someone brought me a chair to sit on. When the police officers, all men, arrived, they spoke to me in calm voices. Nursery workers passed in the corridor, shooting swift glances through the door, frowning and whispering behind their hands to each other. One policeman made phone calls, to his boss and then to you – disturbing you on the golf course – and then to some other people about where I should go. I just sat.

"Are those really necessary?" you said when you arrived, looking at the handcuffs that I wore. Your hair was standing up as though you'd run your hands through it.

"For her own protection," the police officer said quietly.

"Shall I follow behind?" you asked.

"Yes please, sir. They'll need you for the paperwork."

His radio hissed on his belt and he picked it up. You shifted anxiously from foot to foot, unsure of yourself. I'd never seen you not know what to do before. You were always the one taking the lead, ordering the food, booking the flights, tipping the waitress. Suddenly I had an urge for you to put your arms round me, to tell me it would be all right.

"Taking her straight there now, Sarge," the policeman said as he pressed the button on his unit and reattached it to its clip.

"All set, madam?" he said to me and I stood obediently, ready to go.

"Do you know the destination?" he said to you.

"Park Prewett Hospital." You nodded, grey-faced. "Mental health wing."

It was only when I got into the back of the police car that I realised I was still holding the baby's blanket. I hoped she wasn't cold.

Next time I saw her, Ginny looked weirder than ever. Like she'd got dressed in a second-hand shop. She wore a cagoule over a pair of walking trousers tucked into wellies and topped off her look with a full-visor motorbike helmet. Her hands were protected by bright yellow rubber gloves. I obviously looked just as ridiculous; she snorted at my outfit, which I'd found in her garage. An old pair of ski salopettes and a see-through mac that looked like the type you bought on a London street corner for two pounds when it rained. On my head I wore a riding hat, with net curtain stapled to the front.

"Why don't you just buy a beekeeper's suit?" I asked, carrying the smoker. Straw burned slowly in the can and I puffed the handle every now and then to keep it glowing as we walked through the apple trees to the hives.

"Have you seen how much those things cost?" she said, rubbing her thumb against her fingers. I had to admit, I'd never looked into it. The bees got noisier as we got closer and I hunched my shoulders, conscious of my exposed neck above my collar. It was the first time she'd asked for help with the bees and I was slightly apprehensive. I certainly didn't feel protected – I felt more like I was going to a fancy-dress party. Especially knowing that the new bees she'd bought were notorious for being territorial, which was why she was keeping them at the sanctuary rather than one of her other honey homes.

"Don't walk in front of the hive," she warned and I veered left of the buzzing entrance.

"Blow here." She lifted the lid of the hive and indicated inside. I took a hesitant step towards her and aimed the nozzle inwards. The frequency intensified into a frenzy as I funnelled thick grey smoke into the wooden box, sending the bees into an alarm dance. Thousands of them, moving over and into and underneath each other, vibrating. Ginny was unfazed, lifting a frame to assess the honey-loading and brushing the bees from it with a soft brush. They fell away, unharmed.

"Fan-fucking-tastic," she said with a laugh. "Would you look at that."

The lower frames were already stocked, the honey built thick and silky from the bottom.

"I knew they'd pay off."

She'd bought herself two new colonies earlier in the month, a new strain of hybrid bees, apparently better for honey production. She was aiming to sell more honey through the local farm shop, with little handwritten labels that she was very proud of. A love-heart design that said, 'Honey, With Love from G's Bees'. All very cutesy but they'd sell well. With all the extra wax, she was planning on making body butters fragranced with herbs and oils. All extra money for the sanctuary.

"Must be collecting from the fruit blossoms…" She was almost talking to herself. "So early in the season."

I smoked the hive again and bees hovered, changed direction, obviously confused. One landed on my veil, making me go cross-eyed as it walked in front of, but not on, my face. I went to bat it away.

"Don't," Ginny said. "If you kill it, or if it stings you, it will attract the others. Just leave it."

I hardly dared breathe until it took to the air again.

"I'll take a couple of jars to the neighbours for free when I can," she said. "Might keep them sweet."

She'd had a bang on the door recently, her nearest neighbour asking her to move the hives further away from their garden, which to be fair to Ginny was about a quarter of a mile away. A request that she'd quite obviously ignored.

"Apparently they don't like bees on their laurel," she'd snorted. Even when the children had suffered a few stings, she had little sympathy. "They live in the countryside. What do they expect?"

With the top layer of the hive replaced, she wedged the lid back on and we set off up the garden. I was glad to get a few feet away. The stress of the bees was feeding my anxiety, my plastic coat was making me sweat even in the weak March sunshine.

Ginny pulled off her bee-wear and hung it on the hook on the garage wall. I followed suit, rubbing the red ridge on my forehead left by the riding hat.

"What's going on with lover boy?" she said as she put my hat on the shelf. "Shagged him yet?"

"For God's sake, Ginny!" I laughed.

"Does that mean no?" she asked, genuinely disappointed.

I shook my head. "In fact I haven't heard from him since the 'Never Have I Ever' night. Maybe I put him off."

"What did you do?" Ginny asked, stamping out the burning straw from the smoker. By the time all the bee-keeping equipment was back in its rightful place, I'd told her about how the game worked and the funny things we had both confessed to. I paused there, not sure how much more I wanted to say, but then it was only Ginny and I trusted her.

"And then, it was never have I ever been in handcuffs, and only Stephen and I owned up to it… and I told everyone I'd stolen something."

She turned to me. "Did you tell him about stealing the baby?" she said, frowning.

I could feel the air in my open mouth. "How do you know about that?" I said, gobsmacked.

She blinked a couple of times and then shook her head as if it was of no import. "You mentioned it that first day you came. The day you killed the deer."

I couldn't believe it. That day had no details for me. Just the deer's eyes rolling in its head and its back feet kicking against the gravel. But I felt offsided that she knew. It was my secret. What else had I told her that I couldn't even remember? I knew I had talked myself hoarse and it felt like therapy, so maybe I *had* shared more than I normally would. The thought made me nervous. I glanced at Ginny sideways but she was fiddling with some bee kit on the shelf, her back to me. She turned round at the silence, and was surprised to see me looking at her.

"Hey, no worries," she said. "We all do mad things sometimes. I told you, I smashed up old Fuckface's golf clubs when I caught him at it." She chuckled and made a choice sign with her right hand. "So did you? Tell him?" she asked again.

I shook my head.

"So why do you think you've put him off?"

"Well, he hasn't been in touch since." I shrugged as if it was obvious. I wanted to check my phone again just to see. "And he thinks I'm *just* a shoplifter."

"How was it otherwise?" she asked. I remembered the pressure of his knee against mine under the table, the light scratch of his stubble on my cheek as he kissed me goodbye. The fact that I could smell the warmth of his body as well as the lemon of his scent. The pit of my stomach pulled.

"It was good." I nodded. Dammit. I liked him. Really liked him.

"Well then," she said as if I was just being stupid.

It was later that day that he texted. I was on my third walk of the day with a retriever, a spaniel and Roo.

"New Horizons picnic on Saturday. Friends and family welcome. Are you coming? X"

A kiss at the end this time.

Ginny was in the barn when I rang to tell her. I could hear her boots on the cobbled floor.

"He texted," I said.

"Never doubted it," she replied.

"Want to come to a picnic?" I asked.

I spotted Nico as we parked, even though he was at the far side of the green. By the time Ginny and I got out of my car, managing a cool-bag, a deckchair each and a very excited Roo on a lead, he was walking towards us, arms extended to help us carry something. As I gave him the bag, so that I could get full control of the puppy, he leaned across and kissed my cheek. I breathed him in and then nodded towards Ginny.

"You said friends and family were welcome… she counts as both," I said. Ginny looked at me in surprise and then flushed.

Nico shook her hand, almost formally, until she laughed him off with a "Dying of thirst here."

We set up under the trees, laying waterproof blankets on the grass in the circle of our chairs. It wasn't really picnic weather, but at least it was dry and the spring sunshine had a hint of warmth to it. Other members of Coffin Club waved a hello. A handful of kids ran in and out of the muddy river in welly boots that would never keep them dry. I craned my neck to see which one of them might be Magdalena. Roo whined and strained at the lead to join them. She always knew where the fun was at. So did Ginny, who had the wine open before I'd even undone my coat. Nico added his belongings to ours on the rug, including a pair of impossibly small white trainers and a bucket.

Ginny leaned back on her hands and surveyed the scene. Her cleavage spilled liberally out of her checked shirt, sun-freckled and soft-looking. It was the first time I'd seen her out of combat gear. Large black sunglasses covered her eyes and her red-grey hair tumbled around her shoulders. I suddenly realised that it wasn't just me that had made an effort.

She and Nico chatted while I set out the food. Pizzas I'd precooked and sliced. Sausage rolls and pork pies. Wine, white and red. Crisps and cookies. Even a box of ice pops. Seeing it all laid out, it became very obvious I hadn't been packing just for Ginny and me. Glancing at Nico's blanket, I saw his stack of four scuffed Tupperware lunchboxes, but couldn't guess at their contents. There was a pink plastic water bottle next to them, with a purple strap.

A game of Frisbee started on the open space behind us – mainly adults, a few gangly teenage boys. A champagne cork popped somewhere and there was a cheer.

"So, how long have you been here, Nico?" Ginny asked, wolfing down a pork pie before I'd even got the paper plates out.

"Three years now. I like to think of it as home." The inflection in his voice was musical. It made me want to lean in, listen longer.

"You're not pining after the sunny Spanish weather then?" Ginny said, looking at the clouds scudding across the sky.

He shrugged, expressively foreign, glanced at me. Our eyes met and held.

"Not at all," he said. "I would like to stay here very much."

"It's a nice part of the world," Ginny said, filling her drink up again. Nico stood for a moment, scanning the kids back-and-forwarding on the riverbank. There were eight or nine of them, all in shorts and wellingtons, or leggings and hoodies, not old enough to be self-conscious of milk bellies or pigeon chests. He obviously saw what he wanted to see, and sat down again. I followed his gaze, dry-mouthed, wondering which one she was.

Ginny lowered her sunglasses and looked over the top. "Where's all the single men then?" she said, eying the Frisbee-throwers, and Nico laughed. But she was serious. She downed her plastic beaker of wine in one long swallow and heaved herself to her feet.

"Behave yourselves, kids," she said wryly as she went, swinging one of my bottles of wine in her hand.

Nico peeled the lid off the first Tupperware box, unveiling oily black and green olives, with squares of pale cheese and flecks of red chilli. The next was miniature chorizo sausages, followed by a frittata and a tub of salad. It was a feast. I felt like we were on holiday.

He shaded his eyes with his hand, looking again towards the river. The kids were daring each other to run in up to their knees, never mind that their wellies didn't go up that far.

"She lived in a swimming costume until her mum died." It was the first time he'd talked about the "before". He'd only ever told me that Magdalena was born on the Costa Del Sol and that he'd met her mum through work.

"I ran my own boat business, tourist trips and waterskiing – you know?"

I nodded.

"She spent many days at the beach." He smiled, looking at something long ago, and I felt a lurch of envy. Oh my God, I couldn't be jealous of a dead woman.

I popped an olive in my mouth to change the taste.

He laughed suddenly and pushed himself to standing. Extending a hand to me, he pulled me to my feet.

"Come and meet her," he said and my stomach dropped like I was on a first date.

The kids were wet and shrieking on the bank. Several were soaked to their thighs, shorts and all. Others more cautiously made tunnels in the sand, filled buckets and dumped mud around. Roo whined in delight as we approached, whereas I could feel the flush of my face, flooding with blood at the thought that I might scare her. Suddenly terrified that she might look at me and cry, I let my hair swing out from behind my ear, shook it forward to hide my scar.

"Magdalena," Nico said and the name was soft in his mouth.

She stood up. Like a sparrow, her knees were bigger than her thighs. She swung a red bucket, on water-carrying duty.

"I don't want to go yet," she said, one little hand on one little hip, head cocked to the side. But a smile, not a pout.

"We're not going anywhere." He laughed. "I want you to come meet my friend. This is Kat," he said and laced warm fingers though mine, pulling me in. I stumbled with the newness of it, leaned against him.

She considered me for a full five seconds, as though trying to work something out.

"Did a tiger bite your face?" she said and for a split second, I almost laughed. The sheer beauty of children. The open-minded purity of what they see and what they say. No judgement. No fear. Just curious. Nico pulled his breath in as if to say something but I squeezed his fingers.

"No," I said to her and paused, beckoning to her with my finger as if to tell her a secret. She came closer, all eyes. "It was... a... lion!" I jumped down the bank, pretending to pounce, and she squealed in delight. All of a sudden we were playing. I was the killer cat and she was the prey. She dropped her bucket and ran shrieking towards the water, only to be surprised when I ran after her, right up to the edge. When I caught her I made a disgusting chomp-chomp sound and she pretended to be dead, slumping tiny against me and closing her eyes. I looked over her head at Nico. He was laughing on the bank, and I realised: *this*, this is what I've wanted. This feeling of being full inside. A small body to hold. This is what I've longed for my whole life. Just this.

Magdalena ate olives till her mouth was greasy and then laughed and wiped it on the back of her hand. She nibbled frittata and picked at my crisps, dropping them on the blanket and flicking them off. Her hair was the colour of coffee with just the tiniest dash of milk. It hung past her shoulders. She ate and drank just what she needed and then she was gone again. Legs and arms pumping as she raced across the green to catch up with her friends. My adrenaline pounded like I'd been on a rollercoaster as I watched her go.

"She likes you," Nico said and I turned to see him watching me. I knew I was blushing; my scar felt tight and hot.

"She's gorgeous," I replied. "You're obviously doing a good job."

He breathed out as though relieved. "It's hard," he said. "Because it's just us, sometimes I know I give in too much."

"How long has it been?" I asked.

"Three years. Magda was only two when Elena died."

Dammit, Elena sounded like a sexy name. Better than Kat.

"And you said you've been here three years too?" I said. He nodded.

"So how come? Why not stay in Spain with your family? To help with Magdalena?" I shielded my eyes from the sun, keen to know. He paused, glanced away.

"I don't have any family," he said. "My mother died."

A tiny tic appeared in his cheek and I put my hand out automatically, touched his arm.

"I know how that is," I said. He looked at me and it hit me in the pit of my stomach. And in my pants. I wanted to kiss him.

The wail of a police car somewhere made him look away, towards the sound. Then he turned to me with a lopsided smile.

"Are they coming for you? For your stolen goods?" he said and it took me a moment to catch on – he was referring to my admission at the "Never Have I Ever" session. I took a deep breath and it shuddered. God, I wished I could laugh it off but if this was to go anywhere, I had to tell him the truth. He'd been sharing stuff, so I should do the same.

"About that…" I started. He listened without a word, a frown flitting across his face a couple of times. I told him everything. The fibroids and the hysterectomy. The depression. The black hole of loss. The breakdown and the baby. How I watched you walk away at the hospital after I was committed. The three months of hospital routine and how it managed to calm some of the noise in my brain. The therapy. The day you came to pick me up and take me home, and how the sun was shining even though it was cold and frosty. How I felt something like a bubble of excitement inside and you told me that was hope.

When I stopped talking Nico licked his lips, as though considering his words carefully. He flicked a glance over to the children as they tumbled and squealed and I realised I should have told him before he introduced me to his child. He might think I was a danger to her, that he'd exposed her to something bad. My throat closed up, suddenly sure I was going to lose out again. That I'd got it wrong.

But when he looked back at me, he blinked several times, his dark eyes wet and shining.

"Life is cruel, isn't it?" he said. "To take something away from you that you want so much."

I nodded.

"Because I think you'd be a very good mother."

I felt something inside me open up, like a swell of something good, and I hadn't felt that since you. And just when I thought things couldn't get any better – Nico leaned over and very gently, very slowly, kissed me.

So I had a new boyfriend. I could almost hear you laughing at the word – boyfriend – as Nico and I were both in our thirties. But what else was I supposed to call him? My partner? My lover? My man?

It was a wonderfully weird time. All those "first times" that you go through with a new partner felt all the more different because it wasn't like you and I had split up. It was just that you just weren't there any more. So the first time Nico held my hand, I noticed how hard his palms were. Dry from the constant washing and sterilising at the care home. So unlike your soft hands, which never did anything like manual work. The first time he put his arm round me and I fit perfectly into the nook beneath made me remember your height. How when you hugged me I faced into your chest like a bear. Nico's laugh was low and chuckling, not a loud bellow. When he stayed over, he liked the curtains open at night to see the stars and then woke early. Not like you and I; we'd stay in bed till lunchtime and then stagger out like two vampires caught in the sun. I'm not saying that it was right or wrong either way. It was just different. It felt good and bad at different times. Wrong and right simultaneously.

We had to be up early in the mornings anyway, to be ready for Magdalena when she woke in the bedroom next door. Sometimes, I'd creep in to watch her sleeping. To see the actual moment when her eyelids would start to flicker, and when she'd stretch in the bed, as she came to consciousness.

She was always happy to wake. Like every day was a new adventure. When she saw me there, she'd smile. Then she'd holler for Roo and run through the house barefoot till she found her. The perfect beginning to a day. For me, anyway.

It started that they would come over at the weekends, then sometimes after school in the week. Nico slowly took over the kitchen. He pulled out all the pots and pans, wedding presents most of them, hardly used as we used to eat out so much. He reorganised the kitchen so that ingredients and tools were handy to the stove. The crockery cupboard was now next to the dishwasher. I loved to watch him making himself at home. And then he started to cook.

He concocted a paella that stained his fingers saffron-yellow and tasted delicious. Magdalena pulled the heads off prawns and sucked the juices with tiny noises of appreciation, like a small animal. The next time it was a roast chicken, stuffed with herbs and served with dauphinois potatoes thick with cheese.

He made great eggs, with chopped chillis and tomatoes, and smashed avocados on toast. He hammered steaks or marinated prawns. I was eating so well and putting on pounds, making up for the starvation months when tea had been out of a tin with a fork, at best.

While he cooked, Magdalena and I would play.

"You're so patient with her," Nico would say, without realising it wasn't patience that kept me there colouring pictures with her, it was pleasure. She taught me Connect Four, I taught her cat's cradle. We sang nursery rhymes. I chalked a hopscotch on the patio and we took turns hopping and jumping our way up and down the boxes. She showed me her homework, her drawings. We began to pin her pictures to "her" bedroom wall. Sometimes we'd walk Roo together, and I'd let her take the lead as the dog bumbled along.

"Magdalena is such a big name for such a little girl," I said. She stood on one foot and swung the other while Roo waited and wagged.

"No one at school can spell it," she said.

"How about I call you Midge?"

She stopped swinging, foot out in front of her.

"Midge." She tested it out and then laughed a yes, and from then on, she was Midge to me, and me alone.

One Saturday, about five in the afternoon, I put on a film and she leaned against me on the sofa, head on my arm. I hardly dared move in case she went away again. Her hair was like a whisper on my skin and she had no idea of the present she was giving me. I couldn't tell you what happened in the film. I just know that it was one of the best ninety minutes of my life.

Nico and I went to the New Horizons meets together, open about being "a thing" but wanting to keep up the community.

"Sod's law," said Kerry, "the two new members of the group get it on together and the old ones are still single."

But then a few new faces joined, and there was a real buzz back in the group. A weird thing to be happy about really, seeing as it meant their husbands and wives had just died.

One of the new women, blond, petite, seemed to find it hard to take her eyes off Nico across the bar at the Sovereigns one night. Every time I glanced over, she seemed to be staring; but it still took me by surprise when she turned up at my elbow.

"Hi," she said to Nico. A quick glance at me, a half-grin. I was the sideshow, not the main attraction.

"Hi?" he said back, slightly bemused.

"I'm Dee, first-timer," she said. "Sorry to butt in, but I think we've met before?"

Nico faced her, non-committal.

"Your face is so familiar." She scratched her chin. "But I just can't place you!"

"St Bede's infants? My daughter is in reception," Nico suggested, but she shook her head.

"No kids," she said.

"Old Chiselford Nursing Home?" he said. "I work there."

"No old people." She laughed.

Nico shrugged and sipped his wine, almost rude but not quite. He was obviously uncomfortable.

"It will come to me," Dee was bubbling on. "Probably in the middle of the week when I'm doing aerobics or some-thing" – she smiled at me as though I was in on the big puzzle too – "and then I'll be like – *I know who you are!*"

A dull flush was creeping over Nico's collar.

"Maybe I've just seen you on Tinder!" She laughed at her own joke and moved away, waving as she went, completely unaware of the seed she'd planted. Nico rolled his eyes at me and topped up my wine but it didn't wash the bad taste out of my mouth.

It lingered there until the next afternoon, when Nico left for his shift and I had an opportunity to be on my own. The niggle had turned into a nag of anxiety, of insecurity. I'd thought we were on the same page. I couldn't bear to think he might still be in the market for seeing other women. Not knowing quite where to start, I picked up my phone, feeling like a nosy parker, typed his name into the Google search bar and pressed enter.

The list of responses was long. It seemed like it was a common name; loads of different Nico Menendezes downloaded, mostly links to Facebook or social media. I skimmed through some, looking for his profile picture or a photo of him with Magdalena, but he wasn't there. So I clicked on images and tried again. This time I found him, but it was just a blurry newspaper clipping, in Spanish, with a photograph of him and his wife on their wedding day, presumably their wedding announcement. I peered at it to try to see her, but the quality wasn't good. There was a similar clipping in the next link, a wedding photo and a photo of their boat business, so it was definitely them even if the image was too grainy to really see their faces. Anyway, it wasn't what I was looking for. Nothing out of the ordinary. I just wanted to make sure I had him and Midge all to myself, without any scar-free competition. So, I bit the bullet and downloaded Tinder, setting the requirements to match Nico's description and location to see if he was there. I swiped through galleries of guys until I got tired and hungry, but didn't see him.

Ginny can swear better than you ever could and the day she got the letter from the council about the hives, she almost literally turned the air blue.

"Fuckity fuck sakes," she was saying, one spaghetti strap of a very dirty vest top hanging off her freckled shoulder. "You'd think they had better things to do with my council tax." Then she laughed, but it didn't sound like she thought it was funny. "Not that I've fucking paid that, mind."

The letter was very clear. She was instructed to either move the hives to a more rural area of the property, or dispose of them, by the following Tuesday. The surrounding families had all now complained.

"So they want to grow flowers in the their gardens but they don't want fucking bees?" She shook the paper at me, fuming. "It's not as easy as all that to move the hives. We'll have to smoke them first, make them calm, and then move them layer by layer, carefully or they'll be bolshy bastards. It's a tricky business."

I noticed the "we" even though I couldn't recall having offered to help. The thought of moving hives that housed fifty thousand bees each, wearing a riding hat and net curtain, was not appealing; but I knew she couldn't do it on her own.

"They've been producing so much, too," Ginny was saying, giving a stained mug a very cursory rinse before pouring my tea. I tried not to wonder if she had been letting the dog drink out of it, as I'd seen her do before.

"I really don't want to put them off their honey. The farm shop sold out of G's Bees honey last week, it's the only thing that's bringing in any dosh." She opened the fridge, bare except for a couple of tins of cat food and a solitary pint of milk. She pinched open the carton and slopped the milk in. After she passed the cup to me, the cat licked the spill on the worktop.

"Is that a thing, then?" I said. "Do bees go off production, like hens that go off the lay?" My tea had the distinct whiff of off milk and there were little creamy specks spinning in the top.

"Bloody better not be," she said, scanning the letter again. "We'll do it Saturday?" she went on as she read, a deep line between her eyes. "Bring Mr Lover Lover if you want, and the kid."

"Maybe," I said, doubtfully. She looked at me over the paper, one eyebrow raised, waiting.

"Had a funny thing happen at the last meeting," I said. "Some woman kept saying she knew him from somewhere. Was convinced she'd seen his face before."

"Maybe she just fancied him." Ginny shrugged. "He's not bad looking." She pulled a face as she said it, as though he really weren't her type.

"In the end she just made some joke about recognising him from Tinder…"

"And?" Ginny's face was expressionless.

I chewed my lip and shook my head. "I looked. Couldn't find him."

She shrugged.

"Let's face it, Ginny. He could do a lot better than me. I'm just worried he might be on other sites, casting his net wide. Maybe this isn't as serious as I'm hoping."

"You're shagging now, then?" she said with a nudge, but not even that could make me smile. I nodded.

"Well, maybe he *was* on there," she said. "You knew he was looking for someone."

I considered that. She had a point. I knew he'd been lonely in the UK. I knew he wished Midge had a mother figure in her life.

"Maybe he's found what he was looking for?" she said and pointed at me. I couldn't help but smile. She could be right.

"I just thought, as my friend, I'd ask anyway," I said, feeling the flush rising up my neck. "You're on all the sites…" I took a deep breath. "Will you keep an eye out?"

She picked a sesame seed out of her teeth, inspected it and then flicked it on the floor.

"Will do," she said. "But I've never come across him before." Then she snorted a laugh so big that snot came out and she had to wipe her nose on the back of her hand.

"And he's never come across me," she screeched.

2013

I don't think you actually realised what being locked in Park Prewett did to me. It's no wonder I have trust issues.

It finished me off. Inside. But it also made me more determined, more direct.

Any bits of hope that I'd have a baby were scooped out, mashed up and thrown away. And the more hopeless I grew, the more important it became. I still wanted a baby. That didn't change. But I did.

My wing was all women. There was one in there who'd killed her babies. She held them under the water of their evening bath, with her own hands, until there were no more air bubbles. One of them was only six months old, but I wondered whether she'd still struggled. The other was three. That must have taken much more effort, probably made the mum out of breath, to have to lean forward and put her own weight on him to keep him under the surface. I wondered which one she'd killed first. Hopefully the older one, so that he didn't see what she was doing to the baby and get scared.

I wondered about how long it took. How many seconds the babies had their eyes open for, looking for their mother through the watery ceiling. Wondering why she wasn't helping them. I thought about it for days, weeks, the full three months that I was in there. Because she was my definition of mad. She'd had everything I wanted. And she'd killed them.

Watching you leave me there was one of those moments I'll never forget. You kept reaching out to touch me, but not quite making it.

Your hand would drop away just before it made contact with my arm or shoulder. Like you were scared. Didn't know how to be with me. I wanted you more than ever then, to pull me into your chest. To build that wall around me with your arms and talk into my hair. But you didn't.

You did kiss me, though, just once, before you went. And you whispered something in my ear.

"You'll get used to it, you'll see. I love you."

Your stubble scratched against my cheek as you pulled away, and I felt the sting of it after the door had shut. Get used to it? I wasn't sure whether you meant the mental hospital, or life as a barren woman.

The hospital was the easy part to get used to. Built on routine and medication, the days passed in rhythm and drone. Once it was established that I wasn't dangerous – to myself or anyone else – I had the run of the floor. I could watch endless television in the lounge or sit in a window chair and look out across the woods. I didn't make friends. I didn't chat to Maureen who had stabbed someone with a knitting needle. I avoided Sarah who had a breakdown at work and tried to throw herself out of a window. All of the other women, some scarier than others, regarded me but, after a few attempts at talk, left me to my own devices. Some rocked in corners, some chattered to dead partners, some screeched and wailed in the night until the nurses were called in with a big needle. I sat. I watched. I thought.

You visited but you left again. And again. And again. And then it struck me. You didn't love me unconditionally. Your love had boundaries. Things it might not be able to get over. Bits it wouldn't be able to accept.

Not like a mother's love.

I could still feel the strength of my own mother's love, even though she was long dead, and more so than ever while I was alone in Park

Prewett. Memories were as clear as day. The stroke of her hand on my head when I had a nightmare. Her tinkling laugh when I danced. The soft support of her body when I sat on her lap. Then the "life tips" she taught me. Advice she gave when I was seven and I'd lie on the hospital bed next to her, while she had chemicals dripped into her veins.

"Always be polite," she'd say. "Manners go a long way."

"Never talk about politics", she'd whisper, "or money or religion. It only causes arguments."

"Never loan money to friends or family. It always ends badly."

"Learn how to ask questions," she urged. "People like to talk about themselves."

And finally, when her voice was so weak she had to lick her lips to get the words out.

"Don't do as I do, KittyKat. Do as I say. Mother knows best."

U nbelievably quickly, it seemed as if my dreams were
finally coming true.

Nico was loving, tender and thoughtful in lots of little
ways. Not big expensive gestures like you used to make, but
small considerate things. He might not book a surprise
weekend in Paris, but he boiled the kettle for me every day
before he left to take Midge to school so that I could make
tea. He didn't arrange me a personal shopper on a Saturday
afternoon, but he did bake me a stroganoff that would last
me through the week. He didn't buy me air conditioning
when the summer got hot, but he opened the loft hatches
before we went to bed and the hot air rose out of our little
turret bedroom like magic.

Midge edged ever closer to me, slipping her hand into
mine when we walked the puppy, lying against me on the
sofa. Occasionally, she even slipped between Nico and me in
bed, and we would each wrap an arm round her and hold
her safe. He called me a "softie" because I'd let my arm go
dead and numb before I moved it for fear of disturbing her,
and I just smiled, because it was true.

Nico introduced me round at his work at the home's
summer family day, not just to the staff, Kieron and Jamie
and the others, but to the residents in their wheelchairs or
on sticks. They all loved him, beckoning him over, holding
out their hands to clasp at his, rubbing his knuckles against
their own cheeks. He crouched beside them, all the time in

the world to listen to their stories, wipe up their dribble. They all smiled at me when he introduced me as his girl-friend, told me I was a "lucky girl," and I said that "yes, I was," and I knew they were right.

I began to let myself believe that we were more than a gang, we were a family. It was perfect.

One Saturday, at the park, Midge hung on to the roundabout. She stretched both arms out straight and leaned back as it spun.

"Faster, Kat," she shouted, "Faster."

I was laughing with her, it was infectious, and I turned the roundabout again and again, making her squeal. Her knuck-les whitened on the rails as she spun but she shrieked with glee.

"More!" she said, like a little adrenaline junkie.

Nico frowned up from his paper on the bench when he heard her, then tucked the pages into the mouth of the nearest frog-shaped litter bin and headed towards us.

"Slide next!" said Midge breathlessly as the roundabout slowed. Before it had come to a complete stop, she leapt off and sped towards the other side of the park. She pulled herself up the ladder, no fear at five years old, and sat at the top momentarily to wave at us at the bottom.

"What's the latest in the Brexit news?" I asked as we watched her.

"Same," said Nico, with a short shake of his head.

"What will it mean?"

"I still don't know," Nico said on a sigh. "It's so uncertain. They're talking about a process that we can go through, an application to stay."

I bit my cheek.

"But maybe we have not been here long enough," he said.

I hate uncertainty and this was painful, to me as well as to him. Everything about me was tight inside, clenched. It would be so bloody unfair if I'd just found something good and then it was taken away.

"We can work it out," I said and caught his hand. He tried a smile.

"I know," he said. "I want us to." His thumb rubbed against my knuckles. "Because I love you, Kat."

It hit me like a punch and burst like bubbles. The L word. I opened my mouth but Midge decided that was the moment to throw herself against my legs at full pelt. She nearly knocked me off my feet and the moment for me to reply was gone. But I couldn't stop smiling as I caught her shoulders, tiny under my hands, and then tickled her armpits until she collapsed giggling against me.

"What next?" I asked, kneeling beside her and scanning the playground. Kids scaled a climbing frame in the centre, upped and downed on a seesaw, zigzagged a ramp on their scooters and pointed their toes to the sky on the swings.

"Seesaw?" I said and she turned to it, cocked her head – then shook it.

"Climbing frame?" Nico said and she looked at the seething mass of kids that covered it, hanging dangerously upside down like monkeys. To my relief, she wrinkled her nose.

"Swings?" I said and she jumped like she'd been stung. Stopped with one leg in the air, eyes big in her face.

"Is that a yes?" I said and she glanced at Nico and then back at me, biting her lower lip very gently.

"She doesn't like the swings…" Nico said.

But she took a step towards me and tucked her fingers into mine.

"Only if *you* push me," she said. I looked at Nico and there was a flicker of something, annoyance or upset, that flashed across his face before he caught himself and shrugged at me. I held his gaze for just a moment until he smiled, showing him it was okay.

"Have fun," he said.

Midge was already off, tearing ahead of me, checking over her shoulder every few steps that I was actually following. When she was in place, holding tight to the chains, she whispered, "Not too high, Kat," and it was the first time I'd ever heard any doubt from her, about anything at all.

"It's okay. You can tell me when you're high enough," I said and drew the swing back gently towards me, before letting it go. She pointed her plimsolls, legs straight out like soldiers. I caught her on the backward arc and gently pushed again, and again, until she eventually said "Higher!" and leaned back as she swung forward, straining for the sky. It got that I could only just push her on the back each time as she built up her own momentum, forward and back, pointing and tucking her feet under the swing like a little ballerina. Nico watched from his bench on the other side of the park.

"Hold on tight!" I called to Midge and Nico smiled across at me, closed his eyes and leaned his head back to face the sky and I grinned to myself, laughed out loud. He trusted me to keep her safe. So did she. I'd have stood there all day, to be honest, sun warm on my arms, listening to her chatter and whoosh. I didn't even notice the woman next to me pushing her own toddler on the baby swing, until he started crying and she lifted him out. He snuffled into her shoulder and she patted his back.

"He doesn't like the swings quite as much as your daughter," she said, nodding at Midge.

I smiled nervously, hardly daring to reply in case I said something to give the game away. The woman hooked the child round on to her hip and toed the brake off her buggy.

"Maybe it's an age thing?" I suggested, "He'll grow into it."

"Maybe," she said, buckling him into the seat and then straightening with a stretch of her back. Midge turned and grinned at us over her shoulder and I thought for a moment she'd call me Kat and the pretence would be up, but she just leaned as far backwards as she could and let her hair almost sweep the ground as she zoomed for the sky.

"She has your hair, that's for sure," the woman said with a smile and pushed the buggy away towards the ice cream van.

I let my breath out slowly as she went. Midge looked like she was mine. My baby, my girl, my own. Someone to love unconditionally. It was a sign. This was meant to be.

My world changed again on a Thursday.

We were at the sanctuary and Midge was helping me clean out the hedgehogs. When I say helping me, she was mainly oohing and aahing and calling them Mrs Tiggy-Winkle, while I scraped out their boxes and refilled their straw. Roo ate any droppings that fell her way, thinking all her Christmases had come at once.

Ginny and Nico were in the henhouse when we came out of the barn into the sunshine. Ginny was filling a basket with eggs, Nico was helping patch up the wire walls to keep the rats out.

"It's not that easy," he snapped, turning away from Ginny. The look on his face as he saw us made my breath catch. He was really angry.

"What isn't?" I said, with a smile, trying to diffuse the situation, Midge swinging oblivious from my hand. Neither replied. "What isn't that easy?" I said again.

He flicked a look at Ginny and she brushed her hair off her sweaty face.

"Bloody Brexit," she said and he let out a breath, loudly, in exasperation. I was surprised. He hadn't wanted to talk about it last time I mentioned it, saying there was no point and "it would be what it would be." I hadn't pushed it, but it hung over us like a guillotine. None of the MPs seemed to give a monkey's about the families it would affect, the human lives it would change. All the coverage just seemed to be about how trade would work and what borders would be hard or soft, whatever that meant.

"I was just asking Nico what he's doing about trying to stay put. Or will they just move on?" Ginny raised her palms in the air, looking at me, bringing me in, and then shrugged when he didn't say anything. Having dropped that grenade into the conversation, she let herself out of the henhouse and followed Midge, who was throwing a yellow tennis ball for a whole bunch of dogs.

I stepped closer to the henhouse door, wound a finger through the wire mesh. This was the conversation we hadn't had. The one I'd been avoiding. I wasn't ready to let it go yet.

"And?" I said, looking directly at him.

"I want to stay, of course…" he said.

"Why?" I said, forcing the issue.

"This is the best place to live in Europe," he said. "I can work and get good pay." I'd seen his pay packet from the nursing home and believe me, it was not a lot. So things must have been bad where he came from.

"Good schools. Good opportunities for Magdalena," he went on.

I nodded. "Why else?" I said.

"It's safe here. And people mind their own business. I can live my life without worry." He banged the hammer into his own palm, but he looked so hopeless, so desperate, my mouth went dry.

"Is that it?" I asked. He still hadn't said what I was waiting for. Letting the hammer hang by his side, he fully turned to face me.

"And I want to stay with you."

I breathed it in, held on to it in my chest. Somebody else, apart from you, wanted to be with me. And it meant Midge stayed too.

"But maybe I won't be able to," he said, blowing out through his lips.

"What would you do?" I asked, already dreading the answer.

He shrugged, banged another nail, hard.

"I guess you could just go home?" I said, thinking that if that ever happened, maybe I could go with them. My Spanish was limited but I could learn. I could at least order "*dos cervezas, por favor.*"

"To Spain?" He shook his head, definitely. "Never."

I was taken aback.

"Nothing there for me any more, I'd have to go somewhere else. This is why I don't want to speak about it, our 'situation'," he said, suddenly, with a flash of anger. "It doesn't get us anywhere. It is not up to me."

He banged a nail into the post and I winced.

"Maybe I have to try France," he said, almost to himself. He wasn't mentioning me at all in this equation. He obviously wasn't expecting me to tag along.

"How can you just let it happen to you?" I snapped, frustrated.

"We will probably have to leave at the end of the summer, in time to get Midge into a new school." There. He'd said it. He was just leaving with her. I was not part of the picture.

My stomach dropped like a stone at the reality. They'd be gone and the hole in my life would be bigger than it had ever been before. Bigger than the crevasse left by you. Big enough to fall into again. No more tucking Midge into bed.

No little hand in mine and skipping songs. No more tiny PJs in the wash, or nursery rhymes in the car.

Nico banged another nail in, hard. I knew his anger came out of fear. Worry. All he seemed to want was to stay, live here, make a home for Midge.

"Nico…" I said, both hands on the wire, but he kept his back to me.

"Leave it," he said. "There is nothing you can do about it."

2014

I hate people making decisions for me. Always have.

When I got out of Park Prewett you seemed to believe I couldn't think straight and started being really fucking annoying. Ordering for me at dinner, telling me the best route to drive somewhere, suggesting when I'd had enough to drink. I'd feel you looking at me when I was talking to somebody, like you were worried about what I was going to say. I'd catch you staring at me when I was at home, watching the TV or reading a book, like you were scared I was suddenly going to freak out. It was really tiring, trying to look normal for you. I'd been doing it too long. It wore me out.

I probably could have kept it up a bit longer if you hadn't changed your mind about trying to adopt a baby, acknowledging finally that we couldn't have our own, and how important it was to me. I'd broached the subject a couple of times and you hadn't said no. That in itself was enough to set me at the internet, that fire in my belly again, but deeper this time. Hotter.

I scoured websites, looked up processes, worked out timescales. I joined forums to talk to other adoptive parents, understand the journey they'd been through. Every night at dinner I'd tell you a success story, clap my hands in delight at the moment they described taking their baby home. We'd got as far as getting the registration process started. Filled in forms, booked an appointment. You'd gone right along with it, blank-faced but compliant. Until now.

We were out one cold, bright Sunday, driving to the beach for a wrapped-up walk and a lunch by a log fire. It's the kind of indulgent thing we did; after all, we just had ourselves to please. Nobody else to worry about. You probably thought it was a good time to raise the subject. When we could walk, holding hands, along the shore and talk it through.

Only we didn't get that far. The shit hit the fan before we even reached the coast.

"We should probably start looking at booking something for the summer holidays," you said, as we took the exit off the motorway. "Would be good to know what we're doing."

The dual carriageway quickly turned into a B road and the fields opened out around us.

"Bit tricky, though, as we don't know how long the adoption process might take," I said. You turned the wheel casually in your fingers, not looking at me as I carried on, "You never know, we might be booking for more than just the two of us."

The indicator ticked as we turned again towards the coast, bare trees bordering the lane.

"I wanted to talk to you about that," you said, glancing over. "I did some research and it looks like we won't get through the process – won't be accepted as potential parents – because of your episode."

Your voice had gone weird again; it sounded like you were talking to a small child. I waited to see if you were joking. You weren't.

"Nobody is going to give us a baby, Kat. You've just got to face it." You were frowning at the road ahead, oblivious. Then you went one step further: "And also, if I'm honest, I'm not sure I'd want to adopt…"

What? Since when? I shook my head, but you were still talking:

"I'm not sure I'd love the baby. It's not ours. I've said it before and I'm certain of it now."

What were you going on about? You'd never said that before.

"If we can't have our own — and we know we can't — then I don't think we're going to have a family."

My eyes were dry as paper. My jaw hurt.

"But I want a baby," I said, simply.

"I know you do." You reached a hand across the gearstick to find mine. "But I think it's time we accepted it's just not going to happen."

You squeezed my hand, like that would make it better. You patronising bastard.

"It's just going to be you and me. Me and you."

It was then that the hole opened up in front of me. I literally couldn't think of anything worse.

"There's nothing you can do," you said, with a little shrug.

You fucking idiot. Trying to make another decision for me.

But this one was too important. I let myself fall into the hole. A place there was no coming back from.

Well, this time there *was* something I could do. Maybe instead of Brexit taking Nico and Midge away, I could make sure it kept them with me.

Watching Nico in the henhouse, his back rigid with anger and frustration and whatever else, I decided I was not about to just stand by and let everything go. It might have taken a couple of years for me to find Nico, but it only took moments for me to feel like I did about Midge. If this was my chance, I was going to take it.

"Nico," I said, gripping the chicken wire until my fingers went white. He finally stopped banging and let the hammer swing by his side, defeated.

"I don't want you to go," I said when he looked at me, hair flopping over his forehead.

"I want us all to be together," I went on, glancing to Midge running with Roo across the lawn, both chasing the same ball. I would not lose her.

"A proper family," I said.

He shut his eyes, exhaled. "That is all I want too," he said. "I love you, you know that."

"Do you think an application to stay would have more chance if we were married?" There. I'd said it.

I had his attention now.

He tilted his head side to side, as though weighing things up.

"It would mean security for you. A family for Magdalena." I went for the big sell. I knew what was important to him. Maybe he didn't realise quite as much about what was important to me. "Let's make it really hard for them to send you home."

"What if they still come for Midge and me?" His jaw muscles showed through his cheek.

"Then I'll bring in the big guns and get a lawyer," I said, trying a smile. "We'll hire the best."

He looked doubtful.

"Let's face it, there's a great headline in there – widower meets widow and finds happiness that is then torn apart… We'd get loads of coverage if we fought it in court."

He flinched.

"I don't want to be in the papers," he snapped, "I just want to stay."

I backtracked. "I'm sure it won't come to that," I reassured. He was thinking; I could see his brain working. Midge was twirling noisily on the lawn, round and round and round, until she fell in a dizzy heap.

"Why would you do all this for me?" he said, suddenly, his chin lifted as a challenge.

"Because I– I love you – both." I stammered as I said the words for the first time. "And I couldn't bear to lose you."

His hands fell to his sides.

"I'd do anything for them not to come and take you away," I went on.

He flinched and worry flashed across his face.

I carried on, tweaking his fear, "I couldn't stand by and watch them send you back to a country where you don't want to be."

"We don't know that would happen," he said.

"But we don't know it wouldn't, either," I said. "Everything is so uncertain."

I had him. I could tell. He nodded slightly, just a twitch.

"You know I love you," I said.

He nodded.

"You know I'd be the best mum I could ever be to Midge."
I licked my lips with the importance of it.

He held my eye for a long time.

"Then you have to apply today. I'll help you with the
forms," I said, "and after that we'll look at the register office
availability." I put both hands on the fence, like I was in a bad
music video, and delivered my killer line. "Nobody is going
to deport you or take you away from me if we do this right."

The word "deport" did exactly what I hoped. He closed
his eyes at the impact of it. When he opened them again, he
laid the hammer gently on the felted roof of the henhouse.
Dusting his hands off, he walked towards the door and let
himself out. Finally he came to face me.

"Then," he said, "if we are to do this, we do it properly."

He dropped to one knee in front of me on the grass and
reached for my hand.

"Kat. Will you marry me?"

It was nothing like your proposal over a five-course dinner
in a West End restaurant, but it was exactly what I wanted. It
was perfect.

"Yes," I said, and laughed. His grin flashed white against
his tan, his eyes crinkling almost closed.

"You don't know how happy you've made me," he said,
standing and pulling me into a hug.

And I thought, yes, yes I do, because over his shoulder I
could see Midge turning cartwheels in the sun.

I hardly thought of you at all on the day Nico and I got married. But naturally, I couldn't help but make a couple of comparisons.

We stood in a register office and not a church. We signed the documents on an old wooden table, and sat on well-worn chairs. My dress was knee-length and cream. The opposite of the full-on bridal gown with the train that pulled heavy at my temples. It was a hot, bright July day, with no sign of the autumn colours of pumpkins and conkers.

There was only Nico, Midge and me, along with Ginny and Lee, a guy from New Horizons, who were our witnesses. There were no aunts and uncles whose names I never remembered, no family friends or hangers-on. Small and simple. Lovely.

"In Spain, our brides have a mantilla – normally made by their mother. But I knew you wouldn't have one," Nico had said on the morning, handing me a package. It was a lace veil attached to a tortoiseshell comb to fit into my hair. I fixed it immediately, letting the veil fall over my face, over my scar, but he lifted it gently and pushed it backwards over my head.

"You don't need to hide," he said and I loved him very much in that minute.

After we were signed and sealed, husband and wife, he motioned to Midge, who ran up with a small velvet purse and opened it on the table. Thirteen coins clattered out, rolling and knocking each other. She giggled and tried to catch them in her hands.

"This is my *arras* for you," Nico said. "Our unity coins."

"Blimey," said Ginny. "Rich as well as good-looking!" She and Lee had been on the pre-wedding champagne too long.

Nico ignored her and put the coins carefully back into the purse before pressing it into my hand. "It's normally carried by a flower girl. But on this occasion, it is carried by *our* girl."

And just like that, not only was I married again, but I was a mum. All that I'd ever wanted came to be in one day. My cheeks ached from smiling as I drank champagne with Nico and sat with Midge on my knee.

I was far too happy to even consider for one moment that one of Mum's old sayings might come true. "Marry in haste," she used to warn, "repent at leisure."

I was as surprised as anyone to see our wedding photo on the New Horizons Facebook page.

It was taken at Borelli's, the restaurant we went to for dinner after the ceremony. I was smiling into Nico's face, my mouth slightly open like I was talking or about to laugh. His eyes were on mine, and one of his hands was moving my hair away from my cheek. Midge leaned over his shoulder, a flower behind her ear. It was bloody lovely.

Ginny made a smooching noise when I showed her on my phone. "Young love," she said and then pretended to put her finger down her throat. I laughed. Nothing was denting my mood, not even cleaning out the goat pen. Ginny had been happy for me to do it; she was busy marking up items with price tickets for a yard sale to raise funds for the sanctuary.

"Lee must have taken it," I said. "Listen to what they say …" I read her the blurb, how Nico and I were a success story for the group. A wedding was big news. A new family was even better. I knew I had a shit-eating grin on my face when I read that bit. I was a family now.

She paused, black pen in hand. "How much would you pay for this?" she asked, holding up a dented and rather scratched black coal scuttle.

"About a pound?" I laughed. "If I was feeling charitable."

"Two pounds then," she said, writing it on the tag, "then they can haggle."

I rolled my eyes and took in the other items she had pulled out of various cupboards and sheds to sell.

"These should go." She pulled over a box of DVDs, and wrote a sign on the box, '£2 each or three for £5.'

"Nico looks really handsome in it," I said flashing her my phone again, but she only gave it a quick glance and a cursory "mmmm".

"How much are you trying to raise?" I asked, getting the message that she had other things on her mind.

She laughed. "Anything really," she said, rubbing the small of her back. "I've got outstanding bills at the vets, the feed store, the council and the electric."

I slipped my phone back into my pocket, embarrassed. I could hear my mum's advice, "Never talk about money, politics or religion."

"The house roof is leaking and I've got a feeling the gas is going to get cut off just as it gets cold."

I widened my eyes at her but still didn't know what to say. I felt kind of bad, truth be told. It had been so long since I'd had to worry about things like that, I'd kind of forgotten about them. Although I was careful with money, looking for deals and comparing quotes, my bills got paid on direct debit and I knew I had enough to cover expenses.

"So, if I raise enough for a hot-water bottle I'll be happy." She laughed it off and picked up a man's blazer, blue with a grey stripe. "How much for this?" she said and I gave it my full attention, happy to change the subject.

"Nice fabric," I said, rubbing it between my fingers. "Ten pounds?"

"Fifteen." She wrote it down.

After an hour, she had a full table. Remains of her married life, long forgotten, had come out for sale. A silver photo frame, a pair of candlesticks, a set of cutlery. A bag of golf clubs, dusty but in good condition. A box of encyclopaedias. A lazy Susan for the table. All overpriced but up for negotiation, she said. I couldn't imagine this other Ginny. The one who had a husband who, before he became known as "Fuckface", had cooked meals and engaged in leisure activities.

The only things that went back in the shed were things that were useful around the sanctuary: buckets without handles, tubs without lids, a tub of weedkiller, a very old box of rat poison, and a pot of creosote.

"I thought that stuff was illegal now?" I said.

"The rat stuff or the paint?" she asked.

"Both." I looked at the date on the side of the poison and it was positively prehistoric.

"Probably," she said, obviously not bothered in the slightest.

I saw Midge, in her school uniform, before I saw Nico. She rounded the corner of the shed and skipped towards us, school bag slung over her shoulder. Nico followed behind, still looking handsome even in his own uniform for the nursing home. He kissed me and his lemon scent was just there, almost hidden under the disinfectant of work.

"Can I see the hedgehogs?" Midge said, tugging my hand.

"Please," Nico reminded.

"Come on, kiddo," Ginny said, not giving a fig for manners, "I'll show you," and Midge wheeled after her, leaving me behind.

"Don't be long, we need to go," Nico said, jangling my car keys. He took my car every day for work now. It was easier than the bus and I had no need for it. Let's face it, I walked dogs for a living. Plus, I knew he liked driving it.

"Hey," I said, "I almost forgot." I dug my phone out and started scrolling. "We're famous!"

I found the image and showed him the screen. It seemed to take a moment for him to register, and then he took the phone out of my hand.

He clicked on the image and zoomed. I leaned in, keen to see the detail too. I didn't even care that you could see my scar, it was such a happy picture. He zoomed in close enough to see his own face and Midge over his shoulder.

"Why did you do this?" he said, raising his eyes to me.

"I didn't," I said, confused by his tone.

"What site is this on?" he said, frowning as he scrolled.

"Don't worry—" I started, but he cut me off.

"I never agreed to any pictures online," he said, his mouth a tight line.

"It's only our group," I said, suddenly unsure. I took the phone off him and saw that it had, in fact, been posted onto the national network rather than the local page. He glared at me.

"Why are you so angry?" I said, shaking my head. "It's a really nice picture." I put my hand out, to touch him, to reach him. To break whatever was happening. He flinched away from me, but then shook his head as though to clear it.

"Sorry," he said, closing his eyes. "It's just..."

Midge ran out of the barn, arms out like an aeroplane. Roo bounded a foot behind.

"It's her," he said, suddenly. "I don't like pictures of her online. You never know who is looking."

I watched her bank around the yard before climbing onto a bale of straw and jumping off.

"There are so many weirdos online," he said and then, I got it. Totally. I'd just never had to consider a child before. But I did now. And I didn't want any perverts looking at her any more than Nico did.

"I can perhaps ask them to take it down," I suggested, linking his fingers with mine, attempting a smile. He nodded and squeezed.

"Do it now," he said.

It was only after he let go of my hand that I realised my fingers hurt.

Sports Day was a big thing for Midge. She'd been talking about it for weeks, hopping from foot to foot, claiming she wanted to win the sack race, or praying to get chosen for the egg-and-spoon. I'd sent her in that morning with an extra squeeze for luck and a promise that we'd be there to watch. So I wasn't very chuffed when Nico rang at the last minute to say he'd got caught up at work and I'd have to go alone.

"She'll be gutted," I said down the phone, not making it any easier for him.

"I'll be there as soon as I can," he said. "Something's come up."

I wasn't just disappointed for Midge, I was thinking of myself really. You know how much I hate going to places on my own, especially where I don't know anyone. You always used to stick at my side, hand in the small of my back, guiding me round. It was reassuring to know you were always there. Now I felt like everyone was looking at me as I walked across the school playground to the field. I wondered if I had sweat marks under my arms.

The noise levels were deafening. The whole primary school was sat in rows along the track, four deep. All T-shirts and shorts, sticky little arms and legs. I could tell Midge's year was at the front, cross-legged. They were the smallest. The thumb-suckers, the ones that still had milk at bedtime. Behind them, the children got bigger, until the ones on the back row, who looked like they could have been teenagers. Some of the girls even had boobs.

Seats were put out for the parents, arranged in year groups. I headed for the chairs under the reception sign, where there was already a group of women and a few men, chatting, fanning themselves with leaflets and hands. I took a free seat at the edge and threw a smile in their direction, suddenly conscious that they were on my scar side. I was really wishing Nico would hurry up.

"Hot, isn't it?" the woman next to me said, pulling a face as though she were melting. I nodded but had nothing to add. All of a sudden, I was a blank. Until I remembered my mum's advice – ask people questions, they love to talk about themselves.

"Who are you here for?" I said.

"Nate," she said, pointing at a blond crew-cut across the way. He waved back.

"You?"

"Magdalena," I said, scanning the front row. She was five to the right of Nate, whispering in her friend's ear. I waited till she glanced up and then waved. She lifted her hand to wave, then paused in confusion when she saw the empty chair next to me where Nico should be. I put two thumbs up to her, trying to signal everything would be okay and he would be here, and she smiled and did the same back.

"Ah." The woman grinned. "I hear she's good at the egg-and-spoon."

I crossed my fingers and tucked them underneath my thigh. I didn't have anything against her Nate but I hoped Midge left him standing.

"I'm Sal," the woman said. "This is Jen and that's Sharon," she went on, nodding to the women next to her, who craned round to smile a hello, and soon I knew who their children were too: Seb and Josh, one an unfortunate-looking boy and the other a nose-picker.

"Isn't it normally your husband who picks up and drops off?" Sal asked. "Is he coming today?"

"Nico, yes," I said. "Hopefully later."

"Ah, that's his name is it? He keeps himself to himself at the school gate," Jen said.

"I think we terrify him." Sharon laughed.

I smiled. In a weird way, I liked the idea that he wasn't part of the group. It meant I could be, in with "the mums". My stomach was bubbling, but it wasn't nerves any more. More excitement.

The kids were lining up for the egg-and-spoon race. Midge held her spoon out with a set jaw. I'd seen that look of determination before when we played games at home, Jenga or snakes and ladders. She liked to win, my girl. Maybe she was a bit like me after all.

A whistle blew and they were off. Sal nearly gave me a heart attack, springing out of her chair to cheer Nate on. The line of mums were red-faced, shouting, laughing at them-selves as they did. I cupped my hands around my mouth and called, "Go Midge," as loud as I could and hoped she could hear me over the racket. Her eyes never wavered from her spoon. Eggs were falling everywhere – luckily hard-boiled, I noticed – and kids were slowing and dropping away. She just kept going, plimsolled feet steady and sure. Nate had dropped his egg, Seb fell over and Josh was not in this race, and suddenly Jen, Sal and Sharon were all calling for Midge too as she took the lead and strode ahead. As she strode through the ribbon, winning by at least five metres, Sal threw her arm round my shoulder and cheered. My face felt stretched with smiling and it only got better when Midge finally let herself grin, directly at me.

By the time Nico arrived, we'd watched running races, hurdles, high jump and goal-kicking competitions and were chatting about all sorts. Nico slotted into the chair I'd saved for him. I introduced him all round, but his face was tense and the women subtly turned away to chat among themselves. I was peeved he had put a downer on the mood.

"Everything okay?" I whispered.

"I hope so," he said, rubbing my thigh. Whatever it was, he wasn't talking about it.

"Sack race, Kat," Sal said, nudging me.

Midge was already in her sack, so big that only her head showed out the top, her two little hands like kangaroo paws at the front to hold it up.

"Look at her face," I said to Nico and he softened with a chuckle at the set of her chin. She saw him sitting there and nodded at his wave, then licked her lips in concentration.

The teacher blew the starting whistle and we all jumped up again. The kids bounded forwards, some running in their sacks, others jumping. Midge was being traditional, bunny-hopping along.

"Go, Midge," I shouted.

"*Venga*, Magdalena," shouted Nico.

She was about three-quarters of the way along the track when she tripped. Probably her feet had got caught up in the bottom of the sack, and she was propelled forward, fast, mid-bounce. Her hands, tucked inside, had no way of cushioning her fall and I saw her expression change at the last minute, just before she hit the floor face-first.

The whole row of mums made a collective noise, and Sal put her hand automatically on my forearm, as if to reassure me and restrain me at the same time. She was right to do so; my instinct was to run over.

The other kids bounced past Midge in her sack, ran round her – an obstacle in the race – and it was a full ten seconds before she lifted her head and looked up. Her mouth was bloody and open, dark red and oozing. A teacher, young and pink-cheeked, ran on to the track and helped her up, looking into her open mouth and then talking quietly to her.

"God, Nate would be bawling," Sal said.

The teacher, "Mrs Mac" according to Jen, turned towards our group of parents with her arm round Midge's shoulders, steering her our way. Nico put his hand up, registering her as his. I could only clasp my own hands to my chest, although I wanted them round her.

As they got closer, Mrs Mac pulled a face and said, "Looks worse than it is, but she's bitten her lip pretty hard," and it was then that Midge pulled out of her grip and ran towards us. I could see now that her eyes were filling up and she didn't want to cry in front of everyone. She was a tough kid, just like me. Nico and I both stepped forward to lessen the gap between us, him dropping to one knee to be on her level. Midge sobbed once before she reached him, unable to hold it in. But then at the last minute, she swerved his arms and threw herself into my legs, arms around the backs of my thighs, bloodstained face into my skirt. Her shoulders heaved as she let her tears out. I held her against me, a hot bundle of emotion. I didn't care about the blood. I didn't care if I could never get the stain out. I would wear it for the rest of my days with a happy smile. Or pack it in my memory box for ever. Because it marked the day she chose me.

I was still ecstatic on the Saturday, when we helped Ginny set up for the yard sale. I'd never even been to one before, let alone run one. It wasn't the kind of thing you and I would ever do, but, as you well know, sometimes I do the unexpected.

Nico was well up for it. I'd only had to mention that it was to raise money for the sanctuary and he marked it on the family calendar I had bought and hung in the kitchen.

"If you can staff the tables, then I can show punters round the animals. Then they can see what I'm raising the money for, might be worth an extra quid to them," Ginny said, passing me a biscuit tin for the money. "Midge can help me, can't you, kiddo?" Midge was delighted with the idea, swinging on Ginny's hand as they headed off to open the gate. Nico and I sat on our deckchairs behind the tables, ready for customers. It was a slow start. In the first hour a solitary car arrived and a man wearing a waistcoat jumped out.

"Got a leaf-blower?" he asked, through his nose. We all surveyed the sorry display and he shook his head.

"Oh well. Good luck," he said and was gone again.

It was nice enough to sit in the sun and chat with Nico. He'd been quiet all week, work on his mind. Ginny and Midge were hanging around in the barn, sorting out the animals while they had time, and it was nice to just have some time to ourselves. Roo was sleeping the sudden sleep of a puppy under the table.

"I'll make us a cuppa," I said.

Ginny's kitchen was dark after the sunlight and surprisingly cool. The sink was full of pots, plates and glasses. The fireside chair was draped in dog blankets. One breadcrumbed worktop was covered in jam jars she was saving for her beeswax products. Her welly boots stood proud on the other worktop where she'd been cleaning them. Tally, the old Labrador, thumped her tail on the floor as I came in, but didn't bother to get up. I found two chipped mugs in the usual cupboard, rinsed them under the tap and opened another door, looking for teabags.

It was like the cupboard that time forgot. There were dusty rows of herbs and spices, four tins of tomato soup and two of rice pudding. Random tins of beans and pulses, all of them dented, or the labels torn. A half-empty box of porridge oats and a split bag of rice were the only other occupants.

The other shelf contained cans of dog food, neatly lined up. She wasn't short of that.

I found the teabag tin on the windowsill in the end, and was relieved to see it did actually contain teabags, although only a handful. I used one bag for both Nico and me, not wanting to take the piss, and topped them up with just a splash of milk.

As I blinked back out into the sunlight, I saw Ginny eagerly waving in a couple of four-by-fours. News had obviously spread. I knew there were posters in Patches, the local cafe, and in the farm shop, so hopefully this was just the start. I was beginning to understand just how important this was to her.

After a while I was quite enjoying myself. It was nice to meet a few people as a couple and Nico had his public face on again, chatty, smiley, gorgeous. You could absolutely see how he'd been so popular with the tourists back in Spain in his boat business. He just had that friendly face and way about him. I squeezed his hand when I passed him some change. I was surprised to see we had about twenty pounds in the tin already. Soon there was a small crowd at the tables, and Nico and I spread out to cover both ends.

I was trying to interest an out-of-towner in the cutlery set for his second home when two dogs went for each other in the yard, snarling and barking. One of the dogs, a spaniel, was on a red lead held by a sun-hatted woman. The other dog just seemed to come out of nowhere, tore across the yard and went for it. The noise was horrendous, deep-throated growling and snapping; it sounded like they were killing each other. The woman was shouting over the racket, pulling the lead, trying to get her spaniel away; it was definitely the underdog. Anyone nearby scurried out of the vicinity, women pulling children with them.

A man from my table ran over, claiming the other dog – a collie – shouting, "Leave it," and trying ineffectually to get a hold of his collar. The collie now had the spaniel pinned to the floor on its back, squealing and squirming. People were shouting now, "Get him off," and "Do something." But nobody did. Everyone was frozen.

The man, red-faced, tried again to grab his dog but it twisted away, snapping at the spaniel's throat. The woman was desperately trying to pull it out of danger with the lead but she was just dragging the dog on its back.

The man swore, and kicked his dog, hard. The sound of his boot made me flinch.

The collie yelped and bounded away immediately; cowered in front of its master. The spaniel took its chance, scrambled to its feet and ran behind its owner, whining.

The man grabbed his collie by the scruff of its neck. "You bastard," he shouted, shaking it with both hands before throwing it down. "You leave it when I tell you." He swung his foot back and kicked the animal again in the ribs. It tucked its tail and tried to scurry away. He followed it, raised his foot and kicked hard, again, and again. The dog yelped twice and then limped off, but the man was still following it, boots crunching on the gravel. The veins were showing in his neck and he spat as he shouted. It was horrific. There were a few cries from the crowd, of dismay, disgust, but Ginny was the only person to physically step in.

"Leave him alone," she warned, her voice low as she moved in between the man and his dog, her back to the animal.

"Fuck off," he growled.

"I'll call the police," she said. "That's animal cruelty."

"Should have done what I told him to do," the man said, aiming a kick around Ginny's legs. She jumped out of the way, but so did the dog.

"Should have trained him better," she said back. "Ring 999," she shouted towards us and I pulled my phone out of my pocket.

"It's dialling," I shouted back, even though it wasn't yet. My fingers felt like sausages and my hands were shaking. The man, suddenly aware of us – the audience – squared his shoulders.

"You're a fucking madwoman," he snarled at Ginny. "Everyone knows it." She closed her mouth but her nostrils flared.

"The mad animal woman," he jeered, making little quotation marks with his fingers in the air. "That's what everyone calls you." He swiped the back of his hand across his mouth, glancing at the tables again. Nobody said anything. I realised I still hadn't dialled the number and started trying to stab numbers into the phone.

"Ah, fuck off the lot of you," he said again and strode towards his car, a Land Rover Defender, army green. He whistled his dog and it limped after him, hurt but loyal. Something about its expression, the shock, the devotion, the fear all mixed together, made my stomach turn. Brought back memories of you. How you looked that last day I saw you. Confused. Shocked. The dog jumped into the passenger seat when he opened the door and the man slammed it behind him. Stones flew as he spun out of the gate.

Nico, suddenly at my side, rubbed my hand and pulled me against him. He took the phone out of my fingers and ended the call.

"It's okay," he whispered, but it wasn't. I was lost in memory.

People were letting out various noises of relief, blowing out held breath. In the middle of the yard, Ginny shook herself, hair falling out of its clip. Turning towards the group at the tables, she tried a smile.

"And people wonder why I prefer animals?" she said with a short laugh, which didn't sound funny, but others took it as the cue to lighten the tension and laughed along. Someone shuffled back towards the table, happy to move on, and soon they were buying again, and Ginny was taking another group around the barn to see the hedgehogs, the favourite of the day. I shook myself back into the present, but felt an old hollow in my chest that was there to stay.

It was all done and dusted by lunchtime. We still had stuff for sale but nobody in their right mind would buy it. Nico and I counted the tin while Ginny and Midge showed the stragglers around. £49.30.

"Not a lot," he said.

"Better than nothing, though," I said.

He surveyed the table, picking up a terracotta plant pot.

"This would look nice outside our front door, yes?" he said, head on one side. I smiled, seeing where he was going. He was so kind.

He took out his wallet and pulled out a ten-pound note.

"Looks like it was expensive," he said, tucking the note in the tin. I thought about the kitchen and pulled another tenner out of my own pocket.

"Very," I said. Let's face it, it was the least I could do.

2014

You were more like a Labrador, when I look back at it. Loyal. Loving. Dogged in your devotion and steadfastness. When all I wanted was what you wouldn't give me. A baby. A child. The chance to be a mum. You thought you could make the decision for me. And I would comply.

Fuck that.

"There's nothing you can do about it," you said that day in the car.

You didn't hear the click as I released my seatbelt.

You didn't see me coming as I threw myself at the steering wheel. But you heard me, a noise that came from somewhere I'd never been before. The darkest sound of desperation. I sounded like an animal. I didn't recognise myself.

I hit the steering wheel with both hands, jerking it to the left with everything I had. Every childless cell in me pulsing with blood. Every barren bone in my body fused with anger. It wasn't fair. I just wanted to hit something.

You shouted something, my name maybe or a grunt of surprise, and the car veered violently as you tried to straighten up, swinging me back against the passenger door. Bracing my feet against the footwell, I thrust myself into you again, managing to hit your elbow with both hands, and the car hit the verge at 60 miles per hour. I wanted to hurt you like you were hurting me.

You were a good driver but you didn't stand a chance. The uneven ground. The long grass. The car flipped, spun. Somersaulted. And then hit the tree and stopped dead, with the screech of twisted metal and the crunch of your broken body. As I flew through the windscreen and lost my face to a thousand shards of glass.

I'd worked out by now that a bottle of red was a good way to get to the bottom of things with Nico, so after dropping the boarding dogs off I bought a really nice Spanish Rioja home with me. Since the yard sale, when he'd been his best self, he seemed to have receded again. I'd woken the night before and he'd not been in bed beside me, the sheets cool to the touch. I got up to find him and heard him clear his throat, outside in the garden, in the dark. Looking out the open window, I could just make him out, sitting on the patio beneath me, the burning end of a cigarette glowing and fading each time he inhaled. I'd never known him to smoke. But you could say I didn't know him very well at all. Or him me, come to that.

So the next evening, I waited until Midge was asleep before I plucked the bottle from the shelf and suggested he get the glasses. The garden was still warm enough after sunset to be immediately calming; it sounded of evening song and smelled of honeysuckle. After the first sip of wine warmed my throat, I could feel my shoulders dropping. Damn, it was nice.

I talked of the normal stuff for a bit, Midge, school, Ginny, the yard sale. I told him Midge and I had been invited to Jen's for a play date with Seb and I didn't know who was the more excited, Midge or me. I told tales of the new dog I was walking, a Westie, full of piss and vinegar. I rambled on about a painter and decorator I'd found who would transform the ramshackle summer house into something we could actually use. Nico remained withdrawn, talking only when necessary, sipping his wine, until it was more dusk than day.

"You're quiet," I said eventually, leaning towards him.

He swilled his wine and refilled the glass. I couldn't read his face at all.

"Have I done something wrong?" I said, suddenly unsure of myself, although I couldn't think why. Relief flooded through me when he shook his head and put his hand out to reach mine.

"What is it then?" I asked. "You've been distracted since Sports Day." As I said it, I felt again Midge's hands on my legs, the soft shudder of her crying into my lap. How much I'd savoured the moment when she ran to me.

"It's nothing," he said, squeezing my forearm gently.

But a seed of thought was there. What if that had pissed him off? What would that be like for him? His daughter choosing me rather than him? I studied his face in the half-light. Was he jealous?

"Was it Midge?" I said. "When she ran to me?"

He frowned. "Why would that upset me?" he said, looking honestly nonplussed.

"It's just been you two for such a long time," I started, "it must be hard for you sometimes, to share her?"

He shook his head, smiled.

"You don't know," he said, "how happy I am for her to have you."

He refilled our glasses.

"Really?" I checked.

"It is all I want. For her to have someone else if something should happen to me."

It stopped me in my tracks, took me back to my aunt's house after Mum died. I told you how cold that house was, how quiet. There were no blankets draping the sofa, and no toy boxes in the lounge. It was like a magazine article, living in that house. To think now that Nico saw me as a good place for his child, and my house a good home, made my eyes burn hot and wet.

"Nothing is going to happen to you," I soothed, pulling him close. He rested his head against mine and kissed my hair, but didn't reply.

The scream startled us all. Roo jumped up, ears pointed and scanning like radar. Nico and I looked at each other for a split second as we established it was Midge and then ran for the door. He took the stairs two at a time, I followed behind. By the time I got to the bedroom door, he was already kneeling by the bed where Midge sat, cross-legged, in a hot pile of bed-clothes. I hung back in the door, not wanting to get in the way, and flicked on the little nightlight that threw stars onto the ceiling. Midge scrubbed at her eyes with balled fists, sobbing.

"*Querida, querida,*" Nico hushed. I didn't know what he was saying, but it was obviously a term of endearment. He reached out to stroke her hair. As his hand touched her head, she flinched away,

"No, no, no!" she cried.

"It's okay, Magdalena," he said, trying again, but she smacked at his hand and pushed herself towards the wall.

"*Mamá* —" Midge called, looking past Nico and straight through me, to something only she could see. "*Mamá.*"

It wasn't me she wanted. I knew it immediately and my gut hurt. It was the only word I had ever heard her say with a Spanish accent.

She threw herself over on her side, facing the wall, crying. Nico rested his hand on her shoulder but she threw it off and he closed his eyes, hurt.

"There is nothing to be done when she is like this. I cannot reach her," he said quietly as he joined me in the doorway.

"Is she even awake?" I said.

He tilted his head to one side.

"I don't think so," he said. "It is a bad, bad dream. She has it ever since her mamá died."

Her crying was losing its intensity, shuddering breaths replacing the sobs. After a minute she was quiet, just the occasional judder as she slipped back into a deeper sleep. I wanted to go to her, rub her back, smooth her forehead, like my mum had done for me after a nightmare, but Nico tugged gently at my hand and I let him lead me away. We closed the door with a click so quiet it would not disturb her dreams.

I realised, after that night, there was so much I had to learn to be a good mum. Things that if I'd been there from the start, I would have just known, instinctively. But becoming mum to a five-year-old is being thrown in from quite a height.

There were some things that were quite fun to find out as we went. Like the fact that when Midge laughed really hard, she snorted. Which only made her laugh harder, and so it went on. That was a good day, when we were tickling each other with grasses, under the chin, in the ear, lying on a blanket in the garden with Roo.

Or little things like what her favourite colour was. She was very particular about this answer, leading me by the hand to a foxglove in the border of the garden to show me the exact shade of purply-pink that she preferred.

There were other things that I felt I should know which were easily fixed. Her shoe size, found on the sole of her sandals. What age T-shirts she wore, on the label at the neck. How she liked to wear her hair – plaits or bunches; the answer changed daily depending on her mood. And every snippet I would memorise, add it to my Midge file, building her up for ever more.

Some knowledge is vital, though. Some things a mother *needs* to know.

I took her to the doctors for a sore throat and they asked me if she was allergic to penicillin. I stammered something about checking her records, mortified.

"It's important to know," the doctor said, as he held down Midge's tongue with a wooden stick to inspect her throat. "Allergies can be fatal. Especially these days. You hear so much about food allergies and people reacting to packaged sandwiches."

I felt like saying, "I know that, fuckwit." But all the same, when I got home I made it a point to hide the peanut butter until I'd had a chance to ask Nico. He laughed softly and put it back on the shelf.

"No allergies," he said. "Don't you think I would have told you?"

He had a point, I suppose; he was her dad after all. "She's even okay with bees, but my head looks like a beach ball in five minutes if I get stunk."

I laughed. "Stung," I corrected him gently, loving his mistake.

I wanted to know everything at once. I drank it all in. Her best friend at school (Tabitha). Her favourite TV programme (*Hey Duggee*). Most delicious dinner (spaghetti with cheese). Drink of choice (pineapple juice). Most loved animal (Roo, a million times Roo.) These were all the basics. I wanted more.

I tried different caresses to see which one made her smile or purr. Was it when I stroked her hair back from her forehead? Or when I rubbed the skin between her shoulders? Or tickled her gently on the inside of her forearm, wrist to elbow? She didn't seem to be very discerning, making little kitten noises to everything, revelling in the attention. She loved it all.

I watched her silently as she said her prayers at night, kneeling by the bed with Nico. I was quite happy for them to have their religion and they didn't seem to mind the lack of mine. Since you died, I knew I could never step foot in a church again, only managed it for your funeral for the sake of appearances. But watching her face as she prayed was the nearest thing I've ever come to believing in God.

I made her afternoon snacks that looked like faces. Carrots for mouths, hummus blobs for noses, cucumber circles for eyes, just to make her smile. I read her book after book at night, prolonging the bedtime routine, until Nico came in and yanked me out and she waved sleepy from the pillow. I roused her in the morning with butterfly kisses, using just my eyelashes on her cheeks, and she woke giggling with pleasure.

I wanted to know everything about her and be everything to her. Every day I fell deeper in love. It seemed all my life there had been a Midge-shaped hole in my heart. And now it was full. Of flesh, blood, heart and soul. She was the girl I'd always dreamed of. And if anyone hurt her, I'd cheese-grate their fingers.

It was a Tuesday, the day Nico finally told me his secret. Why he was withdrawing. Why the silences between us sat longer.

We'd agreed to meet after his shift in Gostrey Meadows for a picnic. Ginny was coming to join us after she'd checked the farm shop for stock. Honey products were still her best seller and she'd ventured a new range of hand balms and lip salves alongside her candles and body butters, which she wanted to monitor.

"I've gone all la-di-da," she'd said down the phone, "scented them with ginger and mint! Let's see how the posh fuckers like them!"

Midge and I had got there earlier in the afternoon and set up on a blanket next to the stream, in the dappled shade of an old oak. It was lucky we had, as families flowed in during the afternoon, all with the same idea, and had to bake in the open, on the browning grass. The water in the stream was icy-clear and foot-numbing as we paddled in the shallows and used coloured nets on sticks to chase minnows. We ate olives from the pot and threw peanuts into each other's mouths. Played Poohsticks off the bridge and high-fived each other, whoever won. I taught her how to play old maid and we sat facing each other, poker-faced and cross-legged as we tried to pass each other the unwanted card. Everything was fun. She recognised a few friends from school and Jen waved at me from across the park. It was starting to feel like

I was a part of something. I couldn't wait for Nico to get there, to be part of it too. I slathered Midge in suncream and she ran back to the stream to fish with her friends, leaving me alone in the happy noises all around me.

They appeared at the entrance gate together, Nico and Ginny, deep in conversation. I waved to them as they crossed the meadows and when Nico saw me he strode ahead, breaking away, as though he were keen to get to me. He arrived at the blanket a moment ahead of Ginny and threw himself down. Something about the set of his face told me this wasn't a good day. I felt like sighing.

"Good job you got the shade, I'm melting," said Ginny, fanning her face with her hands. She was indeed rather on the red side.

I turned to kiss Nico a welcome but his lips were tight against mine.

"You okay?" I asked and he pursed his lips and did a little tilt of his head, which I knew by now meant things could be better. Work again, probably. Who knew? It was like getting blood out of a stone.

"How's sales?" I turned to Ginny, trying to give him a little space to just sit and enjoy the sunshine, adjust his mood.

"Better than ever," Ginny said, "ten lip salves and four body butters – in ONE DAY. I might even make enough to buy a new hutch this season if this carries on. Or at least get a bit of straw in for the winter."

I wondered whether it would also put some food in her kitchen, or secondary glazing on the farmhouse windows. Probably not.

"Where's Magda?" Nico cut in and I pointed her out down by the river. She was up to her knees, net in the water.

The chimes of an ice cream van rang across the park and the children in the river all stopped instantaneously and looked for it. I laughed as they all waded and splashed and clambered out of the river to find their parents and beg.

I rummaged in the picnic bag and found my purse in readiness, flicking it open to check I had change. I'd been to the cashpoint earlier in the day to get money for the painter and decorator and someone had come to stand behind me as I waited for the machine to discharge my money. I hated that, always made me feel like they were watching how much I was taking out, or as if they might hit me over the head and rob me; so when the notes started to poke their faces out of the slot, I'd grabbed them and stuffed them roughly inside my purse. Now, as I opened my purse, the thick fold of twenties fell out on to my lap. I was mortified.

"For God's sake, Kat," Nico hissed, horrified. His eyes glinted in the sun. I grabbed the bundle of money, and saw Ginny's eyes slide away, looking at something on the other side of the park. Nico gripped my elbow and pulled me to my knees. It was not comfortable or helpful.

"I'll come with you," he said, glaring at me. Magdalena saw our movement as a good sign and diverted straight to the ice cream van, running ahead. We were about halfway across the park before he spoke again.

"You're always flashing your money." The words came out between clenched jaws and my mouth dropped open at his tone – and the unfairness of the accusation. "You're so stupid."

"It just fell out, Nico," I said, taken aback.

"It's not just now," he said, glaring, "there's always money on the sideboard."

The only money on the sideboard was a coin bag for Midge; she'd been collecting money for a sponsored silence at school. I tried to tell him but he wasn't listening.

"Bank letters lying about, account information…" he ground out. I had to concede that was true. I wasn't any good at filing my statements.

"Such big numbers, I've never even seen as much before." He was storming ahead. "You don't know who's looking!" He raised both hands in the air, exasperated. I recalled the slide of Ginny's eyes. Embarrassment hit me as I thought about how little she had.

"You don't think how it makes people feel." He banged his fist on his own chest and lengthened his stride, getting away from me. A woman walking towards us looked at him in alarm and then scurried past.

"It just causes trouble," he said over his shoulder.

What was he talking about? Okay, so I wasn't the best at being careful with bank statements, but I'd never had to be.

I tripped forward a few steps, catching him up, laying a hand on his forearm, but he threw it off. A flush of heat hit my neck. People were watching.

"Nico," I said, part shocked and part pleading. "What's the matter?"

He turned to me and I could see the battle on his face. He was angry, really angry, but, maybe not all about me. He took a deep breath and blew it out.

"What is it?" I said quietly and he finally made eye contact, face taut.

"I got suspended," he said. "From work."

Ginny thought it was hilarious when I told her the details the next day, laughing out loud as she mucked out the goat pen. Only one of the goats was left now as the other two had been rehomed. The animal watched me with his weird eyes, marble-like, protruding from the sides of his head.

When I got to the part about the family making a complaint about Nico's conduct at the home towards a resident, a Mrs Dennison, Ginny snorted so loud that the goat jumped.

"As if he'd mistreat an old woman," she said.

"He's saying Nico's trying to influence their mum," I said, leaning on the fence, glad to be on the outside. I wasn't keen on the goats. You'd have hated them. They stank.

"Who is?" Ginny asked, trying to keep up.

"Mrs Dennison's son. He's saying it's been going on for months. That Nico just keeps chipping away at her."

Ginny shovelled shit with gusto, shaking her head. "But chipping away at her for what?"

"To write her will," I said.

She forked the last bit of muck out and started throwing new, clean straw around. The goat immediately started eating it.

"They're accusing him of will-chasing," I said, helping her to shut the gate. The goat promptly released a pile of steaming poo on the fresh straw and then bleated at us. Ginny laughed.

"Mad old fucker," she said affectionately and scratched his head. We made our way towards the house.

"So he's suspended, pending investigation. But they're so short-staffed down there most of the time that it could take weeks to sort out a date."

"You know it's all lies, Kat. I don't know why you're worrying."

"Because it's horrible for him to have it hanging over his head."

It was true. Nico had dark shadows under his eyes and walked so quietly I hardly heard him when he entered the room. He'd lost his bounce, his chat. It was like the fire had gone out of him, and I didn't know how to bring it back.

"They're saying he gives her special attention."

"Ooo-errr," pantomimed Ginny with a pelvic thrust, until I had to laugh.

"No, so that she'll put him in her will."

"What does he say about it?"

"He says he did encourage her to make a will, but so that she is happy with where her money goes. One of her sons comes to visit all the time. The other hasn't been for years. She just wants to make sure it's the son who visits that gets the money."

"But he's the one making the complaint?" Ginny shook her head. "Talk about shooting yourself in the foot." She laughed again and put the kettle on the Aga.

"I just want it sorted," I said, thinking of Nico's drawn face. I would have done anything to put a smile on it. I wanted my happy family back.

"It's all bollocks, anyway. Let's face it, why would Nico need to chase a will? He's got you!" She shrugged her shoulders like it was obvious. "Come to think of it, maybe that's what I need – a sugar daddy!" She suddenly checked her watch.

"Talking of which – time for my next dose." She lifted a small paper sachet out of a medical box and emptied it onto her tongue.

"What's the hell is that?" I said.

"Sugar. Or a new chemical version of it anyway. I have to dose myself on the hour and then take my pulse and blood pressure and note it down."

She flipped open the old laptop on the wooden kitchen table and it buzzed into life. Rolling up her sleeve, she slipped it into a blood pressure monitor, which had been thrown over the back of the chair, and pumped the valve to inflate it.

"Are you ill?" I said, sitting down next to her.

She punched in some numbers and shook her head. "Clinical trials," she said with a grin. "I'm giving my body to medical science – well, to any trials that pay well, that is."

"Is that safe?" I said, shocked.

"Hasn't done me any harm so far." She shrugged. "Apart from a bit of a rash." She showed me her wrists, scabby with eczema.

I finished making the tea while she took her pulse and entered her data. Looking at the state of the milk, I'd decided black tea might be best. Ginny pressed send and closed the page as I put her cup down in front of her. Her screen saver appeared, a beach scene worthy of a picture postcard. It was then that I realised exactly what I could do to put a smile on Nico's face. A holiday. A honeymoon, in fact.

"Mind if I borrow that?" I asked and slid the computer towards me.

It was so nice to have a secret – a good one – that I didn't tell Nico about the holiday immediately. I hugged it to me in anticipation. I wanted to wait for the brochure to come in the post so we could look at the pictures together when I told him. I could just imagine his face.

In the meantime I put some other things in place to make life easier.

He was cooking when I got home. He cooked every night. It had become one of our things. Funny how quickly these little routines take root, become a way of life. You'd never cooked for me, always ordering takeaways, or at the most heating up a ready meal. "Ping cuisine," you used to say as you popped it in the microwave. But Nico cooked, properly cooked. Chopped a rainbow of vegetables, softened meat with hammers, seasoned and marinated so my mouth watered as I walked in the front door. If I tried to help, he'd pour me a glass of wine and take it to the table, sitting me near enough to talk to him over the sizzle and spit of the hob.

That night was no different. He seemed happier when he cooked. He had purpose.

"Steaks," he promised as I walked into the kitchen and took the wine he offered. Red, Spanish. Another one of our things.

Midge skipped through to show me a picture she'd drawn, a man, a woman, and a child in between them. A dog that was as big as the child. A sun with beams that almost touched their heads. A happy picture.

"That's you," she said, pointing – thankfully – at the one wearing a skirt.

"Looks just like me," I said, pulling her close.

"And that's Dad," she said. "And Roo."

"I can tell by the ears," I said.

"And that's Mamá," she said, pointing at a star in the sky, right next to the sun. I hadn't noticed it at first. I turned to her to read her face, but it was open and happy.

"That's lovely," I said. "Always watching over you." I put a hand to her head, stroked her hair just the once.

"Keeping me safe," she said. The theme tune to *Hey Duggee* sounded in the other room and her eyes widened in excitement. She was gone without another word.

"You're so good with her," Nico said and raised his glass to me. I sipped my wine, smiled to hear her singing along next door.

"Any news on the investigation date?" I asked but Nico shook his head. He was grinding black pepper into the red meat of the steaks, rubbing it in with his thumbs.

There was a salad bowl already prepared on the table, red tomatoes glistening in oil. Once the steaks were in the pan, I took the envelope out of my handbag and passed it to him. It was already open; I'd checked it was all in order when I picked it up.

He pulled out a bank card for my account in his name. He stared at it as if he'd never seen a debit card before, turned it over in his hands.

"Makes sense," I said. "We don't know how long you might not be working for."

"I have a bank account," he said, frowning.

"This is a joint account," I said. "What's mine is yours and all that."

"I didn't ask for this," he said, pushing the card back towards me. I didn't take it, so he put it on the worktop and turned back to the steaks, a red flush on his neck.

I didn't know what to say, and for a moment the meat spat into the silence.

"A man should be able to look after his family," he said eventually without looking at me, and my chest hurt for him and his pride.

"And sometimes a woman should be able to take care of her family too," I said, gently, and put my arms round him from behind.

He was tense until I squeezed and then he relaxed back against me.

"Okay?" I asked. He breathed out slowly. I didn't know if it was acceptance or relief.

"Okay," he said.

The solicitor also seemed a bit hesitant about my request and asked me three times if I was sure. I told him yes: that I was of sound mind and it was my money to do what I wanted with. Well, that's not quite true, I suppose; it's your money. Or was. But it's mine now and if I wanted to give it to Ginny's animal sanctuary then nobody could stop me. Not that I was going to do anything as stupid as that.

The solicitor had long white eyebrows that pointed waywardly upwards and gave him the look of an eagle as he peered across the desk at me. Quite unnerving really. He was obviously assessing whether or not I was mad, but I was used to people from Park Prewett looking at me like that and I faced him down with a calm smile. Cheeky fucker. I was as sane as the next person.

He twitched his nose as he reread the papers, pen poised for signature, but hovering.

"You've thought this through?" he said.

"Thoroughly," I answered. In truth I'd been thinking about nothing else for days.

It was Nico's predicament at the home that had brought it to the front of my mind. I kept thinking about old Mrs Dennison wanting to do right by her family and Nico wanting to help make sure her money went to the right person. Well, so did I want my estate to end up in the right place. The right hands.

I couldn't help but think of you as part of the equation. When we'd made this will, and signed it, we didn't really even believe one of us would die. We were too young and carefree to think it would ever happen. We left the solicitor's office and went out to eat spaghetti in the restaurant with red-and-white check tablecloths. That's how little it meant to us. But it did happen. You died.

So, now I'm making changes. But I think you'd approve, wouldn't you? You'd be happy that I was happy? That's what I'm telling myself anyway. I sniffed and the solicitor looked at me over his half-moon glasses.

"Everything all right, Mrs..." He consulted his notes. "Menendez?" He might as well have been calling me Mrs Shithead, by the look on his face.

"Fine, thank you," I said with a smile that meant, just bloody hurry up.

"So," he said, shaking the papers in front of him. "If you'll just sign here." He handed me the pen and indicated a dotted line. "And here," he went on, flicking forward a page or two. "And, finally, here." He turned to the back page. I signed. My new signature felt strange on the paper.

"And as your witness," he said and signed next to mine.

It was done. He closed the file with a clap.

A pang hit me. A memory of you signing with a flourish, floppy-haired, carefree, happy that all your family money would stay in the family.

Well, I'm just doing the same. I'm just making sure it's going to stay in the family. My new family, that is.

When I told Nico later that I'd changed the will and Midge would never face the insecurity that he worried about, I swear to God he physically had tears in his eyes. And, at that moment I really believed, without a shadow of a doubt, that I had done the right thing.

Who would ever have thought a rubber-duck race would be one of the highlights of my summer? But there we were, back at Gostrey Meadows, Midge almost beside herself with excitement. It's funny, how much I was enjoying these local events, which would have been a last resort in our past lives. We'd always choose bar, restaurant, shops, theatre. Now, sunshine and parks were my daily pleasures, as long as Midge was there.

A loudspeaker crackled into life as we picked our way through the patchwork of picnic blankets to find a space to claim as our own. A voice welcomed everyone to "the event of the summer" and there was a little cheer and some laughter. Nico started unpacking the cool bags he'd filled with food and drink, a bottle of red, tubs of frittata and tuna salad. Midge hopped from foot to foot, trying to see what was going on by the river. The duck stall was mobbed, people waiting three deep to claim their duck and make a note of its number.

"Come on!" she urged.

"Don't worry, they're not going to run out," I said, rolling my eyes at Nico.

"You go with her, I'll get set up here." He was happier than I'd seen him in ages, surrounded by food and bathed in sunshine. Maybe it was the bank card. Maybe it was the knowledge of the will. But he was happier and more secure than he had been in days, even agreeing with me that "no news is good news" about his work hearing. I left him opening a bottle of wine and took Midge's hand.

"I want to get number 377," she was saying, "it's my new lucky number."

Jen and Sal were queueing too and waved me in, tucking me alongside them in the crowd. Midge wriggled through adult legs to stand with Seb and Nate at the front, eagerly pointing at the different colour ducks.

"Every year it's the same," Jen was saying, "Why they don't do two or three duck stalls I just don't know."

"I've never won anyway!" said Sal, fanning her face with a paper programme. "It's more for the day out than the race. I think most of the class is here."

"It's my first time," I said, "so I'm hoping for some beginner's luck."

"You never know, eh!" Jen winked.

"Bit of advice for you newbies though, steer clear of the burger van. Last year half the school were ill on the Monday. Me included," said Sal, mock-vomiting.

"And the coconut shy is rigged, so don't waste your money. Even if you hit one, it never falls off," Jen added.

"The donkey rides are good, though," Sal said, scanning the field.

"They're not here this year," Jen pointed out, "not since what happened last year."

A look passed between them. I took the bait.

"Was there an accident?"

"The opposite actually, it was safe as houses. More of an *incident*," Jen said, jumping at the opportunity to tell me everything. "The rides were really well managed, the children were loving it. It was just five of the old donkeys from Sayers Farm.

He brings them out for fetes and fairs, and one of them even goes to the church for the nativity. They're gorgeous. Anyway, the kids were being good. Only under tens were allowed to ride, you know, so they're not too heavy on the donkeys' backs."

"Mind you, you can get some pretty heavy nine-year-olds these days. Think of Nell Onslow," Sal picked up the story and Jen acknowledged her with a quick nod, keen to carry on.

"Anyway, all of a sudden, there's this madwoman lying down on the ground in the way."

I don't know if you've heard of her, she runs the animal sanctuary at Hollow Farm," Sal chipped in.

"Literally lying down in front of the animals, shouting about animal cruelty…"

Oh God, I didn't know where to put myself. I could absolutely see Ginny doing it too.

"She made it impossible for anyone else to have a go. Spouting on about spinal damage and depressed animals." Jen was loving this story. "Nate was actually riding the donkey she lay down in front of, so we got a ringside view!"

"Right bloody nutter, she is," Sal added.

"Apparently she once attacked someone in town for wearing fur."

"Wouldn't surprise me in the slightest…"

I was cringing for Ginny, but not sure what to do. I didn't want to lose my two new friends, but I had to stand up for Ginny after everything she'd done for me.

"I've met her, more than a few times actually," I started. "She's always been really nice to me."

Both of them shut up abruptly.

"She's kind of my neighbour – I help out at the sanctuary too."

They glanced at each other quickly before catching themselves and laughing it off.

"Well, I wouldn't wear fur around her if I were you!"

"Or suggest a donkey ride."

They both laughed, not bothered at all, happy to be happy, and I blew out my relief.

"Ladies," the guy behind the stall said, "what numbers can I get you?"

Midge was there first, jumping up and down.

"377," she said, "377."

Soon, I had a plastic tumbler of red wine in my hand and the sun on my back. Nico and I stood in the river, downstream of the winning ribbon stretched over the water, bank to bank. Parents clustered around us, drinking, chatting, trousers rolled up, bare feet on the gravelly bottom. Middle England at its best. You would have pissed yourself laughing at the thought of it. Not a cocktail in sight, just lots of farmer types and yummy mummies. But I was amazingly happy there with my husband and daughter. Everyone was smiling and it felt like a good place to be. The children squealed and splashed and jumped in and out. In that stretch the river was only knee-high at its deepest, which felt safe enough for the parents and exciting enough for the kids.

The loudhailer was keeping up a ramble of announcements, raffle ticket sales, rotary club notices, information about the upcoming carnival. The announcer liked hearing his own voice, by the sounds of it.

I'd had my drink topped up twice by the time all the ducks were actually loaded into the river and sat as a bobbing mass under a net at the starting line. People lined the bridge and strained to see if they could spot their own numbers.

The countdown worked the children up into a frenzy of excitement and by the time the whistle blew and the net was lifted, the screams were deafening.

It was pretty impossible to see the numbers on the ducks, but I knew Midge's 377 was purple, so shaded my eyes to better see.

"And they're off!" The pitch of the announcer's voice had risen. "Who will make it round the first bend?"

Already some ducks had nosed their way into the plants on the bank. They bobbed there gently without moving, mostly yellow ones, but a spattering of blue and red ones too.

"...Who will make it down the rapids...?"

The so-called "rapids" were a very shallow stretch where some of the larger stones broke the surface, and the water bubbled crystal clear. Several ducks hit stones and turned upside down, tails in the air. I could see Midge jumping up and down, hands clenched into tiny balls.

"Into the last stretch – the deep waters of doom..." That guy was really making the most of his part. Maybe he didn't get out much.

Hundreds of coloured ducks bobbed towards me, most as a mass, only a few swimming on their own. A sudden current on the left of the river pushed a handful forward, single file, towards the finish line. None of the ducks in front were purple but Midge didn't seem to care; she was holding hands with another girl and running backwards and forwards in the water.

Nico was shouting beside me, a mix of English and Spanish so I didn't know what he was saying half the time, but he was grinning and punching the air. He looked happy, relaxed and, quite frankly, fucking gorgeous. My husband.

The first duck won by a beak and was plucked out of the water by an official.

"Number 83," he said and showed it to the crowd, who cheered. Midge turned round and shrugged at us, not bothered in the slightest, then ran out of the water to play with her friend on the bank.

Nico slung his arm round my shoulders and tapped beakers with me. The sparks in his eyes were very yellow that day, and his smile lit them up.

"Nico," someone said, behind us.

Nico flinched and turned his head, dropping his arm off my shoulder.

"Nico!" someone said again. A man, walking towards us from the bank a few feet away. "It *is* you."

He was maybe a year or two younger than Nico, blonder, sandy-haired, good-looking. He took a step into the water towards us, put out both arms to embrace Nico, who was stiff, taken aback and awkward with a drink in his hand. As he let him go, Nico breathed out slowly; I heard it.

"I can't believe it. It's been so long." He slapped Nico's shoulder. "Great race, eh?" His eyes danced up the river while Nico scanned the bank around us before facing him again. He was obviously feeling caught out.

"Not going to introduce me?" the man said, nodding towards me.

Nico lifted his chin but said nothing, and I rolled my eyes, embarrassed. The wine must have kicked in. He must have forgotten the guy's name, that's why he wasn't introducing me. I stuck my hand out to ease the situation.

"Hi, I'm Kat," I said. "Nico's wife."

The man looked at me and then smiled back at Nico before shaking my hand. His grip was hot and dry and my own palm felt damp in his clasp.

"Matteo," he said to me; and then to Nico, "Everything changes, eh, my friend?" Nico licked his lips but said nothing. I felt the need to say something, it was so awkward.

"Do you live locally?" I asked.

"No. We're on holiday. Such a lovely area. Do *you* live here?" he said directly to me and I opened my mouth to reply, but Nico caught my other hand and tugged me to him.

"No," he said. "We don't." It was the first time he'd spoken and his voice was lower than normal. I saw his glance flick to the bank to where Midge was playing tag.

"Magdalena!" Matteo said, following his gaze "She's grown so big! She was just a toddler last time I saw her. When you and Elena came to Joe's party."

I felt a little stab at the thought of Nico with Elena, dancing, carrying their baby around. But at the same time, a prick of interest at hearing about Midge when she was little, and curiosity about their old life. I still knew so little about it all.

"We were all so sorry about what happened, you know," Matteo said. "And then, when you left, we lost you all." He looked genuinely sad for a second before a big grin split his face. "And now we've found you again. Wait till Maria hears." He scanned the bank, looking towards the bandstand.

"Actually, we're just leaving," Nico said, to my surprise, and started moving out of the water, pulling me with him. "Sorry, we must go."

"But Maria will be…" he said. "Won't you—"

"Another time, maybe," Nico said with a shrug.

Matteo stepped forward and caught his arm as we passed. "They were good times, eh Nico? The boat parties, the sun. I'll be sure to let everyone know at home that I've seen you."

Nico switched into Spanish to say goodbye. The man smiled in return. The whole thing was uncomfortable, to tell the truth. Probably Nico felt wrong-footed about forgetting the guy's name in the first place. I looked over my shoulder as I climbed up the bank, and Matteo waved, once, directly at me. I smiled tentatively and lifted my hand in return.

Nico's silence was telling me it was not the time for questions. I also felt like I'd done something wrong, but had no idea what.

"Magdalena," he called. "Here, now."

Midge pouted but came, disappointed to be leaving so soon. He held her hand tight and she made a little noise, trotting along beside him to keep up. I thought she looked so cute, I wondered why he hadn't wanted to introduce her.

"Nico," I said, completely bewildered, "didn't you want to stay and catch up?"

"Another time," he said. "Let's just go home."

He didn't look back.

I didn't really feel like I could say no when Ginny asked me to run the sanctuary. Especially as she said it was just for a couple of days as she had to go to the hospital. Who could say no to that? I'd done the feeding and cleaning routine with her so many times that I knew it inside out, and I knew Midge would like to come and help too. I nodded and looked at her over my tea.

"Are you okay, Ginny?"

She frowned and then laughed. "Me? I'm as fit as the butcher's dog," she said. "It's another medical trial." She shrugged. I nearly spat my tea out.

"Don't get your knickers in a knot." She rolled her eyes. "I knew you'd react like that."

"You obviously know me too well," I conceded. "What's the trial for?"

"Menopause and how it affects the libido," she said with a snort. "Although Terry from Tinder can tell you there's nothing wrong with mine!" She flashed her phone screen at me and there was Terry, well, *part* of him anyway. A very intimate part. I struggled to swallow my tea before I burst out laughing.

"You can't be showing that around!" I said.

"Why not? He's obviously very proud of it." She looked at it, approvingly. "And rightly so." She flipped her phone shut with a grin.

"So what will they do to you – for the trial?" I asked.

"Truthfully? Two days lying in a bed and getting paid for it, I don't care what they do to me," she said. It was very obvious she hadn't read the information.

"Is it dangerous?"

"Maybe a few new drugs?" she said. "But I've had my fair share of those in the past."

"So you're not worried? It's all above board?"

"The rate they're paying, I'm not worried at all. Might pay the hay bill for another month."

My eyebrows rose but I didn't say anything. Better not to. I rummaged in my pocket for my phone and hit the Facebook symbol, wanting to change the subject.

"What you doing?" she said. "Looking to sign up yourself?"

"Very funny."

I scrolled to the New Horizons page to see if there were any new notifications.

"Surely you should get kicked out of that group now?" she said, looking over my shoulder. "Now that you're all happy and married again."

I laughed. "They're a nice bunch," I said. "Some of them still need a bit of support. A coffee now and then…" I scrolled. "Sometimes just a chat on the phone."

"Saint Kat to the rescue." The sarcastic tone caught me off guard but when I glanced up, she was all smiles.

"Not really," I said. "But if it helps."

I was just about to flick Facebook off when I saw there was a memory to view in my notifications. I loved the old memories they threw up, photos I'd posted long ago. I clicked on it and there you and I both were, four years before, when my face was whole. Before the hysterectomy, before the baby, before Park Prewett. We were in St Lucia and I had freckles that you kissed at night. Your hair had sand in it, and your teeth were white in your face. Our grins stretched our cheeks. It took my breath away and my eyes got hot, wet. God, so much had changed. Everything was so simple then. It was like looking at a photograph of someone else.

I breathed deep and it shuddered on the way out. There was no going back. I couldn't change anything. And I wouldn't anyway, would I? I had Midge and Nico now. This was a different life. It was what I'd always wanted. That little hand in mine. The overpowering love.

I let myself study the photo for just a few more seconds before clicking back to the home screen. It was then that I noticed the red dot that indicated a friend request. I only had a small group of friends on Facebook. Let's face it, I'd lost a lot of people along the way. Most of the people on there now were from New Horizons, and a few of Midge's school mums. There was also a handful of random names from my primary school, which was weird because we weren't even friends then, so why they wanted to know what I did on any given Tuesday was a mystery. I tapped on the request and waited for the image to load.

The square box loaded slowly, from the top down. Rather than being a photograph of someone's face, it was a sunset and a beach. Standard holiday shot. No clue as to the identity. It was only when the image finished downloading that the name appeared underneath it.

Matteo Alvarez has sent you a friend request.

The only Matteo I knew was Nico's friend from the duck race. He must have searched for my name when he got home.

How nice, I thought, and pressed accept.

I planned on showing Nico my new friend on Facebook as soon as I got home, but then Midge tripped coming down the stairs and landed awkwardly on her wrist, so I had to take her to A & E. With painkillers inside her, she was content to sit in the waiting room and play one-handed with the communal toys, which gave me loads of time to scroll through Matteo's photos and read his wall on his page. Call me nosy, but I don't think there's anything wrong with a bit of Facebook stalking. I knew exactly what I was looking for, and eventually, after three patients had been seen and a woman had vomited on the floor, I found it. A photograph of Nico.

It must have been about four years before, as Midge was just a babe in arms. Nico looked every inch the doting dad, holding her against his bare chest, on the beach. His other arm was slung around a bikini-clad Elena. I zoomed in on the photo as much as I could to see her face, beaming and suntanned. Make-up-free and gorgeous. They looked really happy. Midge wore a pink sun hat that almost obscured her face, but I could just see dimples. She was obviously smiling too. It made me feel a bit sick to look at it.

I scrolled to the next picture. Nico and Matteo stood side by side, raising stubby bottles of beer to the person taking the picture. It was a different occasion; they wore shorts and T-shirts and sunglasses, and stood on a patio. Nico leaned an arm on Matteo's shoulder. There were a few more shots with them together, either in the foreground with shoulders touching, or in a background group. They obviously had a big gang of friends.

I had a look at Matteo's friends list while Midge drank a carton of juice. Her colour had come back and I noticed she was using both hands again, to pick up toys and pass them to the other children. We probably could have left at that point, but I decided we should stay just to be on the safe side.

I knew I shouldn't, but I couldn't help myself. I trawled through the friends list looking for Nico. First of all I thought I must have missed him, so I put the friends in alphabetical order and scrolled again. But he wasn't there. Obviously he didn't have a Facebook profile any more. I'd never thought to ask, not being much of a prolific user myself. But it seems Elena had a profile. Or should I say *had* had a profile. Her name was where I thought I would find his. Elena Menendez. In brackets it said Elena Castello. Obviously her maiden name. I clicked, hating myself as I did it. I felt like I was reading someone's diary; forbidden, but irresistible.

I needn't have worried. The page had been put into memorial. I'd heard about this before. It meant the page was still there, but you couldn't post anything on it any more as the person had died. Her profile picture was a shot of her as a bride, full veil pushed back high over her head. Dark eyes, dark hair, in contrast to the white lace. Beautiful. I bit my lip and clicked off the site. Mum used to say, "curiosity killed the cat." Well, in this case, she was right.

Four hours later it was confirmed that nothing was broken, thank God, just a very bruised wrist, which seemed okay judging by the way Midge was waving goodbye to everyone in the waiting room. I was so relieved to get her home and tuck her into bed that the glass of wine Nico offered me when I came downstairs turned into two, or maybe three, and when we went upstairs I was blurry. But I did remember that I had something to tell him.

"I had a friend request today, on Facebook." I pushed the bedding off me. It was hot and the room was still, even with the windows open. "Your friend, the one we met at the park. Matteo."

Nico turned to me in bed, found my eyes in the half-light.

"You didn't accept?" he said and I knew without a shadow of doubt that I'd done the wrong thing.

"Of course not. I don't know him." I turned onto my normal sleeping side so I didn't have to lie to his face. He curved in behind me.

"Do you not like him then?" I asked, innocently.

"I don't know him very well," he said and I thought of the photographs on the Facebook page, the open faces, the beers and buddies. It didn't make sense. But then he continued, "And he knew me when I was with Elena."

All of a sudden it was more understandable. He put an arm round me and pulled me back against him. "I'm with you now," he said. "I want to move on."

It was easier to accept that. I understood how just a little white lie could be exchanged for a peaceful new life. What was wrong with that?

I turned to face him again and let our bodies change the subject.

Only it wasn't that easy to move on. Mum had once told me that one lie leads to another. Turns out she was right.

It was the next day, when I was doing the rounds at the sanctuary, that Messenger beeped on my phone. When I flicked up the screen and saw his name again, Matteo Alvarez, something fluttered in my chest like a trapped butterfly. I'd accepted his request, and I'd lied. Both bad.

I tapped the message, chewed my nail.

"Everyone in Nerja very interested to know Nico is well. Hope to be able to meet up again."

Harmless enough, surely? There were obviously other friends still interested in him and Midge. That was nice, wasn't it? Surely Nico'd like to know that? He must miss people, even if he did want to move on. But I couldn't let him know. Not now that I'd said I'd turned down the friend request… I'd trapped myself in my lie. Maybe I should just come clean when I got home. It might be better. One less secret between us.

Nico was home when I got there, cooking a feast. His fingers were garlicky and a bottle of wine was already decanted to breathe. Still seemingly loved up from the night before, he wrapped me in a bear hug so tight I could almost taste the lemony scent of his skin. I held on tight, putting off the moment I was dreading.

"Nice to be just us for a few days," he said, releasing me and kissing the top of my head. I realised he meant Ginny. She'd been popping over quite a lot – around teatime normally – and often stayed for a bite to eat with us. Maybe he wasn't so keen on having her round all the time. I should have thought of it earlier. Two's company and all that. We *were* still officially newly-weds. Maybe that was why he was in such a good mood. Having dropped Ginny at the hospital, he knew she wasn't going to turn up tonight. It was because he was in such a happy place that I made the decision there and then not to tell him about the Facebook request. Or the message. I just didn't want to spoil it, break the moment. Or that's what I told myself, anyway.

He was there at the stove and his eyes were soft and he smelled so good.

"Where's Midge?" I asked, suddenly conscious of the quiet.

"Sleepover play date at Sal's," he said with a grin. "She was more than a little excited."

When he smiled, I swear to God, the world smiled back. I'd seen it happen to people. He'd be chatting quite normally, passing the time of day at the park or commenting on the weather at the greengrocers, and then he'd smile at them and their own faces would light up in this wondrous way, like a reflection. His smile was infectious, and once they caught it, they couldn't stop it. He could brighten your day in an instant. Looking at him in my own kitchen – *our* own kitchen – I just wanted to enjoy the evening together. Enjoy my husband. So I kept my mouth shut.

He passed me a glass of red and I drank a long, slow mouthful. By the time we'd feasted on garlic chicken thighs and sucked the bones for the juices, we'd opened another bottle and lit some candles. Roo was spark out at my feet, and the jasmine scent drifted through from the garden on the evening air. The world was good.

Nico was on top form, telling me funny stories from his childhood. Dating disasters, trips to accident and emergency as a boy. There was so much that I didn't know about him. So much to learn. He got more Spanish the more he drank; I'd noticed it before. Slipping into Spanish phrasing and becoming more animated with his hands. He moved on to talk about places he'd been in Europe and we discovered we both had a yearning to go to Venice.

"Why have *you* never been?" He spread his hands wide.

"Just never got round to it," I said with a shrug, thinking of all the city breaks I did with you. Berlin, Rome, Seville, Copenhagen, Paris – regularly. "What about you?"

"Couldn't afford it." He laughed and I kicked myself, wishing I'd known this before I booked the trip for our honeymoon. But now felt like a good time to surprise him. I jumped up and plucked the tickets from their hiding place at the back of the drawer.

"Here," I started, "it's not Venice, but I thought the three of us could have a holiday together."

I slid the envelope across the table. He grinned in delight and picked it up, holding it close to his chest, unopened.

"You did this for me?" he asked and I nodded, suddenly shy. He leaned across the table and kissed me, once, twice, his mouth warm, soft, then sat back and opened the envelope.

The tickets inside fell onto the table – flights and a hotel reservation. He picked up the airline confirmation and read it, slowly, having had nearly a full bottle of red to himself. I took a deep breath and found myself holding it.

"Malaga?" he said, a tiny crease between his eyes. I grinned, unable to contain myself, and picked up the hotel reservations.

"And staying at the Marinas de Nerja. Your old part of town," I said.

"Nerja?" he repeated, shaking his head.

"All three of us," I said. "I know it's traditionally a honeymoon after a wedding, but this is a familymoon. We couldn't leave Midge out."

I'd lost him somewhere. He was staring at the tickets, not listening to me. When he looked up again, his eyes were wet.

"Nico, what is it?" I asked. He tried to shake his head but only succeeded in toppling the tears that were brimming, so they trailed down his cheek. My chair scraped as I pushed it back to get to him, put my arms round him. I couldn't bear it. My surprise was not going the way I'd planned.

"What is it?" I said again. "It's not meant to upset you. I thought you'd love it. A chance to go home, show Midge where she was born, visit some old friends." I thought of Matteo's message again, about people being interested in him.

He swiped at his eyes with both hands. When he finally got some words out they were thick with emotion and slurred with wine. "You don't understand," he muttered. "How could you know?"

"Know what?" I said.

"There is nothing there for me now. Nothing and nobody."

I was stunned. Seems I wasn't the only one who occasionally told a lie. He threw the tickets onto the table and put his face in his hands.

"I can never go back," he said. "Never."

I leaned close to his bent head, held him. "Why not, Nico?" I said.

"Too many memories," he whispered. "Too many ghosts."

I was hopeful that a night out would cheer things up a bit. I'd never had a plan backfire so spectacularly before. Nico's tears had been heartbreaking. His back was still shuddering even as we went to sleep. I could have kicked myself. I made a resolution that going forward I would talk to him about things rather than try to pull off big surprises. That way Nico and I could have spent the evening planning a romantic trip to Venice, rather than crying over the kitchen table.

The annual dinner and dance for the National New Horizons Club felt like it could be just what we needed. A swanky evening at the Grosvenor, dressed to the nines and ready to party. Several of our local group had bought tickets, and we were going to share a minibus into London.

"Wow," I spluttered when Nico came into the bedroom in a dinner suit. He looked bloody gorgeous and born to wear it.

He flicked his bow tie and winked. "I might say the same about you," he said, coming to stand behind me in the mirror. I'd had my hair done in town; it swept up at the sides and then cascaded down my back in curls. It was the first time I'd worn it off my face in a long time. My hand wandered to my cheek. It felt so bare.

He caught it between his own and kissed it. "Ready?" he said.

The ballroom was buzzing. The dinner was good, although I did think not as good as Nico's cooking. But then again, it was mass catering, whereas for me he was like a "private chef", I told him.

"With benefits." He grinned. Our whole table was on good form. The ten of us all from the Cheltenham branch of Coffin Club, everyone excited to be out, enjoying a more special occasion than the normal meet at the Sovereigns. Even Stephen was agreeable, although he was hogging the red wine over his side of the table. Nico had his arm round the back of my chair, his thumb occasionally stroking the back of my neck, as the waitressing staff cleared away.

"Thanks," I said to the girl as she took my plate, thinking how I used to hate waitressing. The feel of someone else's food squished under your fingers. The drips of gravy on your shoes. But it paid the bills. A million years ago, it felt like.

'I Gotta Feeling' by the Black Eyed Peas broke the moment as it boomed out of the speakers. Hordes of merry widows and widowers swarmed to the dance floor with whoops and hollers and Nico stood beside me, extending his hand.

That man could dance, believe me. His hips worked as well on the dance floor as they did in the bedroom. I couldn't help but feel proud to be his partner while other people exhibited varying degrees of dad-dancing around us.

It had been so long since I'd been anywhere. Even the minibus ride had been exciting as we drove deeper and deeper into London. I pointed out the lights of Harrods, marvelled at the windows of Harvey Nicks where a thousand brightly coloured windmills turned together in a manufactured wind. I craned my neck to see the names of restaurants that had changed since I was last in town, noticed my favourite shoe shop had closed. I used to know the city centre so well, every short-cut, every good hotel bar. It felt good to be back. With Nico.

I was spinning with excitement. The wine, the lights, the feel of my dress around my thighs as I moved. The man in front of me, smiling only for me. I put my arms in the air and my hair swished around my shoulders.

As the record ended, I fell laughing against Nico. He circled me with his arms, and we kissed, smiling as we did. Then again, longer.

"Get a room, you two!" someone next to us jeered and we laughed, got back to dancing.

It was later that the evening went sour. Flushed with wine and dancing, I made my way out to find the ladies. At the top of the stairs from the ballroom, I paused to take in the whole view. Leaning on the balustrade, I could see everything. The perfect patterning of the round tables, the white tablecloths. The strobe lights and laughter. The dance floor was busy and everyone left seated at the tables had congregated together, moving chairs around to fill gaps left by missing dancers. Nico was back at our table, talking to Kerry and a couple of others. His arm still rested on the back of my empty chair, saving the space for me. The other side of the table was empty. I was breathless with it all.

My heels tapped the high-gloss tiled floor of the long corridor. It was the first time I'd worn heels in I couldn't remember how long. A dress that I hadn't walked the dog in. Make-up and perfume and all-over lotions. I felt elegant, feminine. And thirsty.

I spotted a water fountain outside the cloakroom. A man, just moving away, wiped his mouth on the back of his hand

and I stepped in. I could still hear the faint beat of the music, a peal of laughter, as I dipped my head and pressed the button. The water was cold and delicious, icy cold, and I closed my eyes as I drank.

"Putting on a right show on the dance floor," someone said as they came out of the cloakroom behind me. "As if anyone wants to see that."

Without opening my eyes, I knew that voice. I'd recognise that pompous tone anywhere. Stephen. Someone grunted, in agreement but without comment. I kept my head bowed but stopped drinking. Whose dancing was he moaning about? Honestly, he could always find something to complain about.

"Bloody rubbing it in our faces," he said. "Just because they 'found their second chance at love'." I could almost hear him wagging his fingers in the air around the words, referencing the New Horizon's mission statement. Oh my God. He was talking about Nico and me.

"Shouldn't even be here really. Perhaps I ought to raise it with the administrators?"

Stuffy arsehole. I swallowed another gulp of water and prayed he didn't notice me.

"But I guess he's done well for himself. Bloody foreigner. Not only taking our jobs, taking our women as well."

I couldn't even swallow any more. How dare he talk about Nico like that?

"Lucky bugger, though, literally living the life of Riley. Drives around in her car. Moved into her house. Living off her money." His voice was almost directly behind me. "He could probably give up work tomorrow if he wanted. It's the easy life for him from now on. Not bad, eh?" He paused conspiratorially, then: "All he's got to do is put up with her face," he snorted, and was gone.

Back at the table I felt awkward as Nico slung his arm round me, conscious of Stephen on the other side, quaffing red wine.

"You let it down?" Nico said, indicating my hair, which now swung across my face. He picked up a handful and let it slip through his fingers. I tried not to pull away, cheeks burning. All I could see in my mind's eye was Elena's Facebook profile shot, the beautiful bride. All I could hear was Stephen's voice. I tasted a tang of sick.

"Can we go?" I said, to Nico's surprise.

"You okay?"

I fanned my face with my hands. "Just a bit headachy."

"Probably too much dancing on top of too much wine last night," he said with a smile. It was the first time we'd even mentioned the night before. How emotional and over the top it had been.

I nodded. "So can we? Go?"

"What about the minibus? It's not due till two." Nico checked his watch; it was just after midnight.

"We'll get a cab," I said, remembering you standing on the street after every night out, one hand in the air to hail us a ride home. Nico's eyes widened at the thought. It was a long journey, over an hour in a taxi. It would be expensive.

"More comfortable than the minibus," I said.

"And I get you all to myself," he said with a nod across at Stephen, who had a red-wine smile and glazed eyes.

I couldn't get out of there fast enough.

The taxi was air-conditioned and fast, the driver pleased with a good fare at the end of the night. The radio played low in the background and Nico dozed with his hand on my thigh. We sped through London streets, onto dual carriageways, into roads with less lighting and then through the black banks of the lanes. Every now and then my reflection in the window of the car stared back at me, zigzagged with stitches.

G inny was definitely thinner next time I saw her.
"Hospital food seems to agree with you," I said.

"Yuk," she said with a laugh. "No, I'm on a different type of diet. It's called 'get skinny in forty stressful days'."

Her kitchen counter was spattered in various animal mixtures, dog food and cat kibble, as well as some concoction for the hedgehogs and a dead mouse for the owl. I opened the biscuits I'd brought with me and tried not to cringe as she took one out with her cat-food fingers and crammed it straight into her mouth.

"I'll do the tea," I said, rinsing out the cups first and picking teabags out of the tin. It was one thing she never ran out of. I think she lived on caffeine. By the time the kettle had boiled, she'd wolfed down two-thirds of the biscuits and the animal feeds were all made up.

She swept some papers further along the counter to make room for her cuppa, pushing a load of red bills with teacup rings on them my way.

I sat tentatively on the front of the chair, avoiding a rather dodgy stain that looked like it might be something to do with the cat.

"All well in paradise?" Ginny asked, but didn't wait for an answer. Instead she grabbed a letter from the pile and waved it at me. "Can you believe this?"

I could see the council logo and enough of the wording to see it was a formal communication, which quoted a reference number and started with an indented; **Re: our prior communication**. My heart sank. She was in trouble again. She passed it to me with a choice of words that started in mother and ended in fucker. The letter ordered the immediate removal of the beehives, following numerous complaints from nearby residents.

"Seems my bees are a bit on the feisty side," she said. "I guess that's what you get if you have a territorial strain." She sniffed.

I read the letter through. "It gives you a date – they're coming to check you've got rid of them. Two weeks' time."

"They can come and check," she said with a grin, "they won't find them, but I'm not getting rid of them. They're making me so much honey, they're bringing in the cash."

"Ginny," I warned, looking at the letter again. "You can be fined. £2,000."

"Ha! They can try. But I haven't even got the money for the mortgage this month, so they'll have to join the queue." She saw my shock and waved it away. "Anyway, they won't find them. We'll move them into the back paddock, right next to the hedge."

I was glad that she'd moved away from the money, but noticed the "we" and inwardly my stomach tensed. I've never liked breaking rules, you know that. I couldn't even take the toiletries out of the posh hotels we used to stay in. Not even when they smelled like heaven.

"Bring over lover boy – it won't take long."

I shook my head, thinking about Nico's fear of anything that buzzed due to his allergy. And that was it. I don't know if it was the worry about doing something we weren't supposed to, or the casual way she chucked him into the conversation as though everything were okay, but all of a sudden I was doing noisy crying. The ugly type where snot comes out of everywhere at once.

"Jesus, woman, it's not that bad!" Ginny said with a jolt of shock. "They won't catch me. It will be okay."

I shook my head and tried to get a hold of myself, but didn't succeed. She moved over to me and pulled me into her hot-smelling front, where for a minute or so I really blubbed.

"So I'm thinking this isn't about the bees?" she said when I finally got a grip, and I managed a half-smile, half-hiccup.

"I feel like such an idiot," I said.

She passed my tea and I took a sip. I told her about the way we'd bumped into Matteo at the duck race and Nico had not even introduced me.

"It was embarrassing, Gin, like he couldn't get me out of there fast enough."

Ginny frowned, leaned on her elbows.

"And he doesn't want to go home to Spain – not ever – apparently. He says he's got no one left there when I know, *I know*, that's not true. There's Matteo and a whole gang of friends." She widened her eyes at me and I snapped, "Facebook," by way of explanation.

"I've seen photos of him, partying, at the beach, volleyball. Loads of them. But he doesn't want to introduce me to any of them. And her, Elena, wife *numero uno*, I've seen all I need to of her too." I shook my head to try to clear the memory of olive skin, the perfect cheeks, the veil.

"And do you remember," I said, hitting my stride, "the fuss he made about those photographs on the internet after our wedding? Said it was about Midge, and not having pictures

of little girls online, but I'm not so sure any more..."
Suddenly everything was starting to make sense. My chest
was hurting with the realisation as it grew.

"What are you going on about?"

"Stephen said all he had to do was put up with my face,"
I said and my eyes burned. "Maybe Nico's ashamed of me.
Of my face."

I lifted my chin and squared up to her, daring her to look
away. She didn't.

"Rubbish," she said.

"It all makes sense. It adds up."

"It adds up to a load of bollocks," she said.

"Face it," I said. "He doesn't want me to meet his friends,
have any photos of us, go to his home town. It's obvious."

"The only thing that's obvious is that you've got a screw
loose. Is it a full moon or something?" Ginny stood, scraping
her chair on the dirty floorboards, and pulled out a half-
drunk bottle of whisky from the cupboard. She slopped two
large measures into some misty-looking tumblers and pushed
one in front of me. "Sounds to me like you're having an
attack of the collywobbles."

I slugged back a large mouthful, which burned tongue to
stomach.

"You're jumping to conclusions all over the place," Ginny
said. "Maybe he doesn't like this guy as much as the guy likes
him? You know what it's like in a crowd of friends." She
sipped her own drink. "Maybe he just wants to move on.
Forget the past. He's with you now, in a new country, a new
life. Maybe he wants to stick with that."

I sniffed. It was very close to what Nico himself had said.

"Truthfully, do you talk about Sam to Nico? You don't seem to be running back to London every weekend to meet up with old friends, or revisit old haunts."

Just bringing you into the conversation gave it a different turn. She was right. I'd left London as soon as I could to get away from what had happened. To leave it behind. The visit last night had been the first time I'd been back.

"Have you introduced Nico to anyone from that part of your life?"

I blew out a breath and shook my head. No, I hadn't. But I had lost anyone I might have called a friend when I went mad, and I lost your friends when you died. There wasn't really anyone left.

"Well then. I don't think you can hold it against him if he wants to move on too." She topped the glasses up again, clinking hers against mine before downing it.

"And the photos, I don't blame him – you don't want a kiddie-fiddler looking at Midge, do you?"

"But Stephen—" I started and she banged her glass down a little too hard on the tabletop.

"Balls to Stephen," she said, making an explicit hand gesture. "He's a twat. Tried it on with me at the picnic and took offence when I told him I didn't normally have sex with people that wore pink trousers. He's probably just jealous you're both getting laid."

I snorted despite myself. "So you don't think…?" I said, pointing at my scar, which I knew would be very white against the flush of my face.

"Nope," she said. "I don't."

"He could do so much better," I said, wavering.

"Bollocks," she said again. "I see him all the time, romantic fucker that he is, tucking your hair behind your ear."

I blinked. She was right. He often did it, gentle fingers hooking my hair round my right ear, not letting me hide behind a curtain.

"Makes me want to vomit every time," Ginny said, pouring a third shot and raising it at me with a mischievous laugh.

I couldn't help but giggle and our glasses banged together between us.

"Actually, if it still bothers you so much, I could probably make you a cream that would help with that," she said, nodding at my cheek. She reached out and ran her thumb down my scar, top to bottom. I held my breath, thinking of the ridges and pulls under her fingers. "Beeswax is a great healer."

She held on to my chin, tilted my face left to right, considering.

"I could add some lavender, maybe, some vitamin E."

An unexpected lump rose in my throat and I blinked, twice, before answering. "I'd love that, Ginny. Thanks."

It was probably the sudden act of kindness that made me open my mouth without thinking. "I could pay your mortgage this month for you if it would help, to get you back on the straight and narrow."

As soon as the words were out, I pressed my mouth shut. It went against every piece of advice my mum had ever given me, but Ginny was the best friend I'd ever had and I had the ability to help her. I wanted to do it for her. I really did. Her lips fell slightly open as she stared at me.

"Really?" she asked quietly and I could hear how much it meant by the light quiver in her voice.

I nodded and squeezed her hand. "Tell me how much and I'll write you a cheque." It was as easy as that. I grinned, couldn't believe I'd said it. But it was the right thing to do. I knew that. She'd do the same for me if she could.

"Five thousand?" she said. "I actually owe a bit more than just one month." She closed her eyes as though making a wish. I heard the tiny rush of breath as I gasped, and tried to cover it with a clearing of my throat. It was more than I'd thought it would be.

But looking at her there, with her eyes screwed shut and her fingers crossed, I had the warmest feeling ever in my stomach as I said, "Sure."

Ginny threw her arms roughly around my neck and then the last of her drink down her throat, laughing, and I couldn't wipe the smile from my face.

"So, now that's both of us sorted," she said, wiping her mouth on the back of her hand. "When are we moving these bees?"

After Ginny's pep talk, I let myself be happy. And I was, amazingly so. We stopped going to New Horizons and just let the summer take on its own life. Our life. Some parts of this new life with my new family literally stopped me in my tracks. Made me check myself for a minute and think that you'd not recognise me now. The things that made me happy these days were so different to the things we used to enjoy.

When we first met, I was blown away by how easily you'd call a taxi. Never having to check your wallet first, just pick up the phone and speed-dial. It made me smile with the ease of it. Happy to be free of the droning danger of night buses or running for the last tube. Just a quick call and then a comfy back seat with your arm round me all the way home. Cabs were just the start of the easiness of life. The things that you took for granted that made my eyes widen and my cheeks hurt with smiling. The evenings out, the dinners, the opera, which I didn't understand a word of but which made me cry with the sheer emotion of it. The clubs, holding my hand, skipping the queue, always on the guest list. The holidays, to the sultry heat of Morocco, Dubai, Cape Town, or the icy freshness of Verbier and Helsinki. Places I'd never dreamed of seeing. Hot dogs on the street in New York. Oysters in Copenhagen. The sheer pleasure of life was in the decadence, the novelty – all affordable when you've got money.

But I never really got used to it. I know I've got the money; it's there like a safety net. A cushion to make life comfy. But I'm still careful. And it's the little things I'm enjoying. The things a child brings with them. Sometimes I don't have to spend a penny but my grin is wider than it ever was. You'd probably roll your eyes at the cheesiness of it.

I was thinking along those lines at the lido with Midge a few days later. I'd shown her how to make a daisy chain and watched her patient determination to make her own, chewing her lip in concentration. An hour later she was wearing one around her neck and had put a second one in my hair. It was the most priceless gift I'd ever received.

I was so pleased with it that I forgot to take it off as we left the lido. It was still there when we pulled into the Old Chiselford Nursing Home to collect Nico's things from his locker for him. He'd had a phone call asking him to clear it out – they needed the space for agency staff until after the investigation. I'd offered to do it for him on our way home as I knew he was embarrassed about going in until his name was cleared.

Midge was delighted with our detour. They loved her in the home and she knew it. The few times I'd been in to collect Nico, or for their summer fair, she'd gone chair to chair, delighting the residents with nursery rhymes or smiles. She wasn't fazed at all by wrinkly hands that wanted to hold hers, or smiles that had no teeth in them.

"Nice headdress!" Kieron said as he opened the front door to me. I laughed and touched it there, yellow and white in my hair. As I was explaining what I was there for, Midge threw herself at him for a hug. She then walked directly into the main lounge, where rows of residents sat in armchairs facing the booming television and a five o'clock quiz show. Some were quite frankly terrifying-looking. Some were asleep. Some moaned or whispered to themselves. But Midge went straight in. She certainly didn't lack confidence.

"Midge, stay here and I'll be back in five," I called after her, watching her skip over to a lady in a wheelchair, wearing a cardigan over her blouse despite it being about 103 degrees in there. Midge waved to let me know she'd heard and I turned to Kieron.

"How's Nico?" he asked immediately.

"Worried," I said. "Wanting all this to be over and done with so he can come back to work. You know how he loves working here."

Kieron nodded. "We think it's ridiculous," he said. "The team, I mean." He squeezed my forearm and moved towards the office block. "And the residents are missing him too. Beryl says he does her legs the best – he has to cream them every day" – I couldn't help but marvel at his tenderness, at the thought of him rubbing some old woman's legs – "and Mrs Dennison says nobody listens to her like Nico."

"Will she tell her side of the story at the investigation?" I said, following him towards the office.

He nodded at me over his shoulder. "We're hoping that's what's going to get him back. She can clear it up for everyone. It's just procedure really." He opened the door to the office, empty of people but with a walkie-talkie system on the wall noisily relaying messages from all around the home.

Kieron nudged the volume wheel on the side, turned it down a little. "This is Nico's." He pointed at the top locker. "Do you have his code?"

I nodded and tapped in Midge's birthday – day and month. It was the same code as for his mobile phone and his passwords online.

"Bag?" Kieron rummaged through the desk drawer and pulled out a Sainsbury's carrier, passing it over.

"Thanks, I should have bought one with me," I said, looking at the contents of the locker. I fitted Nico's watch around my wrist. It swung loose but it was safe. There were a few biro pens. A quarter-packet of Polos and a hand sanitiser gel. Finally a small bottle of aftershave, which explained how he always came home smelling good, no matter what he'd had to deal with that day.

I pushed the door shut. "All done," I said.

"It'll all be back in there soon," said Kieron, with another squeeze, this time to my shoulder. "Let's go see what Madam's up to."

Midge was leaning against another chair, playing pat-a-cake with a man dressed in a shirt and tie, with a neat V-neck jumper over the top. "That's Larry," said Kieron. "Never had a visitor as long as he's been here. Look at his face."

Larry was loving it. He was holding his hands up for her to pat, then clapping too late every time, which made her laugh in delight. Kieron and I paused in the doorway to watch, without telling her we were there.

"Ah, Kat," someone said and I turned to see Ellen, the team leader. "That's good timing – I've got post for Nico." She bustled off, holding her hand up to me to stay where I was.

Midge spotted us and waved, as happy as Larry, which made me grin. I must remember to tell Nico later, I thought.

Ellen reappeared and passed me a postcard. "Came a few days ago," she said. Her walkie-talkie buzzed and she rolled her eyes and waved goodbye over her shoulder as she went.

"Come on, Magdalena," said Kieron. "Say goodbye to Larry now." To my amazement, Larry put out his arms to Midge and she climbed in, pressed herself against him as though he were her long-lost grandad. He closed his milky eyes and held on.

"That will have made his day," Kieron said and I suddenly wanted to cry at the power of children. The way they could change your world. She skipped back to me and I couldn't help but touch her, run my hand over her hair and down her back. My girl. My gorgeous girl.

As I strapped Midge into her car seat, the heat of the day and the time at the lido suddenly kicked in and she yawned, long and loud. I got into the driving seat and took the chance to look properly at the postcard. It was a sunny beach scene, which could have been any of a thousand places. There were no identifiable landmarks, just a long stretch of sand at the edge of a town and a sea and sky that merged into blue.

Why was Nico getting post to the home? Perhaps he just hadn't updated people that he'd moved in with me? I knew he'd rented houses beforehand. Maybe it had been easier to get post sent to work. But who was sending him postcards?

I turned it over. It felt wrong, but only mildly so. After all, it wasn't like I was opening a letter, was it? A postcard could be read by everyone – even the postman as he walked up the drive.

The postmark was Nerja. That was the first thing I saw. His home town. Dated a few days ago, as Ellen had said.

But it still didn't tell me who had sent it. There was no name at the bottom. No "Love, Sally" or "See you soon, Grandma". There were only one word on the card, written in Spanish. A blue biro, curly letters.

I glanced at Midge in the back seat, nodding off, eyes drooping. Taking my phone from my handbag, I clicked to the internet and searched for a translation site. The list that came up wasn't exactly what I wanted and I narrowed my search: Spanish to English translation. When the screen refreshed itself, I picked the top one. Clicked onto the site.

I paused again. This felt worse, going to this amount of effort to read a postcard that wasn't mine. But again, it was a *postcard*. It was public. It wasn't as if I was reading his personal email or something.

I typed the Spanish word on the postcard into the site.

Llamame.

Then pressed enter.

I glanced at Midge in the rear-view mirror just as her eyes closed and she melted into sleep.

The internet only wavered for one moment before giving me the answer.

The translation was very clear. One word became two.

Call me.

And then a telephone number. A Spanish one.

Midge slept all the way home, head lolling gently against the back of the car seat, and I drove carefully along the narrow lanes, avoiding the potholes so as not to jolt her. It gave me time to think. I needed that.

So Nico had someone in Spain that he was still in touch with. Someone he still called on the telephone. Best-case scenario it was his dentist and he was overdue a check-up. Worst-case scenario? It was someone he didn't want me to know about.

I couldn't get my head around it. He'd been so clear about not wanting to go back to Nerja. What had he said? *There is nothing there for me now. Nothing and nobody.* Well, that was obviously not true.

A squirrel made a mad dash across the road and I slammed my foot on the brake. It made it safe across the tarmac, scaled a tree on the verge. I checked Midge. She was still sleeping, mouth slightly open. Taking a deep breath, I pulled forward again, gently.

And what about Matteo? Nico saying they weren't friends, when the photos on Matteo's Facebook page showed a very different story. They looked like typical man-friend shots, arms round shoulders, beers in the air. If he had lied about that friendship, what other friendship was he lying about?

Who else might be trying to contact him? Or maybe it *was* Matteo? Trying another method to reach him?

Why did he want to keep his past and his present so separate?

I realised I was just about to miss my turn and swung in without a thought of indicating. The road got narrower, grass showing green in the middle of the track. Oaks overhung, shading the way against the late, low afternoon sun. I slowed again as the patchy surface made the car bounce side to side, conscious of Midge's little neck. Slowing down helped my head, the tension in my back. I let my hands loosen on the steering wheel, stretched out my fingers.

Maybe it was as Ginny had said. Nico just wanted to move on. That's why he wasn't blending the two lives. It was that simple.

And even if it looked like there was someone who still held him between the two, maybe that was none of my business? Just because he'd got a postcard from someone saying "Call me", it didn't mean that he was necessarily going to call them, did it?

For example, if someone from our past life emailed me and said "Let's catch up, it's been too long", I wouldn't necessarily rush to reply. I couldn't think of anyone we used to know that I felt the need to speak to any more, or renew friendship with. It's easier to move on sometimes. Less painful to leave it all behind. It made sense.

Pulling into the drive, I let the engine idle and took the postcard from the glove compartment, read it once more and shook myself. So what? He got a postcard. It didn't mean anything. I slotted it into the Sainsbury's bag with his locker contents. It was his property.

As I turned the car off, Midge woke up as if by magic, a small trail of saliva running from the corner of her mouth.

She stretched and rubbed at it and by the time I opened her door, she was wide awake and clambered out like a puppy.

Nico was at the stove, as always. The smell of lemon in the air, prawns in a shallow bowl marinating on the worktop. He scooped Midge up, noisily kissing her hair, cheeks, neck, until she squealed and wriggled to be put down.

"How was the lido?" he asked her and she nodded a "good"; then she was off, calling Roo, into the garden. Nico turned to me, kissed my mouth, pulled me against him. He smelled delicious. He looked edible. My husband. He chose *me*. That's what I had to remember. He married *me*.

"Wow, you look good," he said and I thought he was referring to the daisy chain still in my hair, but then he skated a thumb down my cheek. "Your skin looks beautiful." I put my hand up and caught his against my face. I'd noticed it too the last few days, since I'd been using the small pot of beeswax face cream that Ginny had made especially for me. Its texture was so gentle and it really seemed to be making a difference. My skin was glowing, my scar softening. I'd have to thank Ginny again, tell her how fantastic it was. I pressed our hands together and then let them drop, smiling.

Leaving the carrier bag on the kitchen table, I said, "I got your stuff," and went through to the utility room to empty my beach bag and tuck the wet towels and swimming costumes into the washing machine. I added the liquid capsule and set the programmer, realising I was working quietly, listening to Nico's movements behind me in the kitchen as he opened the bag, lifted out the contents.

I trod lightly back into the room. He had his back to me, postcard, Polos and hand sanitiser on the table in front of him.

"Was my watch not there?" he asked over his shoulder and I remembered it on my wrist. I held it up to show him and he smiled.

"Thank you," he said, unclasping it and fastening it on his own brown wrist.

I leaned round him and picked up the postcard, peered at the sunny view. "Ooh, looks nice," I said, keeping my voice as level as possible. "Who's that's from?" I lifted interested eyes his way. Waited. He took the card from my fingers, read the back, frowned momentarily.

"Just a marketing card from one of the old boat contractors I used to use," he said. "Looking for work."

"You'd think they would have taken you off their books by now," I said.

"Must be desperate." He shrugged. "Maybe business is bad." He tore the card in half and tossed it on the table. "Was it okay at the home?" he said, obviously changing the subject.

"They were very positive," I said. "Kieron said you'd be back to work soon, hopefully. That Mrs Dennison herself misses you. Doesn't sound like you're a will-chaser to me. Or whatever her son said."

He smiled. "Crossing my fingers," he said. "That's what you do for luck, isn't it?"

I nodded, glanced at the ripped-up postcard.

"Yes, it is," I said out loud, thinking to myself: it *is* what you do for luck. It's also what I do when I tell a lie.

I found the postcard the next day, the pieces thrown in the kitchen bin with a handful of junk mail.

The picture of a beach peeked at me from under an outdoor clothing catalogue as I lifted the lid to scrape Midge's cereal bowl. Blue sky taunted me. I let the soggy cereal fall on top, splatter it, rubbish that it obviously was. So it hadn't meant enough to him to hold on to. That was a good sign, wasn't it?

I slammed the lid shut, fed up with myself. I'd slept badly, after a terrible dream that Nico left me; off he had gone with a postcard in his hand. I'd chased him, following his back as he walked across the drive, pulled at his arm to hold him, but he'd disappeared. Literally – he was gone and I was left holding air. Then I was looking for Midge but he'd taken her too. I was running through the house, even more frantic. Looking for her in places that she wouldn't even fit, the bread bin, the dresser drawers, the wood-burning stove. The house was back to its derelict state, like before I moved in, creepy and broken, and I startled mice and got caught in cobwebs as I searched. Ridiculous when you look back at it, but in the dream I shouted for her until my throat was raw and bleeding. I woke up feeling worn out and empty.

Nico had gone out already, and I was glad I had the house to myself for a couple of hours. He'd taken Midge to town for new school shoes for September. I'd been worried that she'd grow out of them by then, it was still ages away, but apparently if you didn't get them early then you had to go miles for them in the week before school. Everywhere sold out.

I couldn't argue. I knew nothing about this. This was my first year at all this stuff. But I'd know for next year. I'd be the best mum known to man. Or known to Midge, anyway.

I finished tidying the remnants of their breakfast away while the kettle boiled, then took my tea to the patio. The morning was already warm, bright. Roo played at my feet, chewing the head off a stuffed toy. A woodpecker was busy somewhere. Bees buzzed on the honeysuckle. The paddling pool was full and still. Everything looked perfect. But I had a nagging feeling that all was not as it seemed.

The silence was broken by the crunch of gravel. The Audi pulled in and I watched Nico walk round the car to let Midge free of her car seat. I waved from the garden and she skipped towards me, wearing new Converse boots. Bright pink with a rainbow on the side.

"They don't look much like school shoes to me!" I said with a laugh.

"Dad's got those," she said, jabbing her thumb over her shoulder at Nico as though he were her staff. He followed her up the garden towards me carrying a shoebox, hips rolling slowly. Damn, he was a sexy man.

"She persuaded me," he said with a "what could I do" kind of shrug. "Hope that's okay?" he added.

"Course," I said reassuringly. He was as thrifty as me. Always looking at the sale rail first. Not that we needed to.

"Kettle's hot," I said as he went through the French doors. Midge was sitting next to the paddling pool untying her laces, bottom lip held behind her teeth in concentration.

Roo left me and stood patiently beside her, knowing where the fun was at. She followed Midge around all day.

Midge grunted in annoyance and threw her hands in the air, suddenly looking very exasperated and very foreign. I watched her struggle for another moment or so, thinking it good for her to practise her patience and learn to do things on her own. Then I went to her.

"Need some help?" I squatted in front of her on the grass so that our heads almost touched as we both looked at her boots. "Pull the tails," I said. "Like we talked about, remember."

I showed her the ends of the two laces. We'd been trying to get to grips with laces. I called the loose ends the "tails", and the loops were the "bunny ears". She'd giggled and hopped about when I said that.

"It doesn't work," she said.

"Let me see," I knelt and Roo nudged me with her nose, loving having everyone on her level.

The laces were double-knotted. That was the problem. We hadn't ever got as far as that in our lessons, so it was no wonder she was confused. I undid the first knot for her.

"Now try," I said and she pulled the tails. The bow slid undone and she breathed out in pleasure.

I undid the knot on her other shoe while she loosened the criss-cross laces and slipped the first one off, then peeled off her sock.

"This is a different type of knot, it's called a double," I said. "That's why you were finding it difficult."

"She said it would stop them coming undone," Midge said, tongue poking out as she set about the second bow.

"Who did?" I asked, curiosity piqued.

"The lady. In the shop. She did them up for me." She grinned at me as she got the second shoe off and threw her sock after it. Roo immediately picked it up in her mouth and ran off with it.

I ruffled Midge's hair, feeling stupid. She only had to mention a woman and I was immediately suspicious. It was just everything that had been going on. Get a grip, Kat.

"And she played rock, paper, scissors," Midge went on, making a scissor shape with her two fingers and snipping them together.

"Did you win?"

"Yep!" she said, stepping into the paddling pool. "Lots of times!" She made a little "o" with her mouth; the pool water had chilled overnight.

"Wow!" I said. "She liked playing with you." Everyone seemed to fall under her spell. She was just so friendly, open.

"We were just waiting for Dad," she said, cupping her hands under a butterfly on the water's surface and lifting it to the rubber edge.

"Was he paying?" I said, imagining him at the till, worrying about how expensive shoes were.

"No, he was outside," she said, blowing on the butterfly, oh so gently, to dry it. "On the phone."

Call me, the postcard had said. And lo and behold, the first chance he gets, away from me, he makes a phone call. My world felt like it was falling apart while Midge splashed in and out of the pool, or threw water at Roo, who snapped her jaws trying to catch it, both of them oblivious to me sitting there, feeling my life crumbling around me.

Who had Nico been talking to when he was safely alone, and out of earshot of Midge? Had he taken the opportunity to ring the Spanish number? Anxiety moved slick in my belly like a snake, slowly turning, twisting against itself.

"Kaaaa-aaaat!" Midge called, poking her face near to mine and making me realise it wasn't the first time she'd said my name. "Look!" She jumped over the tiny edge of the pool into the water and Roo followed her, part of the game. I smiled enough that she left me alone again.

Nico's shadow fell over me.

"Fresh tea?" he said, nodding at the table where the teapot sat next to his cafetière and cup. He stretched down a hand to help me up and I took it, unable to meet his eyes or say a word.

"Did you sleep badly last night? You were thrashing around, calling out." His eyes were velvety brown in the sunshine. They were really focused on me, holding me.

"Bad dream," I muttered, feeling again the emptiness I'd felt as I ran chasing him, looking for Midge.

"What about?" he asked, pouring his coffee. Suddenly I felt overwhelmingly tired and desperate.

"That you had someone else," I said. He stopped the cafetière mid-pour, his cup only half-full, his mouth slightly open.

"You left me." My eyes got hot and I pressed my lips together to stop anything else leaking out.

Putting the cafetière down, he pulled his chair closer to mine, our knees touching.

"That's the last thing I'm going to do, believe me," he said, tucking my hair behind my ear. "And there is no one else." I could see the yellow flecks in his eyes, he was so close. "It was just a bad dream." He laughed lightly, kissed my cheek and pushed himself back to finish pouring his coffee.

I licked my lips, took a breath. Unsure as to whether to mention the postcard. The phone call? Should I ask him? I opened my mouth.

"By the way," he said, "Ginny rang when we were in town. Said she tried you but you didn't answer."

He took a long swallow from his coffee.

"Just wanted to remind you of the dog show tomorrow. Starts at two. Said if Roo wins best puppy, she should get half the prize money because she was her puppy first."

I picked up my mobile from where it lay face-down on the table. Sure enough, Ginny's name was there, with two missed calls signalled beside it. The calls had come in about an hour ago. When I was making tea or clearing the kitchen. Or sitting out here listening to the birds. About the same time that Nico and Midge would have been in the shoe shop. When Midge was having her laces tied by the shop assistant. It all added up.

"I think she was only half-joking," he said, with a chuckle, and I laughed too. At Ginny, and at the same time myself. I had to chill out. This was ridiculous. I'd be back in Park Prewett by Christmas at this rate.

He couldn't look at me the way he was looking at me, he couldn't tuck my hair so gently behind my ear, if he didn't love me. I smiled and poured tea, leaning back in the chair and tilting my face to the sun, determined to forget about the postcard. After all, everyone's allowed a few secrets, aren't they?

I don't know who was more excited for the dog show, Midge or Roo – or Ginny, who almost ran at us from the bus stop across the car park at the recreation ground.

She looked a sight – cut-off denim shorts to the knee, a camouflage vest and a rucksack that had seen better days, one strap hanging. Roo bounded to her and jumped up, paws already reaching Ginny's stomach.

"Where's your car?" I asked.

"Garage," she said. "Starter motor's gone."

She scratched the dog behind her still-massive ears before telling her to sit – three times – to assess her. Nico nudged me.

"There's my girl," said Ginny.

Roo, who had been groomed to within an inch of her life, was far too excited to keep still and managed five whole seconds before wagging herself back to standing.

"Looking good," Ginny acknowledged, opening her rucksack. "Finishing touches," she said, pulling out a red-and-white patterned bandana, which she tied around Roo's neck. Roo cocked her head comically and looked at me as if to say, "Really?" I laughed and Midge giggled. She did look cute.

We found a place near the arena rope-side to watch the other categories, close to a group from school. There was an agility class already on and Midge sat cross-legged at the front to watch a sheepdog jumping over small gates, balancing on beams and dashing through tunnels. Leaving her there spellbound, with Nico setting up the blanket and baskets, Ginny and I went to register Roo and pay the entrance fee – the princely sum of five pounds. As we picked our way around people and dogs and picnic blankets, she told me of a new resident at the sanctuary, a young squirrel that had lost its tail in a traffic accident. She said it looked much like a rat and I shuddered.

"Will it survive?" I said.

"Yup. Will just have to learn better climbing – without its tail to balance it out." She lifted her arm to re-pin a loose strand of hair, giving me a glimpse of an unshaven underarm, curly and ginger, and a light waft of hot woman. I looked away quickly, embarrassed; not that she'd care.

It took us twice as long to reach the registration tent as it would if I'd gone on my own. Ginny had to stop and talk to every dog she saw, from the biggest Great Dane I'd ever seen to the dachshund whose tummy nearly touched the grass. As much as she loved dogs, when I heard her ask the dog, "And what category are you in today?" several times and wait for the owner to answer, I realised she was also sussing out the competition. I had to swallow my giggles. There were quite a few of my doggy daycare clients there too, who Roo made a beeline for, dragging me across the grass. Doggy heaven.

The registration form was simple enough. Category, Name, Breed, Age, Owner. A few details about favourite foods and activities to give a bit of colour. I filled everything in and rifled for a fiver in my purse. Ginny squinted at it over my shoulder.

"They might read out from this when Roo walks round the ring," she said, putting a hot hand on my arm. "Can you add me in as breeder? Give the sanctuary a mention?"

I saw what she was getting at and nodded, handing over the pen while I opened my purse. She made the most of the opportunity, adding in capitals at the top of the form, 'Bred at Hollow Farm Animal Sanctuary as part of a litter taken for police dogs.' Then, at the end of the form, she added a: 'Come and see the other animals at the sanctuary!'

"It's not an advert!" I laughed, handing it over with the five-pound note, but she just shrugged.

"It all helps," she said.

The agility class was followed by the obedience session. I watched in awe, praying my training with Roo every day would turn her into such a well-behaved dog. It wasn't that she was naughty, just young, and overexcited most of the time. She sat on command nine times out of ten, came to me on demand about seventy per cent of the time and, since being fully house-trained, would bark at the back door to go out – every single time. Pretty good, but looking at the obedience of the dogs in the ring, I knew I had to keep going. She lay between my feet, watching the dogs too, ears twitching like antennae.

Puppy category was last on the agenda. The big finale, as Ginny kept calling it. By the time they called us to the ring, Midge had been recoated with suncream twice and had eaten two ice creams. She hopped from foot to foot beside me as we waited to take our turn, fuelled by sugar as much as excitement. Nico held her hand at the ringside, making sure she was front row.

It was just meant to be a lap of the arena, not much bigger than a tennis court. We were motioned in, Roo walking pretty well to heel beside me, ears pointing the way forward. I turned the first corner.

"Welcome to Roo, the German shepherd," the guy on the loudspeaker announced. "The biggest puppy in this category for sure." He was right. So far, they'd been mainly handbag-sized; like Bella, owned by two gorgeous gay guys who both kissed the top of her head at the end of their circuit. Or they'd been fluffy and cute, like Treacle, a cockapoo the colour of maple syrup.

Roo paused, sniffed the air as we passed a family with hot dogs sitting close to the roped edge. I pulled her lead very slightly towards me and thankfully she moved on.

"Only eight months old, but already looking good on the lead," the man was saying. His voice sounded very much like he might be the same bloke who had commentated on the duck race. Maybe he did the local event circuit.

"Apparently not so well behaved in the garden, digging the occasional hole in the flower beds!" he continued. Roo strained at her lead towards the middle of the arena and I tightened my grip.

"Loves peanut butter!" he said, "but who doesn't?!" A ripple of laughter went through the crowd. The marshall at the corner nodded at me to walk to the centre of the ring, where I knew I had to instruct Roo to sit. It was all going so well. Midge waved at me as we got to the middle.

"Roo, sit," I said.

Her ears pointed straight upwards, listening, but she didn't react.

"Sit," I said again, but instead of complying she turned in a circle, pressing her nose to the grass. My stomach dropped. I knew what she was going to do. I recognised the signs. Sure enough, she did kind of sit down. But only enough to do the biggest poo any puppy has ever done. I'm sure Bella's owners must have been appalled at the sheer size of it. I pulled a horrified face and got the crowd laughing as I stood there, waiting for her to finish, after which she kicked grass wildly with her back feet as if to cover it up, and the crowd laughed louder.

"There's a time and a place, Roo, don't you know?!" the man on the loudspeaker chuckled. I pulled a poo bag out of my shorts pocket – always prepared – and bent to start collecting the pile. Roo took that opportunity, when I was least expecting it, to pull on the lead, and bounded off, much to the crowd's amusement. She ran straight back to the point where she'd smelled the delicious hot dogs and stole one straight from an unsuspecting child's hand. She ran back towards me with a sausage poking out of her mouth and stopped a safe ten feet away to wolf it down.

"Seems like she missed breakfast!" the commentator said and the crowd roared. Roo finally padded back to me, pleased with herself, and I secured her lead. She then decided to sit, perfectly, as I had asked her to do a few minutes before, adding a quizzical tilt of her head. The crowd clapped.

As I led her across the grass to the exit, the commentator said, "Apparently she was bred at the animal sanctuary at Hollow Farm. Pop in there to see the other animals – any time."

Ginny grinned and gave me a thumbs-up as we crossed the rope boundary again, and Midge threw herself at Roo. Nico pulled me to him as we made our way back to the blanket, kissed my head.

It didn't surprise me that we didn't win Best Puppy, although I saw Ginny's face drop. But it did surprise me when the commentator announced a special prize for funniest dog, and called for Roo to do another turn of the arena. They pinned a rosette on her bandana, which Roo tried to eat, but she did make her way around the ring without too much of a problem.

"No prize money?" Ginny asked as I made my way back. I shook my head. "But they did read out your advert," I said, giving her a quick squeeze. She snorted.

Midge was playing on a neighbouring blanket with a little boy she'd made friends with. As we got closer, Roo straining at the lead, Midge spotted us and pointed.

"That's my puppy," she said to the boy, "she won a prize." She nodded at him, smugly. "She's the funniest dog in the world." The boy considered Roo, and me, then asked. "Is that her trainer?"

Midge looked at him, then at us, and laughed. "No silly," she said as she pointed at me, "that's my mummy!"

That was the exact moment that I realised this was the best day of my life.

*M*y mum would have done anything for me. Anything at all. I told you this. You said you would too, but I think that was proven wrong.

There was never anyone in between Mum and me. No dad. No other children. She was mine and I was hers. We could play all day, or watch TV curled up as close as two kittens. That's why she called me her KittyKat. She'd make fairy cakes for me and let me eat the icing from the tub. We'd build dens in the sitting room, hiding under the hanging blankets to read books or colour pictures. She'd wipe crumbs from the kitchen table for me to spread out my homework. She didn't mind me singing, or dancing, not like Aunt Belinda. I could make as much noise as I liked, as long as it wasn't one of the nights when an uncle visited. But I was normally in bed by then. She always made me a hot chocolate that tasted extra sweet, smoky almost, before one of the uncles rang the doorbell. The drink made my eyelids heavy and my tongue big and I "slept like a log". Or so Mum used to say. She had a saying for everything.

I loved to watch her put her make-up on at the dressing table before an uncle arrived. She'd outline her eyes with a thick black crayon, humming along to the music centre. She'd dab perfume between her breasts, behind her ears, and wink at me in the mirror. Once she said, "Put perfume where you want to be kissed." I jokingly put some on my fingers and rubbed it all over my face and she rained kisses on me that stained me red with lipstick. When she was dressed up, in her party wear, she was the most beautiful mummy in the world. Younger than any of the other school mummies who waited in the playground, who wore anoraks and stood in little circles of beige. My mummy stood to the edge, in a red coat, or pointed heels. Bold. Bright. Beautiful.

I loved school, until Olivia James joined our class and was given a seat at the Butterflies table, next to me. High, brown pigtails pulled her cheeks tight, and missing front teeth made her lisp. I was drawn to her, pulled my chair closer and smiled. We played hop-scotch at break and then sat next to each other for lunch. By the time we left at the end of the day, her hand was hot in mine and we ran together breathlessly into the playground. She was going to be my friend.

Her mum had been making friends too and was with the circle. Mine stood by the gate, smoking, grinding the butt under her foot when she saw me.

The next day in class, Olivia moved her chair away.

"Don't want to catch anything," she said.

"I haven't got anything," I said, confused.

"Your mum's a tart," she said.

I didn't understand. Tarts are nice. Jam. Apple. But I knew she was being mean.

She didn't talk to me again, closing her lips like a line. My face got hot, eyes watery. I coloured in my sheet, careful to keep in the lines. But school was different after that. The girls poked their tongues out at me. They refused to hold my hand in the dinner queue.

When I told Mummy about it, her face went very still and then she hugged me tighter than the normal tight.

"You remember in the future, KittyKat," she said, "it's not what you do, it's who you are that's counts."

The next day she said was Baking Day. We made a special tart for Olivia's mum as a welcome present. We both spat in the stewed apple mix, for luck apparently, before carefully putting on the pastry lid. It was a secret ingredient.

"Best served cold," Mum said to a flushed-looking Mrs James in the playground.

After the dog show, the weekend had been a happy blur, me literally smiling till my face ached every time Midge called me Mummy. Roo got away with blue murder: stealing cake from the table, digging a hole in the roses. We all just laughed and called her the "funniest dog in the world". Nico barbecued steaks and chilled wine, then took me to bed early at night without any intention of sleeping. I was happy in my bones.

Monday came around too quickly, and with it Nico's interview at the care home.

He was quiet in the morning, pensive, when I left to take Midge to school. When I got back he was still at the table, brooding. I rubbed his shoulders as I passed him, felt the rigidity of them, the buzz of tension under the skin.

"It will be okay," I reassured, breezy. Still happy with life.

"How do you know?" he snapped.

"I just feel it. Kieron said they thought it would all get sorted out." I tried a smile but he didn't return it.

"He doesn't know either. If they believe the family…" He paused, eyebrows low.

"There's no evidence?"

"Sometimes there doesn't have to be evidence for people to say you're guilty."

He pushed his cereal bowl away, unfinished, and I picked it up and put it in the sink.

"Look, let's not get this out of proportion. It's just a job at the end of the day. Nobody died." I cringed even as the words left my mouth. It was the wrong phrase, with two dead spouses between us. I smacked my own forehead with my hand.

"Sorry," I said. "You know what I mean."

"You don't get it!" he said, grabbing the car keys. "If I get found guilty, I lose my job."

I hesitated. There was a bit of me that wanted to say, "So what? You can get another one if you want to." After all, it was a job in a care home, it wasn't rocket science or curing cancer or something; but he loved it. There was also a part of me that wanted to say, "Never mind, you don't need to work." Neither of us needed to. I'd already thought to myself that maybe we could grow the dog-walking business if he wanted to. Build a kennel in the back paddock, expand to kennel stays. The business, now known as Kat and Dogs, was getting quite a name for itself. But I didn't say any of this, not wanting him to think his job was unimportant. He was quite traditional. He took great pride in being able to contribute and I didn't want him to feel any less of a man.

"Let's not jump to that yet," I said instead, following him to the car.

"My settled-status application says I have a job. If I lose my job, they might not let us stay," he said, striding across the drive to the car. "They might say Midge and I have to leave." He didn't mention me. Just him and Midge. His daughter. I twisted my ankle on the gravel, landing sideways on the edge of my foot. I limped after him, suddenly desperate not to be left behind.

The disciplinary investigation was in Ellen's office. The general manager of the home was there, a bearded man, as well as a woman from Gloucester social services. They would talk to both Nico and the Dennison family, separately. Old Mrs Dennison had already been interviewed, although nobody was allowed to tell us what she'd said. Nico and I sat outside on plastic chairs, as though we were at the dentist's, awaiting his turn.

Ellen called him in with a nod and a smile of encouragement, which I thought was kind. I heard the deep breath he took as he stood. I saw the way he squared his shoulders as he walked through the door. It clicked shut behind him and all I could hear, however much I strained my ears, was a low hum of conversation. I could tell which parts of the conversation were Nico's, though, by the low tone of his voice; he seemed to be talking a lot. Good – hopefully he was explaining himself and all of this would soon be over. Not a blight on his application to stay in the country. I hadn't thought about that being an issue. But yes, having a full-time job, and an important one in the community, could help his case – maybe.

A middle-aged couple were shown in and sat in the chairs on the other side of the door. The woman tapped her fingertips together in her lap; the man looked like he'd had a few pints the night before. And the night before that. His face was red and his shirt stretched across his stomach, showing a glimpse of wiry black hair. Neither of them looked my way. In fact, they made a point of looking anywhere but. The Dennisons, I presumed. I guessed we wouldn't be making small talk.

My phone pinged. A text from Ginny. "I need it now. Fucking hurry up."

I frowned. What was she going on about? I started to reply, with a "what?", but just before I'd added the question mark, another text came through. "Sorry! Not for you!" Before I had a chance to wonder what she did want and from whom, another ping said: "Meant for Tinder!" She put an emoji of an aubergine next to it and I suppressed a smile, conscious of the Dennisons sitting next to me.

"Dirty cow," I texted back with a laughing face.

The door opened and we all looked up. Nico shook hands with the bearded man in the doorway and stepped out.

"We'll be with you in one minute, Mr Dennison," the man said. The door closed. My phone pinged again and Mr Dennison huffed and rolled his eyes. I glanced at it. "Too damn right," said Ginny. I flicked the volume off and threw the phone in my bag.

I knew Nico wouldn't speak in front of the family, so I stood up silently and prepared to leave with him. I held his hand as he brushed past me. We were almost out of the room when Mr Dennison clearly couldn't hold back any more.

"Money-grabbing bastard," he spluttered, loud enough for us to hear. "Go back where you came from." Nico pulled the door open with one hand, hard and fast, and squeezed my fingers in the other so hard that my bones grated. I know he didn't mean to, but it really hurt.

We knew we'd have to wait a few weeks until we got a decision from the care home. Apparently the local decision may well have been made then and there on the day, but it had to be reviewed and agreed at a social services monthly meeting, scheduled for later in August. I could understand it. It was a serious issue. But I didn't doubt for a moment that he was innocent. It just wasn't him. Or the him I knew, anyway.

"Let's make the most of your last few days of holiday, then," I said, presuming he'd be back at work by the end of the month. The weather was so beautiful for the UK, it seemed a shame to waste it.

I found a last-minute break; a suite in a beachfront hotel on the south coast. The carpets were thick enough to make Nico's eyes widen when he first felt them under his bare feet, and Midge ran whooping round the suite, large enough for sofas and lounge spaces, before finding her room, which linked to ours. It was luxury I was used to, but still nice to have. Someone else's cancellation was our lucky break. We spent three days making sandcastles, which Midge loved, and watching Punch and Judy, which she loved even more, shouting bloodthirstily whenever Mr Punch battered the crocodile with a frying pan. We spent the nights waiting until she was asleep in her own room so we could sneak out on the balcony and drink a bottle of wine, giggling like teenagers, telling stories of past holidays; sharing thoughts for the future.

It was our last evening. I pulled my cardigan around my shoulders, the breeze from the sea enough to raise the hairs on my arms. Nico stared out to the horizon, watching the waves.

"It would be nice to have a holiday home somewhere, wouldn't it?" I suggested. "On the coast here in Dorset – or maybe across the Channel in France?"

Nico switched his gaze to me, took a long drink of wine.

"Somewhere we could take Roo with us." It had been hard leaving her with Ginny even for a few days. "Not now, maybe," I corrected, seeing his hesitancy. "Perhaps when Midge is older."

"I'm happy to just have one home," he said. "It means everything to have somewhere you can shut the door on the world." He put his hand between the two chairs and caught my fingers. The gentle rub of his thumb strayed from my hand, to my wrist, to the white softness of my inner elbow, and soon we snuck back into the room and made love very quietly, shushing each other, smiling in the dark.

I remembered the wine bottle, the open balcony doors, later as Nico slipped into sleep. Leaving him snoring, I padded out of the room, wrapped myself in a robe and went to close everything up. Our wine glasses clinked quietly together as I set them on the table inside. The lamplit hotel room was quiet, calm, and I stood for a moment, watching the white tips on the dark sea, my family sleeping around me.

A noise – a moan – made me jump and turn towards our door. It came again: a moan, a cry, not Nico, but Midge. I slipped through our room and headed for the connecting one. Nico's breathing stayed steady, deep and slow, sedated by the wine he'd drunk and the love we'd made. He grunted and turned onto his side as I opened the door.

Midge's night light threw stars on the ceiling; they turned and circled above my head. She lay on her back, duvet twisted around her legs. She looked so tiny, not even reaching halfway down the sheet, and I felt an overwhelming surge of love. Her eyes were closed, but her face was agitated, like she was watching a film she didn't like. She threw her head backwards and forwards on the pillow. Again, the moan. A word.

"No."

I edged towards the bed, perched on the side, not wanting to frighten her. I was conscious of the fact that Nico could never get near her when she had a nightmare, that she shrieked and got hysterical. I didn't want her to react badly if I woke her, but I had to try to calm her. She was thrashing her arms, contorting her face like she was going to cry.

"No," she whispered again, chin trembling.

I put my hand on her shoulder, shook her gently. "Midge."

She woke and sat in one movement, shrinking back against the headboard, driven by fear.

"Midge," I said again but she shook her head and pulled away, edging into the corner.

"Honey, it's me," I said, pushing my face into the glow of the night light. Her eyes widened in a split second of recognition and then brimmed with tears. She crawled to me on her knees, snaked her arms round my neck. Her breath was hot through my robe, face to my breast. I held her tight as she sobbed.

It was a full couple of seconds before I could make out the words she repeated as she cried.

"Don't leave me," she said.

I kissed the top of her head, one, two, three, pressed them there so that she could feel them.

"I won't," I promised. No vow had ever meant that much. Her crying quietened slowly as I sat with her, until her breathing was quiet and even again.

"And I don't like secrets," she sniffed, leaning into me.

"That's okay." I chuckled. "I haven't got any."

"Daddy has a secret," she said, against my chest. "But I'm not allowed to tell."

My skin turned to gooseflesh and I couldn't help but look over my shoulder, weirdly expecting to see Nico behind me in the doorway. But there was nothing. Just darkness. I shook myself, gave her a squeeze.

"Let's go back to sleep now," I said, "There's nothing to be scared of."

As I lay her back down on the pillow and stroked her hair, Mum's voice came into my head. Her words of wisdom. "Out of the mouths of babes," she used to say.

Midge dozed all the way home in the car, worn out from the beach and her bad night's sleep. Although she hadn't mentioned her dream again, she was quiet at breakfast and stayed close to my side, ghost-like, on the sands for our last morning. She didn't wake as we parked at The Nook or when we turned off the engine, as she usually would, and Nico carried her straight to her bed to continue her nap. I watched them go in, hoping she wouldn't wake as he carried her and startle. Only when I saw him pulling her curtains in the upstairs window did I breathe out. Her words from the night before echoed in my head, had been there throughout the journey. *Daddy has a secret.*

The lawn under my sandals was brown and the hanging baskets were wilted. I kept meaning to ring an irrigation firm to come and automate the watering, but I hadn't got round to it yet. I filled a watering can and gave the plants a much-needed soaking to perk them up, pledging to call the company tomorrow, changing the worries in my head.

Other everyday things needed doing. The bird table was empty and by the time I'd filled the wire feeder and walked away, the regulars were already swooping down to eat. A few dead butterflies needed scooping out of the paddling pool before Midge saw them. The ice-maker needed replenishing, which I did with thoughts of a gin and tonic later in the day. The postbox was stuffed and I dumped the pile of envelopes, brochures and junk mail on the kitchen counter.

Nico offered to collect Roo from Ginny's and picked up the car keys, kissing the back of my head as he went. The short holiday seemed to have done him good.

It was actually lovely to be home. The drone of bees in the garden. The ticking of the kitchen clock. The sound of a tractor somewhere in the fields. Nico's words about having a home to shut the door on the world came back to me as I looked out the window. The Nook felt like home now. The three of us living in it had turned it from a house to a home. I knew which floorboard creaked outside the bathroom. I anticipated the hum of the wind around our turret bedroom when it came in from the west. Midge would grow up recognising the seasons by the fields outside her window: spring green, summer yellow, autumn stubble, winter dirt. The house held us, together. Whatever was worrying Midge, I could sort it. I would make this place her haven. Her safe place. I was her mum after all.

The kettle whistled on the Aga and I poured tea to tackle the post, spreading it out fan-like, to assess.

First, I scanned it for anything with a Gloucester County Council stamp, just in case the decision had been made early and Nico could relax. Nothing.

Secondly, the junk mail went in the recycling. Flyers for estate agents, adverts for double glazing. Rubbish.

Thirdly, I looked for anything official. Tax bills, motoring offences. You could tell any of these by the postmark. I always opened them first, as they usually demanded action. Pay your council rates or your car tax. Things that were necessary evils. Nico told me I should be more aware of when that kind of bill was coming in, to be prepared for it. I'd agreed with him, because I knew he was only trying to help, but there was no need really. I'd always considered the cost up front, knew I had the best deal or had selected the best quote.

That day there was very little of interest. A reminder from Midge's school about the uniform for the next year. A bill for me on the flat I owned in London, you remember the one. We bought it shortly after getting married. You loved the fact it had a concierge service and a lift direct to our front door, like a penthouse. The bill was for the service charges, and a note to say the tenants had requested to extend their stay for another year. Good news.

Finally a bank statement.

My new married name on the envelope still looked weird, foreign, which it was. But I liked it. New name. New life. New me. Maybe I really had put everything behind me. Maybe a leopard could change its spots.

I only opened the bank statement because I was sitting there. I never normally bother with those things. Rows of numbers and details of where I'd spent what. It didn't really matter. I knew how carefully I used my money.

But that day, I shook out the pages and read the first one. There were all my usual everyday purchases: pizza restaurants with Midge, cinema night, car service, fuel and takeaways. A vet bill for Roo's injections. Nothing out of the ordinary – until a cashpoint withdrawal for £500. I always chose even numbers with withdrawals, for no real reason, £200 or £400 usually. I checked the date. It was after the Coffin Club picnic when I'd lost my purse. Nico, then. I flicked to the next page and there was another one. £300 transfer. A few other random payments of a few hundred pounds and some other cashpoint withdrawals. Midge's school shoes – and her

Converse, probably. I had no idea how much they had cost – I hadn't even asked.

It was on the last page that I saw the £1,000. It was the number of zeros that drew my eye. Again, it hadn't been me. I strained my brain to remember any big purchases we'd had to make. The summer house. The holiday. The patio being relaid. What else would he be spending money on? Especially that amount?

My train of thought was interrupted when Roo bounded into the kitchen, so happy to see me, overjoyed to be home. I lost my train of thought, bent to stroke her, to scratch her back. The car door slammed outside and there was a crunch of footsteps across the gravel. I shuffled the papers into a pile, bank statement at the bottom.

"How's Ginny?" I asked.

"Her usual charming self," Nico said, throwing the keys back on the hook, without a laugh.

"All okay?" I asked. I know Ginny could be a bit obnoxious sometimes, but he normally seemed to rub along with her pretty well. She sometimes called him direct now if she needed a fence panel holding or something heavy shifting.

"She asked for a donation to the sanctuary for looking after Roo for you."

I snorted. I couldn't help it. I was always round there, feeding animals for her, helping her to move this, that or the other. Paying her flipping mortgage for her too, come to think of it.

"Did you give her something?"

"I only had a twenty in my wallet, so I stuffed that in her tin." He turned to face me. "Hope that's okay?"

I wanted to laugh, but I knew I shouldn't. "Some people are just all about the money," I said, attempting a smile.

He looked back at me and caught my eye and I saw his lips twitch.

"Money-grabbing bastard," he said. The words hung for a moment in the air, before they popped and we both laughed. Midge wandered in, rubbing the sleep out of her eyes.

I swept the papers away into the recycling.

Ginny was after my help again the next day. She wanted new posters for the sanctuary. I thought about charging her for my time but didn't think she'd see the funny side.

The kitchen was a pigsty, but she took me through to the "office", a room in the farm I'd never seen before. The walls were lined with old cardboard boxes, overflowing with box files, spewing out paper. In the middle there was a desk, hidden under coloured folders and animal-feed brochures.

"Don't think much of your filing system, Ginny," I said, but she just shoved a cat off the seat and wheeled it out for me, positioning me in front of an ageing computer. Just looking at the keyboard made me cringe – it was caked with dirt and sticky under my fingertips – but I knew I had anti-bacterial gel in my bag, so I took a deep breath and started up the computer.

"You're better at this stuff than me," she said. "I just want new promotional posters. Going to put them in the vets, the doctors, the cafes. I think people must have gotten too used to seeing the old ones, they don't even notice them any more. I've only had two visitors this week."

I waited for the computer to buzz into life. Nico and Midge wandered past the window with Roo and Cleo. The dogs followed Midge like kids skipping after the ice cream van, sure of something fun if they did. The view out of this window was new to me, looking out towards the orchards, away from the sanctuary. The apple trees were full and heavy in the paddock, the field to the right empty except for two donkeys and a makeshift shelter. Midge was heading straight for them, delighted.

"Where did they come from?" I said, nodding at them through the window.

"Advertised the field for rent and their owners took it. Ned and Bluebell," Ginny said. "Thought the pay would help, but they've cost me way more than they've earned so far. Bluebell managed to eat a plastic bag that blew into the field and I had to call out the emergency vet. Thought she was going to snuff it." She shook her head. "Not that she thanked me for the medical help. Grumpy fucker." She lifted her T-shirt at the side and showed me a large red welt, a bite the size of my fist.

"Jesus," I said and she let her top drop. I was kind of relieved. Her skin was startling in its whiteness, and baggy-looking.

"Giving her a wide berth next time I feed her," she said.

"So, what does this poster want to say?" I asked.

"All the usual stuff," she said. "Come and visit, blah blah. Opening times. And then, sponsorship opportunities available!"

This was new. She looked pretty excited about it. I pulled up a Word document and she talked me through the proposition.

"You can choose an animal category to sponsor: mammals, birds or amphibians – although I don't get many of those. It might be the hedgehogs, or the owls, or the squirrels." She smelled lightly of straw and dung as she moved around the desk behind me.

"I might even do an offer that you can sponsor the animal of the month – someone like Al Pacino, remember him? Someone with a bit of special appeal, a story behind them."

I started dragging and dropping, lifting pictures from her desktop.

"Have you got a pic of a hedgehog? People like those," I said. She pointed at a folder called "Family Album", and I clicked it open. Hundreds of thumbnail pictures opened, one after the other, every animal she'd ever helped. She indicated for me to scroll down past pigeons and foxes and badgers to hedgehogs, the biggest category. I lifted a picture of a hedgehog looking particularly cute, curled into a ball and lying on his back, looking at the camera.

"I'd just ask for a one-off payment for the 'rescue of the month', but perhaps the sponsor could have their photo taken with them or something? As a keepsake."

I nodded, thinking about a catchy headline.

"But the *main* sponsors, they'd pay regularly *every* month. That's the beauty of it. A regular income. Which ones are *your* favourites?" she said to me as I scrolled back up the page. I paused for a moment at a handful of pictures of deer, but my stomach tensed as I flashed back to the day Ginny and I had met. The deer I'd hit. I carried on past. God, that felt a long time ago, but the pull in my stomach told me it was still too close.

"The owls, probably," I offered, typing the copy and considering it. Did it grab the attention? I bit my lip.

"The owls!" she said, licking her dirty finger and flicking through her notebook. "Yes, beautiful birds."

I retyped the advert, emboldening the free entry and opening times, appraising it as if I was seeing it for the first time. It looked good, like a fun thing to do. Well, if you were into that kind of thing. You and I would never have done it, but now that I had Midge, I could see the appeal for parents. The animals were a real draw.

"Let me see…" Ginny muttered to herself. I sat back in my chair and rolled my shoulders back, glancing out the window.

Nico was on the phone under the shade of the apple trees. I could see Midge standing on the bar of the fence, watching the donkeys. Nico was listening, then talking, eyes shut, phone clenched to his ear. Even without being able to hear a word, his face told me everything. It was wretched. Desperate. God, was this news about the job? Or, no – what if this was the decision on his application for settled status? He opened his eyes but was looking at something a long way away, as though wanting to be somewhere else. He put one hand to his hair like he'd pull it from his scalp.

"Kat!" Ginny said, obviously not for the first time. "I said, you could sponsor the owls for £100 per month," she said with a nudge, her elbow pointed into the fleshy bicep area of my arm. "It's normally £120 but I'd do a deal for you."

I opened my mouth to answer but could only blink. I'd just given her five grand! Outside, Nico spoke a few words and his face was blurred with emotion. He pocketed his phone and turned away. Just as I thought it was over, he smashed his hand against the trunk of the tree.

"What do you think?" Ginny said, like a bad second-hand car salesman.

A scream sounded outside and I jumped. Midge streaked across the garden, still screaming, with her hands to her face, and Nico caught her. By the time he'd picked her up and started running towards the house, I was already on my feet, pushing the chair away and heading for the door. Ginny was right behind me. We met in the kitchen, Midge crying noisily, face hidden in Nico's front.

"Don't tell me that donkey bit her?" Ginny said nervously, but Nico shook his head.

"Bee sting," he said, sitting Midge on the draining board. I gasped. Her eyelid was already so swollen that her eye was shut. The sting was still in her skin, sticking out from just above her eyelid. It looked like she'd been hit by a cricket bat. Nico pulled his bank card from his pocket and told her to sit still, murmuring gently and occasionally in Spanish.

"Bloody hell. Is she allergic?" Ginny said. 'That's some reaction."

"No," he said. "Not like me." Using the flat of the card, Nico scraped the sting clean out of the skin without squeezing any more venom out. Midge sobbed steadily, clutching at his T-shirt, but sat still, good as gold.

"All done," he said, kissing her forehead. I moistened a tissue under the cold tap and pressed it onto her hot face. Her eye was purple. She shuddered a few more breaths.

"Maybe your neighbours are right?" Nico said, "Those bees are spiteful little bastards."

"Sorry, kiddo," Ginny said, rubbing Midge's leg but speaking to Nico. "They might be spiteful little bastards but they're worth their weight in gold."

We didn't hang around after that. Ginny huffed a bit, worried about her poster, but it was pretty much finished. She could print it as it was. Thankfully, she didn't mention the sponsorship opportunity again.

In the car on the way home, even though it was just five minutes, Midge nodded off, worn out with shock and crying. The car bumped along, putting distance between us and the bees, the shock.

"Who were you on the phone to?" I asked casually as we pulled into the lane. "When Midge got stung?"

The car hit a pothole, hard.

"Shit," Nico muttered, twisting the steering wheel away.

"You looked sad." I said, turning in the passenger seat to face him. Understatement of the year.

"Just work," he said, eyes focusing on the road. "No news yet."

I decided the next morning that I didn't believe him.

I tested it out overnight, gave him the benefit of the doubt for a few hours, that yes it had been a work call. I knew he was frustrated about Mrs Dennison, that the decision by the care authority was taking too long. Of course he would be upset on the phone to them.

But then I replayed the scene in my head, saw his face, saw the violence in his hand as he slammed it against the tree trunk. It wasn't just frustration that I'd seen. Over the course of that minute, there had been anguish, anger, shock – and, at the end, love. Yes, in the split second before he ended the call, as he uttered his goodbyes, that had been love. I recognised it like a punch in my gut. When I accepted that, I knew it wasn't work. He was lying.

So I did what any suspicious wife does, apparently; if you watch any movie, or read any book, if she's got doubts she checks his phone. I didn't even have to do it surreptitiously; I did it right there in the open. In the kitchen. With him doing the washing up. It just kind of happened.

The home phone had rung, a customer for Kat and Dogs. The woman was a talker. She had a beagle called Mavis who wanted walking on certain days, and doggy daycare on others, as well as potential overnight stays. I was trying to keep up with her, decided I needed to make some notes and grabbed a pad from the worktop, found a pen in the pot, all while giving appropriate responses to her million questions.

I clamped the phone between my shoulder and ear and flipped the notepad to find a clean page. Grocery lists, Midge's drawings, phone numbers for the garden watering system.

The woman was still talking. Could she bring her own dog meat, Mavis preferred raw food. What about Christmas – would I consider it? How much for a certain combination of stays and walks? My head was so full with her demands, I couldn't even think about arithmetic; I dug in my pocket for my mobile to use its calculator, but it wasn't there.

"Let me just work that out for you," I said, motioning to Nico to lend me his phone.

He nodded, up to his wrists in soapy washing-up water. I grabbed it off the counter with a smile and punched his code in. Midge's birthday. Going straight to the calculator, I ran through the requirements again with Mavis's owner and added up the total. She then asked for another combination of stays and walks per week and I worked that out too. By the time I'd finished, she had three options to consider, and I had brain-ache.

She thanked me and started on arranging a trial walk together the following Tuesday. I flicked the phone back to the home screen to look at the diary to check the date. It wasn't until I got to the diary and saw that it was blank that I remembered it wasn't my phone.

Nico was still washing up, as quietly as possible, being considerate of me being on the phone. Scrubbing a pan with a Brillo pad, trying to remove baked-on sauce. I carried on the conversation with Mrs Mavis, at the same time flicking Nico's mobile to call history. Last numbers dialled or received. I didn't even really question myself for doing it.

There it was, yesterday's number, and it definitely wasn't the care home. That much was blindingly obvious; it started with 00 for an overseas number. And if I was a betting person I would have put my house on the dialling code that followed being for Spain.

"Sorry – are you still there?" Mrs Mavis said down the phone and I stammered an apology, muttered something about losing the line for a moment. She carried on, reassured.

I clicked on the call itself to look at the history of that number. Sure enough, he'd rung it before. He'd been ringing it every week, for about five minutes. Every Sunday at 2p.m., or as near as dammit. Where was I usually then? In the garden with Midge? Walking Roo? Picking something up from the farm shop for tea? Where did he go to make that five-minute call? That last-minute dash to pick up some wine from the off-licence would cover it. The desire to fill the car up with fuel for the week ahead, or the weekly trip to the car wash? Five minutes was fairly easy to fit in. Let's face it, he could probably make it from the end of the garden when I was in the house.

"Thanks, see you then. Mavis is looking forward to it already!" the woman on the phone was saying. I didn't reply straight away, even though she had hung up; I deliberately let Nico think I was still on the phone as I flicked to his messages. Kept up an occasional, "Yes, I think we'd be able to manage that" or, "Sometimes we have several boarders at once, how is Mavis with other dogs?"

The message history was clear. In fact it was squeaky clean. Just a text chain between me and him, with a lot of "I love yous" and smiley face emojis. A text or two from Kieron at work, asking him for a pint. And one from Ginny: "Animals are hungry. Hurry up." Charming as always. Nothing out of the ordinary. Nothing to worry about.

Apart from a weekly phone call to someone, apparently.

I pretended to wind the call up, thanking the woman down an empty line and saying I was "looking forward to meeting you and Mavis," before I hung up. It gave me time to flick Nico's phone back on to the home screen and pop it down on the counter.

"New customer?" he said, stacking the remaining plates in the dishwasher, to all intents and purposes the perfect husband. My second chance. A sexy, gentle, funny man who didn't care about my scar, my past, my money. Who gave me his child. Who loved me.

The same man who withdrew big chunks of money from the bank, yet I never saw anything he spent it on. The man who made a secret phone call every week. The man who couldn't go back to his homeland.

And again it was Mum's words that came back to me, echoing round my head.

"If something looks too good to be true, it probably is."

Things didn't feel quite the same after that. Because once I'd seen Nico's call history, I couldn't unsee it, and it put him in a different light.

He still tucked my hair behind my ear. He cooked the most mouth-watering meals. He made love to me and murmured Spanish words in my ear that I didn't care what they meant. He looked at his daughter with a wonder that never ceased.

But he also had a habit of picking at his hangnails until they bled. Of shouting at the news, swearing at politicians and thumping the sofa with his fist. Other times, he'd be so lost in thought, with a frown on his face, that he'd physically jump when I spoke to him. Little things seemed to take on a bigger importance. I suddenly realised how little I really knew about him. What a short time we'd known each other.

"What do you think of Nico?"

It came out of my mouth without me knowing I was going to say it. Ginny was filling a feeding bottle with milk mixture for an injured fawn, and paused, jug in one hand and bottle in the other.

"Why?" she asked. "Had a row?"

I scrunched up my face and shook my head. "Just feel like maybe I don't know him as well as I thought..."

She sat back on a bale of hay, shaking the bottle to mix it. "Come on, then," she said, "what's he done?"

I told her about the chunks of money going from the account, hundreds at a time, the latest yesterday. She sniffed.

Then about the phone call I'd seen him on, the fact that he called someone regularly. She tilted her head, listening properly. Finally, the time I discovered he'd cleared the search history on the computer.

Ginny grinned. "Porn?" she asked.

"No!" I said, realising that that hadn't even crossed my mind.

"What then?"

"He just smiled and said, 'Can't a man plan a surprise for his wife?'"

She rolled her eyes at me and I realised it sounded ridiculous.

"But what do you think of him?" I kicked a stone across to the drain gulley of the barn.

"Well, he's not my type, but I think he's all right," she said and I sighed. "What exactly is it you're worried about?" she asked.

"That he's after my money?"

"Have you ever told him how much you've actually got? Shown him a balance?" she said and I shook my head.

"Well, we're married, so we don't have secrets," I said with a slight twinge. "Not financial ones, even though normally I would never talk about money—"

"– politics or religion," Ginny finished for me. "I know. So you're just worrying about the fact he's using the debit card you gave him to use?"

She had a point.

"Or that he's got someone else in Spain?" I said.

"What, that country he's never going back to?" she replied. "The one he wants to stay away from?"

I nodded. Again, she had a point.

"So what is it then?"

"That he might leave me for this other person?" I said, knowing I sounded pathetic. "That he might be taking money to make his escape?"

"He won't do that," Ginny said. "Anyone can see he loves you and I don't even believe in all that shit. His home is here. With you. That's exactly what he wants." She got up and turned to the fawn, which was waiting patiently for the bottle. As she offered the feed and the fawn took it between its lips, Ginny's face looked as gentle as my mum's.

I took a deep breath, trying to let her reassurance run over me, but it didn't quiet the nagging in my gut. That something wasn't right. But at that exact moment Midge skipped into the barn, leading a sheep on a rope, oblivious, and my stomach turned over with the realisation that if Nico went, Midge went too. And that could never happen, not now I was a "proper mum" at last.

I realised then that it was up to me to make this work, for Nico not to leave me. That I would do anything, literally anything, to keep us together. I had to look at the bigger picture. After all, I might think he was spending a bit much, and he might have an old flame in Spain he couldn't let go of, but it wasn't as though he were dangerous or anything, was it?

You never met my Aunt Belinda. She was definitely not ever a "proper mum".

You thought we invited her to the wedding and she couldn't make it. Shame, you said, seeing as she was my only family. But in truth, as I dropped all the other white envelopes into the mouth of the postbox, I put hers in the bin instead. She didn't deserve to come. I didn't want her there.

Being a mum is an active thing. It's a choice you make. My Aunt Belinda decided she didn't want to be one when my mummy died. But I had to live with her anyway, even though I'd never met her before. She carried my bag into the smallest, plainest bedroom in her three-bedroomed semi, and I wished I'd bought my posters to put on the wall.

I sat on the perfectly made guest bed and watched while she put my clothes in different drawers. She tutted at socks with holes in. She sniffed T-shirts and put them in the wash. She was very busy while I sat. I just wanted her to stop doing things. Stop touching things. Just sit with me. But she didn't. She always had a chore to do. Or a phone call to make. Anything that wasn't being with me.

She didn't swing hands between us and sing when we crossed roads; she'd yank me by the bicep. She'd vacuum under my chair at the table while I ate. She said goodnight from the door, not from the pillow. Occasionally, I'd catch her looking at me like she was seeing someone else. Sometimes she'd have wet eyes. Mostly she just looked cross. Over time I got used to it. I just thought aunts were different. They just weren't mummies.

It was on my fourteenth birthday that she said The Thing. The words that made me realise just how much she didn't want me. I'd rolled my skirt up at school like the other girls for the first time, trying to make friends with people who thought I was the odd kid, the kid who didn't have a family. The loner. Apparently I always said the wrong thing or tried too hard. I rolled it over one more time than they did, to try to win their favour, it was short enough to show more than a couple of inches of white skin above my knee. As I walked home past the new estate, a builder hung off the scaffolding and whistled, low and long. I made myself focus on the pavement as I scurried past, red-cheeked, half shocked, half proud.

Aunt Belinda was coming out of the baker's on the parade as I passed. Her pinch on my elbow as she marched me home was as sharp as her tongue.

"Making a show of yourself," she hissed in my ear. "Why am I surprised? Like mother, like daughter."

I didn't feel like I had a lot to say to her after that.

On my eighteenth birthday she asked me to move out.

A mum would never have done that.

Matteo popped up again, like a bad penny. Right when I was least expecting it, sitting on the patio, chilled glass of wine in front of me. Midge was watching TV inside, worn out from another day of being five. I was enjoying the sunset, the quiet – a chance to just sit. My phone beeped. Facebook message.

It wasn't that I'd forgotten about him; I still felt bad I'd accepted the friend request and hadn't replied to his first message. I'd hoped he had just "gone away".

As I picked my phone up, I certainly wasn't expecting to see his name on the message bar. My wine went sour in my mouth.

Matteo Alvarez.

Dammit. It made me feel guilty just to see his name. It wasn't that I just hadn't told Nico about it, I'd actually lied about it – that was something completely different.

I clicked the link.

Please ask Nico to call me. I am worried for him. His telephone number followed. The dialling code I had seen before in Nico's phone. It was for Spain.

Matteo obviously wasn't going to disappear, then. But what about the second sentence? I frowned. Maybe it was simply the wrong phrase – had it just got lost in translation somewhere? Did he mean he was worried *about* Nico, because he hadn't heard from him? I mean, why would he be worried *for* him?

Holding the phone in my hand, I could imagine Matteo in Spain, holding his own phone, staring at the screen, seeing his message sending to me. He might still be waiting, imagining me reading the words, hoping I'd reply straight away. But I had no idea what to say.

With the doubts already in my stomach, I really didn't want to add to them by worrying myself about Nico's old life in Spain. I had enough worries about his life here. And with Nico's fears about Brexit and his job at the care home, I didn't want to add to his burden either. Any time I mentioned Nerja, he shut me down. He'd made it clear he wanted to move on from everyone. No, I think the last thing we needed was to add another worry into the mix. I could certainly do without that. I turned my phone off and laid it face-down on the table.

In hindsight, I should have replied.

Two letters came the next day. The first one was for Nico. He found it lying innocently enough in the postbox and brought it into the kitchen, where I was getting ready to go to Ginny's.

"It's from immigration." He showed me the government postmark and his eyes held mine. My breath caught in my throat. This could be it, his notice to leave or refusal of application. What the hell would we do then? I swallowed to wet my mouth, and again.

He ripped open the envelope and scanned the letter. I had to clear my throat before speaking.

"What's it say?"

He exhaled loudly. "Nothing," he said and I let my own breath out. "*Your application is being reviewed.*"

"No news is good news, my mum used to say." I tried a smile as I poured him a coffee, but he didn't join in.

"How long do these things take?" he said, exasperated. He pointed at the text, "for them to 'do *relevant checks*'?" I buttered him some toast, passed him Ginny's honey, wanting to sweeten the mood.

"What even are 'relevant checks'?" he said, chomping the toast.

"All the normal things, I guess – tax payment, criminal record, employment history – but you haven't got anything to worry about, have you?"

He drummed his fingers on the worktop, chewing, then suddenly stopped, swallowed.

"What about speeding tickets? Would that be on a criminal record?" We held each other's eyes again. "I had two speeding fines in Spain. When Magda was small."

"I don't know," I said, already reaching for my phone to google it. He pushed his toast to one side and looked over my shoulder. I typed "what shows on your criminal record?" into the search bar and pressed go. The results could change everything. I couldn't hear Nico breathing as I clicked through onto a site: Basic Disclosures.

I scrolled past some blurb about who might access the information and why, government bodies, potential employers in certain industries, and zoomed in on a bullet point.

- unspent criminal records. For each, it discloses the date of the convictions, the court, the offence committed, the date of the offence and the sentence received.

"Doesn't say anything about speeding?" Nico muttered. I scrolled down again to the next bullet point.

"What they don't disclose," I read out loud. "*Spent criminal records, fixed penalty notices, or allegations.*"

I scanned on again. "Found it! Fixed penalty notices such as speeding fines won't show – well, they will on your driving licence, but not on your criminal record." I grinned, but Nico was still frowning.

"What's the other thing – allegations? Is that the same as the Dennisons at the nursing home, accusing me of something I didn't do?"

"Yep, so anything you've been wrongly accused of won't show either."

He took a moment and then his face melted into the first full smile of the morning. "So my record is totally clear." He kissed me, long and slow and left me with a taste of honey. Whether my husband was a liar or not, he was still a damned good kisser. And immigration was not taking him, or Midge, away from me.

Ginny got the second letter. It had arrived at the farm that morning and, by the time I got there, she'd opened and read it and was spoiling for a fight. She met me in the drive as I pulled in, crunching across the gravel to pull open my car door.

"Two fucking weeks they've given me!" she said, thrusting the letter at me. "They can't do that."

"Bees again?" I said, presuming the worst.

"Ha! I wish!" She waved the letter at me again and I took it, reading it aloud, half to myself, half to her.

"Dear Mrs Brookes. Re: Mortgage arrears." My stomach dropped, a sense of foreboding kicking in. Not again. "In the matter of the property, Hollow Farm, Lower Doyle. Blah blah blah…" I skimmed the legal wording, trying to make sense of it. "This is to notify you that full and complete payment of your mortgage arrears must be deposited by 31st August 2016. If arrears are not cleared by then, proceedings will be started by your lender to repossess the property."

I stopped. It was as bad as I'd thought. Worse. Ginny glared at me, like it was my fault, and I felt awkward, uncomfortable and, more than anything, angry.

"What happened to the money I gave you for the mortgage?"

She flushed, but bit back at me. "That bloody donkey happened. You know, with the plastic bag."

You can't be serious?" I rolled my eyes.

"I couldn't let her die, could I?" She looked at me as if I was missing the point entirely.

"All of it?" I asked, incredulous.

No," she said and I felt a glimmer of hope that died in the next second. "The rest of it went on a starter motor."

I made a sound of exasperation. She threw both her hands in the air.

"I have to be able to get about. Collect feed. Pick up the injured animals. Get to the vets."

I pressed my lips together to stop myself saying anything else. I'd really tried to help her. I had. But I should never have gone against the advice I'd stuck to all my life. *Never loan money to friends or family.* But come to think of it, I hadn't even lent it to her. I'd *given* her the five thousand pounds. And she'd cocked it up. I was livid. At her – and at myself.

"They can't just spring this on me, can they?" she said, poking the letter with her finger, completely oblivious to the fact that she'd spent the money on the wrong thing.

"I think they can, actually," I said with a grimace and she kicked at the driveway stones. One flew up and pinged off my car but I didn't dare say anything. A crimson flush was spreading up her neck.

"They don't normally do this kind of thing out of the blue, though, Gin," I said. "How many letters have you had exactly?"

She shook her head impatiently and turned on her heel, stomping to the barn. I took a couple of deep breaths and followed. I found her feeding a brood of ducklings in their new pen, scattering grain on the ground where they waddled and quacked.

"I take it you've had a few, then?" I said. She opened a delivery box from the grocers, took out some leafy greens and threw them in. The ducks immediately left the grain and turned to the treats.

"You never told me it had gone this far. When did you get the first one?" I said, trying a different tactic.

"A few months ago," she muttered and moved to the first of the hedgehogs in their crates, lifted the lid to start clearing it out. "Nobody donates to charities any more, not even animal ones. Everything just dried up."

"Have you spoken to the mortgage people about it?"

"What's to talk about?" she said. "I haven't got the money, or I'd have paid them wouldn't I?" She lifted out a hoglet and placed him in a holding cage while she scraped out his normal home. "It seems bees don't pay the bills, no matter how much honey they make."

"They might have given you a bit more time, or worked out a new payment plan or something?" I'd heard that Money Saving Expert on the radio recommending trying to organise a payment holiday if you needed it; not that I was sure if it would have been relevant in Ginny's case. I'd never had a mortgage. I felt out of my depth. But I knew what repossession was. I knew she could lose her home.

"They might have let you pay just a bit a month for a while," I said.

"I haven't paid for months, maybe nearly a year. Whatever cash I get is needed in here," she said, throwing her arms wide. I took in the stock of hay, the stacked tinned foods, the shiny wheelbarrow. Many of the old cages with broken latches had been replaced with new plastic crates with air vents and removable bottoms, easier to clean out. The barn was swept and clean. The medicine cabinet was full of bottles and tinctures. Certainly she'd been spending money in here; it was clear to see. Maybe some of my money had been put to use here too. Some of the more curious animals – the goats, the sheep with a dog bite – stood at the front of their pens, eyes on Ginny, waiting for her to come to them. They bleated for her. Trusted her. I could see where her money went. On them. In fact, it looked like they were living in the lap of luxury now compared to her shithole of a house.

There were slates missing from the roof that must be letting in the weather, and the window frames were rotting away to dust. Last time I'd been in her kitchen, I'd seen a new bloom of damp spreading down the inside wall. When I opened the fridge on the hunt for milk, there was only a tin of dog meat, almost empty, a fork sticking out of it. There was certainly no money being wasted in there.

Ginny picked up the hoglet and let it lie on its back in her gloved hand. It squinted up at her, nose twitching. Her face softened. "There you go, my little mangy mate." She had the same clothes on I'd seen her in the other day. Her hair had a piece of straw sticking out of the bun. She stretched out her arms to pop him back into his cage and it was then I saw the fresh red scratch lines running horizontally along her arm, elbow to wrist, each one a slit a couple of centimetres long. Too concise to be an accident. Too uniform to be anything but man-made. I looked away. Poor Ginny. I'd thought those days were long gone.

"Come on," I said, aching for my friend, still wanting to help her like she'd helped me. "We can ring the Citizens' Advice Bureau first. Let's see what options you've got."

Ginny blinked quickly.

"It's not me I'm worried about," she said. "The animals don't stand a chance without me." I closed my mouth, not wanting to say the wrong thing. But I was thinking that they'd just get transported somewhere, another sanctuary would take them in. But it was more than that to Ginny. I realised that. They filled the hole for her. The one that Midge filled for me.

She closed the latch and turned to me, ready to start.

"They're not taking them away from me," she said through her teeth as we walked back out into the sunlight. Then, almost to herself, "Over my fucking dead body."

"Night night, sleep tight," I said to Midge later that evening from her bedroom door.

"See you in the morning," she replied, with a sleepy smile. She loved our little bedtime routine, the same one my mum had done with me. I remember the stripy softness of brushed cotton sheets, the smell of her hair as she kissed my cheek. I pulled the door slowly closed until I heard Midge say "stop" and then left it there. She, like me as a child, was reassured by the landing light. I watched her shift in her bed in the shadows, turn onto her side, ready to sleep. I wondered if my mum had watched me the same, just stealing an extra moment of time. I bet she had.

As I crept down the stairs, Nico sped into the drive, gravel flying in the dusk. I moved quickly to the front door, waved to get his attention and then motioned with a finger to my lips and a nod to upstairs. He acknowledged me with a brusque nod. Face like thunder. My stomach dropped.

Opening the boot, he started pulling out shopping bags from the farmers' market. He didn't look like he'd had the best day. Join the club. I went to open some red wine, pouring it into a carafe to breathe, polishing two glasses. Looked like we both needed it.

"Hey," he said, loading the table with dog food. I poured the wine and passed him a glass and he glugged a good few mouthfuls of it without a thank-you. Maybe a worse day than I'd thought. I sipped at mine and felt the warmth run through my chest, releasing my shoulders.

"I've just seen Ginny at the feed store," he said. "She was having her credit denied in front of everyone, so I paid for her shopping. Just a bag of dog food," he clarified, then, "She told me everything."

"A right mess, isn't it?" I said, pulling out a chair and sitting down, ready to talk. He refilled his own glass and sat down too. It was obviously going to be a heavy night. I told him about the afternoon, the letter Ginny had showed me. How the rest of the day had been spent, on the internet at first, sitting in her cluttered office, googling help available and reading articles. None of which gave me an increase in optimism. After that, I'd spent hours on the phone in her kitchen, mainly on hold while I watched a trail of ants march between the bin and the windowsill. Listening to muzak while I waited for someone from the Citizens' Advice Bureau to tell us what to do. When I finally got through to the right person, it had been pretty disheartening. Question after question. Had we been in touch with our mortgage provider when we first got a warning letter of arrears? Ginny shook her head. Had we organised a late payment plan or a payment holiday? Ginny sneered. Did we have any savings we could offer as part or full payment now? Ginny laughed but it didn't sound like she was amused.

At the end of the call, the only advice we could use was to contact the mortgage provider and ask for more time. I did that, getting through to an account manager in the right team. They were very nice, extraordinarily polite, but very firm. The time for token gestures had passed. Unless Ginny could pay the full amount in a fortnight, the farm would be repossessed.

It was at that point that Ginny grabbed the phone from me and put it on speaker, leaning over it and shouting down at it.

"What about the animals?" A small glob of spit sat on her lip. "You can't do this!"

The person on the other end attempted a polite response, but once Ginny started calling them "a heartless fucker", they clicked into full automaton mode, recited their anti-abuse policy to her and hung up. She didn't even realise they'd gone for a full twenty seconds. When she finally heard the static of empty air at the other end, she smacked the phone on the table a couple of times before putting it down.

"I'm not sure it will ever work again," I said to Nico now, with a shake of my head. It was good to be able to talk about it. It had been a pretty intense afternoon. Ginny had been manic almost, picking at her scabby arm, not caring that I could see the slits. Just scratch, scratch, scratching at the tiny marks. The noise gave me trouble swallowing.

"The thing is, after I paid for the dog food, she asked me straight out if we could help," Nico said, pouring me more wine. We were almost through the bottle already. I threw him a look, bemused.

"What do you think I've been doing all afternoon?" I laughed, but he didn't join in.

"That's not what I meant," he said, fixing me with his eyes. "Or what she meant."

I swallowed my wine, but this time it didn't go down as smoothly. Please don't let him say what I thought he was going to.

"I meant, can we give her some more money."

Damn. He'd said it.

I refilled our glasses, playing for time, letting the last drips run from the bottle before setting it back on the table. He took my silence as consideration, leaned forward on his elbows.

"We have so much," he said. "We could give some to her. She's your friend."

I nodded then, at the word friend. He was right. She was the best friend I'd ever had. Maybe the only true one. Totally mad and like nobody I'd ever met before, but she had been there when nobody else was. The things I'd told her about my past hadn't put her off. She'd stood by, regardless. That had to count for something. I bit my lip, hard.

"That's exactly why I've helped her out once already," I said. "And look where that got me."

Nico took a long swallow of his wine. "We could just pay it off," he said then, and I flinched.

"The arrears?" I said.

"No," Nico said. "The whole mortgage."

I sat back in my chair, like I'd been pushed. He leaned toward me.

"Why not?" he said. "It's not like you don't have it." He sounded angry all of a sudden.

"You don't just go buying a house for your friends, Nico," I said, and then caught myself. It sounded as though I were explaining something to Midge. I cleared my throat.

"But we have everything we could ever need." He threw his arms wide. My gorgeous husband in my hand-made kitchen, in my mortgage-free nineteenth-century home, with other properties dotted around the country – and abroad – that I'd never even slept the night in. He was right, but even so.

"That doesn't mean—" I started.

"For God's sake, Kat, what's the point in having money if you don't do the right thing with it?" His shoulders slumped. "You know she's eating dog food in there."

I grimaced. The tin in the fridge. The dirty fork sticking out of it. I'd presumed it was for Cleo.

Nico's eyes were burning into me and I couldn't meet them. I felt for Ginny, I really did. Hadn't I already gone against my better judgement once and written her a cheque? Hadn't I always gone out of my way for her? Not just physically at the sanctuary, feeding animals, shovelling shit, but financially, tucking donations into the box whenever I had change. A little bit here, a little bit there. "It all helped" – that's what Ginny always said when she emptied the donation box. But however sorry I felt for her, I just couldn't pay off her mortgage. It wouldn't be right. Mum's voice was ringing in my ears. And this time I was going to listen to it.

"It's just not a good idea," I said, standing to open another bottle of wine.

Nico slapped the table and I jumped. "What's stopping you?" he said. "I thought you cared about her."

I spun to face him then. "That's not fair, Nico. You know I do."

"Give me one good reason then?" he pushed.

"Never loan money to friends or family," I said. "It always leads to trouble. So Mum used to say. And look, it's already caused tension between Ginny and me, and now it's causing an argument between you and me because we're talking about it."

He licked his lower lip, thinking. "Maybe you should listen to me and not your mum?"

The challenge was open and I made myself look him straight in the eye, even though my stomach was churning.

"What's yours is mine, you said." His eyes blazed.

I nodded, weakly. I couldn't directly tell him that no, he could not take this decision without me. I said: "It's a big decision though, Nico. Mum's advice has always stood me in good stead in the past. The one time I ignored it, Ginny abused it."

"But if I wanted to, I could just take it." The air between us fizzed. My guts churned. Was this really what it all came down to? Money?

"You could. But I would hope you don't." I forced a tiny smile on to my lips, trying to diffuse the situation. "Besides, a withdrawal that big on a joint account would need both of us to sign it off."

He slumped, like his bones had collapsed, ran his fingers through his hair.

I pulled the cork from the bottle and took it back, topping up our glasses in the silence.

"Why do you feel so strongly about it?" I said. I sipped the wine, but it tasted sour in my mouth. "The money for Ginny?" I wanted to know his reasons, to convince myself he wasn't just trying to assert himself.

"I just think it would solve a lot of problems," he said. "Give a new start—" He shut his mouth, shook his head, dismissing whatever else he had been going to add. It didn't convince me. I wasn't going to give money to Ginny just because he wanted to start controlling the money. My money.

His hand, feverishly hot, found mine across the table. My knuckles grated together in his grip.

"I think this time your mum might be wrong," he said. "I just don't want it to be something you regret later."

"I won't." I shook my head.

He looked at me for a long time. "In that case, leave it to me. I will tell her."

Looking back on it, he was right, of course. Mum's advice *was* wrong this time. If she'd been there she'd probably have advised me differently. I think she may well instead have used that old adage, "sometimes it's better to cut and run."

I avoided going over to Ginny's for a few days after that, not knowing quite what to say. I was happier to avoid her and believe that Nico had deferred to me where money was concerned and that he'd have the tricky conversation on our behalf. Can't say I wasn't relieved about that. I'd rather have poked myself in the eye than talk about money again with Ginny.

I let myself be easily distracted by the Scarecrow Festival that was taking over the village. Every house on the through road had one in their front garden, stuck on poles above the hedge. Tourists came from miles around, cars crawling through the town while children leaned out of windows and pointed.

Midge was fascinated. She had chosen her favourite one, dressed in a tartan coat and wearing a trilby. He resided on North Street and we visited him daily.

"He's called Bucklemuck," she said, waving to him as we drove past on our way to the recreation ground, where all of the other entries were being judged.

"Did he wave back?" Nico asked.

"Yes," she said. "Did you miss it?" She giggled. We couldn't help but smile.

The car park was jammed and we crawled around looking for a space. My nerves jittered when I spotted Ginny's car. Nico saw it too. Mud-splattered and with a newly broken wing mirror.

"Ginny must be here with her honey," he said.

Nico navigated the last corner spot, expertly edging into a gap I'd never have tried. His brown hands on the wheel suddenly made me think of you driving the convertible, sun-tanned in the summer. I took a deep breath, enjoyed the memory, and then let it go.

Midge clambered out and we went to the tent to collect our three judging pebbles. It was a clever idea; all visitors judged the exhibits, leaving a bright-red painted stone at the feet of their three favourite scarecrows. Whoever had the most stones at the end of the day won the annual prize – dinner at the pub.

With our stones in our pockets, Midge took my hand and we were off.

"Shame we can't vote for Bumblefum," I said to her.

"Muuuuuuum!" She laughed, swinging on my arm. "He's called Bucklemuck!" The crowd parted ahead and we dived into the gap, nudging our way to the front. The scarecrow was called Boris Johnson and had a sprout of golden straw for hair. The adults laughed but the children were not very impressed. Midge kept her stones in her hand. Nico snorted. We moved swiftly on to the next, called Worzel. Highly uno-riginal. I rolled my stone in my pocket, smooth and cool.

Visitors were three or four deep at every entry and it made for slow going. One scarecrow wore a German army uniform and was called Herr Crow. He had lots of pebbles in front of him. Midge didn't get the joke but I put one of my pebbles down. But the next effort made her laugh out loud and put two of her pebbles down at once. Haircrow wore a long blond wig, back-combed high, looking every inch like a member of an eighties American rock band.

Midge wrapped her final pebble tightly in her fist and pulled me forward. The crowd parted and I saw the next stand was not a scarecrow, it was G's Bees. There was Ginny behind the stall, hot-looking, talking to a customer.

Not interested in honey, Midge pulled me onwards to the next exhibit. I felt like I was sneaking past, but at the same time I was relieved that Ginny hadn't seen me. It was only when we got to the next scarecrow, the scare-eagle, which had an eagle head and was quite frankly weird, that I turned to laugh at it with Nico and realised he wasn't there.

I craned my neck to see over the crowd and saw the glint of his black hair – at the honey stall. He was standing slightly to the side while Ginny served a tweed-wearing day-tripper who wanted a taste of the country. Half of me wanted to go over and see her, the other half just couldn't face it. Midge pulled me further into the crowd, surprisingly wanting to give her last pebble to the eagle-faced scarecrow. From my hiding place, I could still see them clearly, although I couldn't hear a word. Ginny's customer left, honey jar in hand, and Nico stepped closer.

He was obviously talking as Ginny opened a tin and put the customer's money inside. I could tell by the shake of his head, the shrug of his shoulders, he was telling her that I wouldn't help with the mortgage. She closed the tin before she looked at him. And when she did, it was with such a fierce anger that my breath caught in my throat. She banged the table in frustration. He spoke to her again, leaning in, put a hand on her forearm, and she slumped, closed her eyes, breathed out through parted lips. It was like she was giving up. She asked him something else, but Nico shook his head again. I knew he was apologising.

Suddenly, she straightened. She smiled. Said a few words, and Nico relaxed slightly; I could see his shoulders drop. He thrust his hand out towards her and she looked at it a moment, surprised, but then took it. Shook it. My own breath came out slowly. I hadn't realised I was holding it. It was going to be okay. Thank God. I didn't want to lose her. She was my best friend.

"How many have you got left?" Midge asked, pulling at my hand. "Can I have one of yours?" I smiled and pulled out my remaining two stones and handed them over, much to her delight.

I turned back to see what was happening with Nico. He'd left Ginny and was making his way through the crowds back to me. She was watching him go, thoughtful. I lifted my hand to get his attention. His face broke into a smile when he spotted me, full of happiness and love – and relief – and I smiled in return.

"Best to leave Ginny alone for a while," Nico had said after the Scarecrow Festival. "Just give her some space." Wise words probably, but I missed her. And I had a plan that might help. So I ignored him, and went anyway. Sometimes, I should probably do as I'm told.

It had been three days since she'd found out about the repossession. The farm, even in sunlight, looked ramshackle as I opened the gate to drive in. The donations notice was hanging off the gate and the box was missing. I couldn't help but feel nervous; I really didn't want to talk about money again. Another couple of hundred had come out of the account the day before.

Ginny had shorts and wellies on, teamed with a tank top of some sort that looked like it had done military service. But I was so pleased to see her that I couldn't care less what she was wearing. She waved a saw at me, then steadied a plank of wood with her knee and started cutting.

"What you making?" I asked, sheltering from the sun under the barn canopy.

"New donation box," she said. "Some fucker stole the old one."

"For God's sake," I said. Talk about kicking a woman when she's down.

"Hope he has a blast on the £1.63 or however much was in it this week," she said, but she didn't laugh. The plank fell into two as she finished the cut.

"How's things?" I said, hoping she wouldn't tell me.

"I've trained the dog to do a trick," she said, whistling for Cleo, who came loping over from her spot under the apple tree.

"GET THEM," Ginny shouted, pointing at me. Cleo changed in the blink of an eye, hackles up, teeth bared. She growled at me, ears flat back on her head. Instinctively I took a step backwards. Ginny cackled.

"Good girl," she said to the dog, scratching her ears. Cleo wagged her tail and licked her hand, back to her old self.

"Bloody hell," I said, stunned.

"They'll have to get past her – and me."

The dog sat and proceeded to lick her bottom, not looking so fierce now.

"Look – about the repossession," I said. "I've been think-ing about it…" I had her attention now. She faced me, saw hanging by her side.

"You're my best friend and I know how important this is to you."

She worried her lip with her teeth, waiting.

"I want to help you."

Her face lifted with a surge of hope and then burst into a smile. She dropped the saw and grabbed me in a hot hug that smelled of woman and dog in one.

"But Nico said it was a 'no'," she muttered into my hair. I froze. Oh God. She thought I was giving her the money. I was such an idiot. I'd said it wrong. Gently, I disentangled myself.

"No, I didn't mean, not the money…" Her arms dropped to her sides and she took a step back, incredulous.

"I've had an idea to *raise* the money," I stammered, words rushing over each other to show her I really did want to help. "I want to start a public appeal. Let's get the media involved.

The TV, radio, local papers. I can write you a press release. I used to do it at work."

I wasn't sure she was listening. She was looking at my lips moving, but it was like she was lost in thought. Her face contorting, one expression morphing into the next. Considering.

"I'll write a sponsorship letter for you, send it to all the big firms in Cheltenham and Gloucester. Let's get them involved in the appeal too." I gabbled on about how I'd do it, and who I'd contact first, and would she do the interviews?

It looked like it was sinking in. She seemed to come back to me and then nodded. She'd obviously made a decision.

"Worth a try," she said finally and relief made me feel slightly dizzy.

"Right," I said. "I'll crack on, then. The sooner we get started the better." I turned to leave.

"Hold on," she said. "I've got something for you."

She disappeared into the house and came back with a face cream refill for me, my name written on the top of the pot in red pen.

"Improved version," she said. "I added balm mint for its soothing properties. Let me know how it feels."

My eyes got hot and wet in a rush. She was still my friend.

"Thank you," I managed, feeling quite overcome.

"No worries," she said. "You deserve it."

I meant to tell Nico about it when I got home, I was so touched. But when I got back, Midge was sitting quietly watching *Peppa Pig* and there was no sign of him anywhere in the house. I thought maybe he'd dozed off; it was such a hot day. I made my way to our bedroom but the bed was perfectly made and empty. It was as I turned to come back downstairs that I saw a movement in the garden. Nico was right at the end, pacing the hedge by the barley field, phone clamped to his ear.

Every now and then he flicked a glance towards the house. I stayed away from the window so that he didn't see me.

I kept my promise to Ginny and rang the local paper, the *Gloucester Herald*, the next morning. It gave me something to focus on, keep my mind off Nico. The reporter I spoke to sounded fairly bored until I mentioned the idea of a public appeal, something the paper could really get behind. The sound of typing paused at the other end as he considered it, before admitting they could do with another community focus now that the Scarecrow Festival was over.

"Send over some background," he suggested. "August is silly season in the media, after all. There's never any real news." I scribbled down his email address and hung up, quickly, before he could change his mind.

I started a new document on the computer, titled it Hollow Farm Animal Sanctuary in big bold type, then let flow with everything I knew about Ginny and the animals she saved. I talked about the variety of creatures, the barn owls and the dormice. I noted the numbers of rescues, how each season brought new problems. I went to town on the terrible types of injury, the hedgehogs with legs mown off, the sheep with dog bites. I googled other animal sanctuaries to see where the closest ones were, and found one about thirty miles to the north. It specialised in hedgehogs but didn't seem to accept other animals. I made a note of that for the newspaper. Hollow Farm was the only local resource of its kind. That must make it important.

I explained how Ginny had devoted her life to the animals, raising the funds to feed and house them while they recuperated, forging links with local vets who gave their time voluntarily to stitch or sew or splint. Then I ground to a stand-still. What else could I put? What else did I know? I made a point to say she was a part of the community, selling local honey and making pottery. Then I tapped my fingers on the keyboard, racking my brains. Was it enough? I added her contact details at the bottom so that they could call her direct for interview.

Reading it back through, I figured it was a good start and the reporter should do his job and bring it to life. I suggested an appeal fund name: "SOS: Save Our Sanctuary!" and rec-ommended they did a visual of the fund jar being filled up as the donations came flooding in. I cheekily hinted at it being front-page stuff, with a little update every day. I pressed send, pleased to have done my part. I checked my watch, noticing it was nearly lunchtime. I'd been busy for a good hour. Nobody could say I hadn't tried to help.

As my email flashed off into web world and I shut down the computer, Midge squealed and streaked past the window. She was holding a water pistol but running away from Nico, who was obviously a better aim. Roo bounded alongside, jaws snapping at the stream of water as it shot from the nozzle. They were having a ball. All of them. My gorgeous girl, my dog and my husband.

I could write pages of information about Midge and I'd never run out of things to say. Her likes and dislikes, her little phrases. Her cute mispronunciations and facial expressions, "hoggable" instead of "horrible", with a quick wrinkle of her nose. "Gubblebum". I could describe how soft her skin was. How she smelled of fresh laundry and biscuits, of my hopes and dreams for our future together. Our trips and holidays when I could show her the world. I wouldn't struggle at all. I could fill a book.

Nico was another matter. I was married to him, but what did I actually know about him? The residents at the care home would say he was kind. He was patient. He rubbed cream into their legs gently. But one of them also said he was a will-chaser. I'd admit he was loving and caring and cooked like a dream. I'd swear to him being a good dad who would do anything for his daughter. But I didn't know much more about his past. What did I actually know about his life in Spain apart from the snippets he'd told me? Midge wouldn't go near him at night when she had a nightmare. And she'd also said he had secrets. What was that all about?

They ran past the window again. Midge had lost her water pistol along the way and was now sprinting as fast as she could, arms like pistons, her back soaked. Roo bounded beside her, equally wet and bedraggled-looking, but tail wagging non-stop. Nico stopped in the middle of the lawn, panting, hands on his thighs. I pushed myself back from the computer so he wouldn't sense my eyes on him. But I wasn't quick enough.

He stood, shading his eyes with his hand, and caught me looking through the window; waved, smiled. Beckoned me to come out and join them, before running after Midge again, causing fresh screams.

My jaw clenched, wishing, really wishing I could just take him at face value, but the nagging in my gut wouldn't let me. Whatever it was he was hiding, I wouldn't let it take them away from me. I had my family at last, and I'd overcome anything for that.

Things didn't quite go to plan. Story of my life.

The article, when it ran a few days later, was hardly the big community fundraising campaign I'd envisaged. It took me two flicks through the local paper to find it, a small, single-column story on page fourteen. The only addition the journalist had put in was a quote from Ginny. Lazy bugger. And there was me thinking he'd do some research of his own. Maybe send a photographer along, get a shot of Ginny surrounded by her animals. But no, the tiny picture they used was a stock photograph of a ferret. I didn't even know if Ginny had ever rescued a ferret.

Nico put his arms round me from behind, pulled me to him. "You did that. My wife, the campaigner," he said. "You should be proud of yourself."

"It's so small," I said, sounding small myself.

"But it has everything it needs," he said, pointing at the donation line. At least the paper had done that right. It said that people could call in and pledge money, or drop it in to the newspaper office.

"But look at that." I pointed to a neighbouring article, bigger, bolder, with the title 'decrease noticed in charity donations nationally'. I threw the paper down on the table, frustrated. "Do you think people will donate?"

"If they read it, maybe yes," he said, giving me a squeeze.

I couldn't even pick out the tiny article in the paper, and I had been looking for it. Someone would have to read it cover to cover to stumble across it. It wasn't enough.

"I need to reach more people," I said. "Get the message out there."

An hour later, I'd set up a GoFundMe page for the sanctuary, linked to my Facebook page. I scrolled through my phone for a photograph of Ginny with the animals to include, but she was holding a glass of wine in every single one, which I didn't think gave the right impression. In the end, I went with a stock photograph of a hedgehog. At least it wasn't a ferret.

I started the fundraising off with a donation of twenty pounds, just to get the ball rolling. People never like to be first with these things, it's like going into an empty restaurant. I made the page public and crossed my fingers. Let the donations flood in.

Midge wandered by outside the window, wearing my headphones. They were way too big for her and she held them to her ears to stop them slipping. I could hear her singing, loudly and out of tune. Daydreaming of being a world-famous singer. Roo followed behind, tail wagging, just happy to be alive.

It was music that gave me the idea of ringing the local radio station, Gloucester Sounds. All the parents at school listened to it because it was the best for local information, traffic problems, school closures, that sort of thing. I found their number on the internet, took a deep breath, and dialled.

The reporter there was much more interested than the lazy pillock at the *Herald*. Said the only other news at the moment was a local outbreak of stomach flu and she'd be glad to get her teeth into something more meaty. She was young and excitable. She started talking about how they were currently interviewing local heroes, and that Ginny would fit perfectly for saving the local wildlife. I matched her enthusiasm, told her everything I knew and gave her Ginny's mobile number before hanging up.

"Lunch is ready," Nico said behind me and I jumped. But when I turned to him, he was smiling.

"Wow," he said. "Look at you! You're glowing."

I caught a glimpse of myself in the mirror behind him on the wall and he was right; my skin looked wonderful, although maybe my scar looked a little redder than usual. Maybe it was a new stage of the healing process. Nico put his hand on my face, rubbed his thumb on my cheek. My skin tingled under his fingers, just like the very first time he'd touched me.

"Come and eat," he said, tucking my hair behind my ear. "I've made you something special."

I let him lead the way.

I had obviously had too much sun that afternoon, playing with Midge in the garden. By teatime I was nauseous and headachy. I retreated into the shade of the house. Nico seemed unaffected, maybe from having grown up in sunnier climes. Midge was wearing a sun hat and smothered in factor fifty, playing in the shade of the apple tree. I had no worries about her.

The kitchen tiles were cold against my bare feet and I had an urge to lie down and put my face against them to cool down. Instead, I downed two paracetamol, poured myself a lemonade and took it to the window seat, where I could see what was going on outside. Roo flopped onto the floor beside me. I didn't want Nico to think I was keeping an eye on him, so I held my book in my lap, but deep down I knew I was watching to see if he made a phone call.

My own phone buzzed in my pocket and I nearly had a heart attack. Guilty conscience showing itself. I flicked to messages, expecting it to be Ginny. It was Matteo. Damn, this guy was persistent. I glanced outside, checking that Nico wasn't looking, then opened the link.

I need to talk to Nico. Elena's brothers are coming to the UK.

He knows what they are like. It could mean trouble. For him and for you.

He printed his telephone number again at the bottom and signed off with an M. Like we knew each other. Like we were friends. I guess I had nobody to blame for that but myself. I had accepted his friend request. Fuck.

It could mean trouble. What did that mean? What kind of trouble?

Absently I stared out of the window, watching Nico as he threw a ball for Midge. What had happened between him and Elena's family? Maybe they just wanted to see Midge. I could understand that – she was part of their family. But that one word was bothering me. Trouble. It sounded threatening. It had a tang of violence to it.

Should I tell Nico? I immediately pushed the thought away, not wanting to have to admit to being in touch with Matteo. He had been so adamant about it. I caught my lip between my teeth, pulled at it, thinking.

Anyhow, even if they did come to the UK, how were they going to find us? It was a big place and, let's face it, The Nook was a hidden cottage, in a tiny lane, surrounded by fields and farms, in rural England. If you blinked, you'd drive straight past.

And then my mistake hit me like a bag of sand, knocking the air from my chest. Anyone who was Facebook friends with Matteo could look me up and look for clues in my posts. My teeth pressed too hard on my lip and tore off a tiny peel of skin.

My fingertips felt numb, making me fumble to open my profile page on Facebook to see what they could see. I didn't post a lot ever since I'd learned how Nico felt about pictures of Midge. The most recent post was a week before, a photograph of Ginny and me at the farm shop. Could you tell where that was? Not really, it could be anywhere.

I scrolled to the next. A picture of me and Annie from New Horizons at the local pub. I bit my lip hard. The pub sign was very clearly visible in the background. That gave someone a very small catchment area. The pub in the next village to us was the only one within miles. I worried my lip again and tasted blood.

Then a post I'd forgotten about. A small message about my dog-walking services, saying I was open for business. It had the name of the business and my mobile phone number. I'd posted it at the same time I'd put cards in the vets and the animal-feed shop. Everyone who had a dog locally knew who I was and where I lived. All you had to do was ask.

My head was pounding and I could hear my own breath. Whatever trouble was heading towards Nico might find him because of me. And if it found him, that meant it found me too. And Midge. Dammit.

My fingers shook as I opened up my friends list on the home page and scrolled to Matteo's name. I needed to get rid of him, get him off my list, out of my life. I clicked for the options on what to do. There: block Matteo Alvarez. It meant not only were we not friends any more but he couldn't see me or anything about me on Facebook. My fingertips fizzed as I clicked it. Done. Now they couldn't find us. Could they? Unease crawled over my neck like a spider, made me flick a glance behind me, check nobody was there.

A shout outside. Midge on Nico's shoulders, waving at me.

"Are you feeling better?" Nico called.

I licked the blood from my lip. "No," I said.

Never had I said a truer word.

I vomited a couple of times, later that afternoon. Hot frothy water that tasted like acid. The sun had obviously cooked my stomach juices to a yellow broth. I flushed it away and closed the toilet lid, sat down to rest. My skin was hot to touch and my scar itched. I buried my face in a cool flannel. I thought it must be sunstroke at first, until I remembered the radio journalist saying how a tummy bug was doing the rounds. The mirror told me I looked as bad as I felt. My skin was goosebumped with shivers but my blood was boiling. My face was puffy, and I looked like I had slap-cheek. There was no way I was going anywhere except bed.

The sheets were beautifully cool at first and then freezing and uncomfortable, and I pulled my knees in, curled up like a baby. The bedroom window was open, curtains wide, but I didn't have the energy to close them. I lay watching bats flit from eaves to trees in the garden and back again in the dusk. Normally we'd be outside at this time, enjoying a glass of red on the patio. Midge would be trying to tell the bats apart from the birds, or showing us her handstands. Anything to put off going to bed.

She and Nico had come inside too now, though, their sounds drifting up the staircase. Murmured conversations, occasional bursts of singing, the rumbling of the TV. I wondered how long it would be before one of them came to see where I was, for someone to miss me, and it was only minutes later that small feet padded on the floor-boards and a brown face peeked round the door. I was glad it was her.

"You say tomayyyyyto," giggled Midge, seeing me under the covers.

"And I say tomarrrrto," I rasped back.

She sprang on to the bed, but was careful to avoid my legs.

"You say potayyyyyyto," she said as she curled in front of me. I slung an arm over her and pulled her in. She was like my medicine.

"I say potarrrrrrrto," I whispered in her ear and she snug-gled back against me.

"Are you sick?" she said, around the thumb she'd stuck in her mouth. I nodded and she craned her neck to look over her shoulder at me.

"I'll ask Daddy to make your favourite tea," she said.

"What might that be?"

"Prawn gaspetti." She edged off the side of the bed and the gap she left was cold. My stomach turned in on itself at the thought of food.

"You know me so well," I said as she scampered out the door. "But just tell Daddy I'm not hungry tonight."

The room was quiet again without her in it. The light had dimmed and the bats were harder to spot. A breeze rustled the trees in the garden. Everything was calm, apart from me. My mind was spinning. Words went round and round in my head, mixed up: my message earlier with Matteo, my con-versations during the day.

Trouble. I could feel it brewing. Building. Something was coming. Something was wrong. However much I tried to ignore it, I couldn't any more.

You know me so well. True in some ways. I knew Nico well enough now to know that although he stroked my hair with the gentlest fingers, he hurt my hand when he held it sometimes. That although he would do anything for Midge, I saw anger flash across his face when she didn't put her shoes on fast enough.

He knows what they are like.

I wanted to shout, throw something. He knows what *who* is like? I didn't even know who they were, what they looked like, let alone what they might do. I felt blind and that made me vulnerable. The thought stopped me in my tracks and I sat up, mind racing. I didn't even know what the trouble looked like.

Stumbling out of bed, I went round to Nico's nightstand. Checking the door first, I eased open his drawer and rummaged, looking for anything that might give me a clue. I had to see what these people looked like. I needed a group shot that showed Elena's family, maybe a wedding photo; but it was just a jumble of receipts, a Spanish to English dictionary, books of matches. Nothing of help. I pushed it shut, careful to be quiet.

I crawled back on to the bed with my laptop, fired it up and waited for the patchy internet to kick in. The screen lit up my face in the darkening room, the brightness made my head pound.

I entered his name in the search bar, as I had before. Nico Menendez.

The results came up in a long list, the same links to people of the same name who had Facebook profiles. I knew he wouldn't be one of them. I scrolled further this time, ignoring links to Twitter and other social media, knowing it was not what I wanted. There was apparently an aspiring singer of the same name, listed with links to music videos and reviews. Nothing.

Again, I typed his name into images. The Spanish newspaper article with his wedding picture came up and this time I paused. Something about it didn't sit right but I couldn't put my finger on it. I clicked on it to see the detail. The article loaded and was all in Spanish, but a quick flick down the page showed me a wedding picture of Nico and Elena, clearer now I'd enlarged it on a laptop and not my phone. It wasn't a picture I'd seen before and I could see why perhaps Nico wouldn't have chosen it for his family album. Elena looked every inch the bride, beaming at the camera, but Nico was caught unsmiling, frowning fiercely as he looked at her. He was holding her hand and I wondered if he was just about to squeeze it too hard.

The words were indecipherable. Just looking at them hurt my head. But the article was clearly not just a wedding announcement; it was quite long and included dates and quotes and the photograph of the boats at sea. I checked the date of publication. Just over three years ago. Right around the time that Elena died. Not when they got married at all. This was something important, something that I should know.

Returning to the headline, I used my cursor to highlight it, copying the words. It only took me a moment to find a Spanish–English translation site, and paste the phrase into the search. I licked my lips, swallowed loudly as I waited. I wasn't ready for what came up.

Groom accused of foul play in bride's death.

My breath stopped in my throat.

"How are you feeling?" Nico said from the doorway. Startled, I closed the screen with a snap. I hadn't heard him coming and the light from my laptop would have hidden him in darkness. How long had he been there watching?

"You scared me," I gasped.

"Guilty conscience," he joked, sitting on the side of the bed. When he took my hand I could feel my own sweat slick on his skin. "I know you. You're just pretending to be sick so you can look at Facebook."

I tried to smile but it fell off. He flicked on the bedside lamp.

"You don't look so good actually," he said, examining my face.

"I've been sick," I managed.

"You must have really overdone the sun," he said. "I'll make you some soup."

I shook my head, the thought of it turning my stomach to hot water, but he ignored me.

"It's important to keep your fluids up," he said. "I won't be long."

For the next couple of days it was like living with Florence Nightingale. Nico was always there, to all intents and purposes looking like the perfect husband.

If he wasn't plumping my pillows, he was opening the window to let fresh air in. Whenever I pretended to fall asleep, he crept out of the room. When I woke again, he'd bring in a jug of water rattling with ice cubes. When I sweated, he'd sponge me down. He brushed my hair off my face. He even applied Ginny's cream to my face and dotted salve on my chapped lips.

By day two we had agreed that it was stomach flu. My temperature was soaring and yet, on a seventy-degree day, I shivered even under a blanket. Nico started bringing me a boiled broth, a family recipe apparently, which was yellow and reminded me of my own sick. He offered it to me at least five times a day, lifting my head and tipping the cup.

"I'm worried about you," he said. "Shall I call the doctor?"

I shook my head, "It's doing the rounds. I'll be fine."

"Don't want you to get dehydrated," he kept on. I'd try to keep him happy by sipping a mouthful or two, until I gagged, and then he'd take it away. Eventually, I satisfied him by sipping the water he brought me. He'd smile and nod like an old woman.

I had too much time to think, to worry, chewing my cheek, but unable to do anything about it. It was infuriating. I just wanted Nico to go away so that I could translate some

more of the article. Did it mean what I thought it did? Was
it saying that Nico had had a hand in Elena's death? It was
the last thing I'd ever expected. Naïve of me, of course; I
know more than most people that it does happen. Sometimes,
things are not as straightforward as they first appear. Look
what happened to you, after all, when I launched myself at
you in the car. It was my fault the car came off the road,
although nobody ever knew that. It's not the kind of thing
that comes up in conversation.

"I'm going to take Midge to the park," said Nico, from
the doorway. "She's going stir-mad."

I didn't have the energy to correct his phrasing, but I grabbed
the opportunity to have the house to myself. "Could you bring
my phone up before you go. Just in case I need you?"

I left it five minutes after I heard the car crunching over
the gravel, to be sure they were not going to pop back for
sunscreen or a forgotten wallet. Then I pulled myself out of
bed.

Everything about my body hurt. My joints felt as though
they didn't fit properly, bones grating against each other as I
moved. Paracetamol didn't even take the edge off the ache. I
rubbed at my skin and it prickled and puckered under my
fingers. The strangest sensation.

From the window, I could keep a lookout. The driveway was
clear, the track to the lane empty. Birds were busy at the feeding
table and a squirrel tightroped along the phone line to the oaks.
My hand trembled lightly as I dialled Matteo's number.

It rang the long alien beep of a foreign number, not the
normal double burr of a local call. I tapped the sill, waiting.
It rang again, and then he was there, answering in Spanish.

"Hello?" I cleared my throat. "Matteo? It's Kat. Nico's wife." A tiny pause before he spoke.

"Are you okay?" he asked and I heard him exhale when I replied yes.

"Thank God," he said.

I took a breath and went for it. "I need to know what's going on."

For a moment it was only air on the line.

"What has he told you?" he asked.

"That Elena died in an accident." Static buzzed and I gripped the phone tighter, worried I might lose the connection. "Is that true?"

Again, a pause while I imagined him at the other end, considering his words.

"The court says yes," he said, and my shoulders slumped with relief, but it was short-lived. "But her family think no."

"They think he killed her?" I whispered and I could hear him suck his teeth. Someone called his name, a woman. He was needed.

"There are only two people that know what really happened and one of them is dead."

"But why?"

"I don't know. It's a rumour. But her family are a big deal. You don't want to be on the wrong side of them." The woman called him again and he shouted back in Spanish. "*Un momento.*" He'd have to go. I didn't have long.

"What happens if they find him?" I asked, supporting myself on the windowsill. His silence told me everything I needed to know. It wasn't going to end well. Nico was in danger. And that meant Midge was too.

"Thank you," I stammered, knowing nothing else could be said.

"The way he left after Elena…" he said, suddenly. "The fact that he never comes home. Has left all his friends. It makes you think."

I held my breath.

"Maybe it *is* true."

The phone went dead.

B y the next afternoon, as well as feeling ill I was starting to feel like a prisoner in my own house. A very well-kept prisoner, it had to be said, as Nico was still waiting on me hand and foot, but contained – like a well-fed animal. Or a creature at the zoo. Watched. Observed. It was making me uncomfortable.

At the same time, I couldn't help but think that if Nico was staying home with me, then at least he couldn't be spotted by Elena's family if they were in the area. Maybe I should be thankful that he wanted to play nursemaid. It kept him out of sight. Anyway, when Ginny turned up it was like a breath of fresh air. I heard her car pull into the drive, exhaust rattling, and went to meet her, not even caring that I was still wearing my pyjamas. I leaned against the porch, not wanting to walk any further.

Ginny secured the handbrake with a loud creak and bundled out, hair everywhere, cleavage massive in a too-tight, too-young long-sleeved top, which didn't quite reach the jeans that hung low on her hips without the aid of a belt. She hitched them up as she crossed the drive.

"All right, Nico?" She called to him where he sat at the patio table with Midge as she headed to me. "Fuckkkkkkkkkkin 'ell," she said. "You look awful."

It was probably the funniest thing anyone had said to me in days and I couldn't help but smile, even though it hurt my face to move. I put my finger to my lips and nodded towards Midge.

I stumbled back into the kitchen and she followed me through.

"Nico said you'd been sick," she said. She handed me a bunch of magazines and I flicked through the covers. *Woman's Own. Country Living. Dogs Today. People's Friend.*

"Nicked them from the hospital," she said. "Had to have a blood test for my latest trial."

The thought of her giving blood reminded me of the scratches on her arms and I wondered if that was why she was wearing that top on such a hot day. She tugged at her sleeves and I knew they were still there. Probably worse.

"How do you feel?" she said, leaning forward, interested.

"Horrible," I admitted. Everything ached. My stomach hurt. My throat was raw from vomiting.

"You went down fast," she said and I nodded. "Do you feel like you're getting better?"

"Not yet," I said. "Worse if anything."

She pulled a face and pretended to move away.

"How's the appeal going?" I asked, realising I hadn't checked the totaliser in the last few days. In fact, I hadn't seen my laptop for the past few days, not since I found the article. She shrugged.

"Well, let's put it this way," she said, "I think three people have donated so far. And one of them was you."

My mouth fell open. I couldn't believe it. After a newspaper article and a radio interview and posters in every shop. I was gobsmacked.

"Tight bastards round here." She sneered. "Care more about themselves than they do the animals."

An awkward knot was tying itself in my gut. But I'd tried. I'd really tried.

"Anyway," she said, standing up. "I'll find a way."

"You're not giving up then?" I said, following her to the door.

"Nope," she said, stretching her shoulders back so that her top rose up again. "There's more than one way to skin a cat. See ya, Florence," she shouted at Nico as she went. His eyes followed her until she was out of the drive, and then I was alone with him again.

I woke up sometime a few mornings later, disorientated and drenched in sweat. My tongue was swollen in my mouth, raw with ulcers, and my eyelids scratched on my eyeballs with each blink. I hadn't ever felt so ill. It took me a moment to realise I was awake; my sleep had been so light it felt like hallucinating. A string of nightmares leading me one to the other.

Midge's stripy pyjamas made a small pile on the floor where she must have stepped out of them. Her plastic cup was forgotten on the bedside table. I made myself sit up and reached for it, my mouth parched of any moisture. It was empty.

Daddy has a secret.

The memory hit me like a punch to the gut.

Daddy has a secret.

That night felt like a dream, fragments of it coming back to me. The smell of wine on Nico's breath. Midge's back heaving with sobs. The way she held on to me so fiercely. My hand stroking her hair, soothing her to sleep under the revolving stars on the ceiling. I'd stayed long after her breathing slowed and her eyelids stopped flickering. Until she was dreaming another dream. Even then, I couldn't sleep for watching her face. I would do anything for her. To keep her safe, to make her happy.

Had I dreamed what she said? Had I imagined it? Her mouth pressed against my chest, her eyes shut like confession.

Had I made it up? Everything felt unreal to me; maybe I was misremembering. A false memory or whatever they call it.

The room swam around me and my stomach turned in on itself as I tried to stand. Like a drunk, I clutched the wall, waiting for things to settle.

My mouth tasted like milk that had been left in the sun too long. I needed a drink so badly. I had to go and get water.

My bare feet didn't make a sound as I walked gingerly along the corridor, arms wrapped round my aching gut. My stomach felt concave; the only thing I'd been able to keep down for days were sips of broth or water, and sometimes even that came back up.

I made it to the top of the stairs, caught a glimpse of myself in the mirror there and stumbled back, shocked at my bruised-looking eye sockets, my angry scar.

Holding on to the bannister with both hands, I put my head down between them for support as a wave of black threatened to overtake me. After it lifted I sat on the landing to wait it out, feeling the roll of seasickness as the room spun.

As the fog cleared, I could see down to the hall, where Roo was asleep on the rug. I could hear the sounds of morning from the kitchen; the radio was playing, a whisk whirred, the fridge door opened and shut. Nico was cooking. He was always bloody cooking. Plates were being stacked in the sink; he liked to clear up as he went along. The silence afterwards would be him wiping the chopping board clean ready for the next job.

"But – Mummy's – not – feeling – well," Midge said, in the quiet. Her voice was punctuated by little thuds. She was skipping or jumping, the air being knocked out of her each time she landed.

"I know," Nico said. "Poor Mummy." He sounded distracted, maybe reading a recipe or testing a consistency. A cupboard door squeaked open and, a few seconds later, banged shut. The rhythmic thump of Midge's jumps stopped.

"Will we still go?" Midge said.

Go where? I leaned my head against the bannister, wood hard and square against my skull. Nico ran the tap, rinsing something in the sink.

"We'll have to," he said.

Where were we going? Had I forgotten something? Thinking was like walking through treacle. Every time I got halfway through a thought it clogged, faltered. Had we been going somewhere? The last time I could properly remember being out of the house was when I went to Ginny's. We were going to support an appeal, weren't we? Or launch one? I did that, didn't I? Yes. I'm sure.

The blender screeched and then slowed. I heard him opening the lid. He tapped a spoon against a bowl, one, two, three. My head pounded against the bannister, bang, bang, bang. Was it inside my head or outside?

"Look Magda, it's just a few more days," he said. "I know you're good at keeping secrets." Secrets – my whole life was starting to feel like it was built on them. There was a silence but I knew how she'd look, solemn, wide-eyed. She took her responsibilities very seriously. My lips peeled apart. I really needed a drink.

"It will all be over by Saturday and then we'll be gone," he said. "Then you don't have to keep it a secret any more."

My gasp made Roo lift her head off the rug below. She thumped her tail on the floor when she saw me. I stared at her, willing her to stop, to not give my presence away. Keep my secret, Roo, until I find out Nico's. What was he talking about? Where were they going? What were they keeping from me? God, was he planning to leave me? I could hardly breathe.

Roo wagged herself to upright, stood facing me, gazing up the stairs. She yawned comically, waiting for me to do something.

There was a silence in the kitchen, a pause.

I made a shooing motion at Roo, trying to encourage her to go into the kitchen, but she remained, happy, tail swinging, fixated on me. I hadn't been downstairs for days and she was obviously pleased to see me.

Roo barked once and it echoed in the hall. Footsteps across the kitchen and then Nico's head around the door frame to see what Roo was barking at. A flicker of something across his face – shock – when he saw it was me.

"How long have you been there?" he said, taking the stairs towards me two at a time, helping me to my feet.

"Just a minute," I said, not wanting to let on that I'd heard. His hands felt cool on my skin. "I wanted a drink."

"I would have brought you one, all you have to do is call," he said. "Are you feeling any better?"

I licked my lips, forced myself to straighten up.

"A bit," I lied.

"That's great," he said, squeezing me against his side, making my bones ache under my skin. "Better for the weekend then?"

By the weekend they'd be gone.

He obviously had plans and they didn't include me. I nodded and forced a smile even while everything inside me hardened against him. He steered me through to the kitchen and I sat on the chair he pulled out for me. He didn't expect me to answer him as he chatted about his day, and Midge's, and I watched him as he tidied, wiped, chopped, with just one thought in my head.

If he thought he was going to leave me – and take Midge with him?

He had another think coming.

It felt like everyone chose to leave me. Except Mum of course. She had no choice.

Aunt Belinda helped me move into my bedsit a few weeks after my eighteenth birthday. She efficiently unpacked my clothes into a different set of drawers, and then washed her hands happily of me as she left. You know I always told you how independent I'd been? How I loved my own space? How I depended on me? It's true, in some respects, I suppose.

But I was lonely. Desperately lonely. I wasn't part of the crowd and friends were hard to come by. Apparently I was "intense". Sometimes even "weird". Maybe I was just trying too hard. To belong to someone. To be part of something. "Try to be more normal," one acquaintance said, laughing, as we headed to a party; but having grown up with a dead mum and a bitch of an aunt, I didn't really have much experience of that. People I met never seemed to stick. They made plans with other friends without including me. They were never available when I called.

*The only good thing I'd ever had was Mum. If she'd been alive, everything would be different. She loved me without thought or reason. And so, slowly, as I got older and realised my mum was never coming back, I began to want to **be** a mum instead. That would be how I could find the love that I was missing. Fill the hole inside me.*

It was a feeling that grew slowly and over time. And it never went away. Not even for a moment. The few girlfriends I had over the years all laughed at the thought. My short-lived boyfriends shuddered at the prospect and stopped answering the phone when I called.

Although nothing changed, I got more used to pretending that everything was okay. By the time I was twenty-five, you'd be for-given for thinking I had a life. I was earning better money in a day job, with waitressing on the side. I had a small room in a shared flat in Balham, although still the dodgy end. I joined a book club, took trips to the cinema, tried speed dating. But still the evenings were long, the nights were empty and so was my bed. And the hole just kept growing inside me. It was a dark place that I knew I had to fill with something. Someone. A baby.

I cut a coupon from a magazine and secretly filled it in. Sent off my order and waited for the postman for a week. A newborn doll arrived, surprisingly heavy, realistic-looking but somehow horrific. I named her Ruby and thought she would fill the void. Something to look after. Someone to hold. I swaddled her, rocked her to plastic sleep in my bedroom. But it was pointless. There was no love in return. Not a smile or a hug. Eventually I hid her in the cupboard, face-down, under a blanket, and never looked at her again.

The thought of having my own real live baby controlled me, but month after month my period reminded me that time was running out. My own mother was not coming back. My eggs, every one of them my own potential baby, were being wasted and flushed down the toilet every twenty-eight days, regular as clockwork. I grieved for them all.

It was May when my period started during a waitressing job. I cleaned myself up in the Grand Hotel toilets, pinched my inner thighs so hard as to leave bruises, swallowed the scream that was building. As I navigated the dining room with my tray of hors d'oeuvres, I'd never felt so lonely. So empty. The hole inside me was big enough to fall into completely.

And then, Sam, I felt someone watching me and when I scanned the room, there you were. A few tables away, you raised your glass.

Handsome and rich and relaxed and happy. Everything I was not. Your eyes burned into me, asking a question already. My womb said yes.

I put everything I had into being a normal person while we dated. It was exhausting. But it worked. Nothing would stand in my way. It was going to be you, me and our family.

If I'd known you were going to fuck it all up the way you did, I'd never have bothered.

This chance of a family was not going to escape me. But I had to work fast if I stood a chance of keeping them. I settled in the kitchen, curled on the window seat, preventing them from any opportunity to plan or plot against me. Nico offered me spoonfuls of marinade to taste, and poured me water instead when I couldn't stomach it. To all appearances he was in fine form, seemingly pleased I was feeling a bit brighter. He tucked my hair back, told me it was nice to see me downstairs again. Midge skidded around on the floor, chattering, singing. It was the kind of morning I'd grown to love, the type I'd always wanted. Damned if I was going to give up on that.

I sipped at my drink, letting the water cool my raw throat. I forced myself to finish the glass; every sip made me stronger – and I needed my strength. This was a battle I had to win.

Roo gave me the opportunity I was looking for, whining at the door until Nico gave in and picked up the lead.

"Will you be okay for an hour or so?" he said. The look on his face, you'd really think he cared. Not that he was planning to leave me on my own for ever. I nodded, even raised a smile, and waved him off. His feet crunched across the gravel as Roo danced around him in excitement. At the gate, before he turned on to the lane, he raised his right hand in a final goodbye. I wondered if he was already fishing his phone from his pocket with his left.

I didn't have long. I had to be quick. I had an idea that might just keep him – them – with me and I was going to give it my best shot.

"I bet you can't run upstairs and find my mobile phone and run back down in less than a minute!" I said to Midge, biting my lip as though it were impossible. She took the bait immediately, as I knew she would.

"Go!" I shouted, and she was off, bare feet slapping on the tiles. "One, two, three, four…" I counted aloud as she ran out of the kitchen.

"Fifty-one, fifty-two, fifty-three!" I said as she landed back against me with a thud. "Well done!"

"Told you I could do it," she puffed, delighted, and I smoothed the hair off her hot cheeks.

I checked my messages. Nothing from Matteo. But I guess he had nothing else to say. One message from Ginny, sent yesterday.

"Any better?"

I didn't have time to reply to that now. I started drafting a new message to Sal. It was still early days, but I had definitely felt like one of the gang of mums at the school gate before we broke up for the holidays. I just had to hope she'd help. She seemed like the type that liked being the centre of the group. The one that people turned to in an hour of need. Let's hope I was right.

"Hi Sal, you home? Can I beg a favour? Could Midge come to you for a sleepover with Nate? I'm not well and Nico has had to go out."

I was just about to press send, but paused and added:

I feel terrrrrrrrrrrrrible! With a crying face emoji.

Send.

Please let this work. I was literally drumming my fingers.

"What challenge shall I do next?" Midge jumped in front of me, one foot to the other. I glanced round the room, looking for something to distract her, nodded at the skipping rope hanging over the back of the chair. That was obviously the sound I'd heard earlier.

"Skip to the bottom of the garden and back in less than a minute. Go!"

After a slight delay to roll her eyes and pull on her trainers – "I can't skip on stones with bare feet, Mummy" – she was just out the front door when Sal's reply came in.

"Poor you! Of course. Nate will love it. I'll come now and then you can go back to bed."

Exactly what I'd hoped. Saint Sal to the rescue. It would give her a story to tell the other mums at the park, gossiping round the baby swings. How she'd swooped in to help a sick friend. I texted a thanks and our address and a million xxxxxxxxx's so that she'd hurry up and by the time Midge skipped back in the front door, I had her next challenge ready.

"You've got two minutes to pack your rucksack for a sleepover!" Her eyes widened with excitement. "You can take your favourite toy and don't forget your toothbrush and PJs! Go!"

Sal pulled slowly into the drive, peering over the steering wheel. In the back, Nate had his nose pressed to the window. Midge jumped up and down in welcome in the porch, where we stood waiting. Her Dora rucksack, at my feet, was crammed full with much more than I'd instructed. I could definitely see a water pistol sticking out of the side pocket. Poor Nate. He might not be so happy to have her over in half an hour.

"God, I've never been out here before," Sal said as if we lived in Alaska, and I realised I'd always dropped Midge over at hers. "Such a beautiful spot."

She slammed the car door and turned round in a slow circle, taking in the fields that enveloped us, the trees that kept us hidden. I prayed silently she didn't think she was staying long. I needed her gone before Nico came back. He normally only went out for an hour with Roo, a quick circuit around Long Down Woods. I was running out of time.

"Thanks so much, Sal," I said and was pleased with the way my voice rasped.

"God, you sound awful," she said, scurrying over to me. She put her hand on my forearm, but then quickly removed it when she felt the heat rising from my skin.

"I just need to go back to bed," I said and leaned against the wooden upright beam of the ancient porch. "Midge will have so much more fun with you and Nate."

Nate was waving manically out the window.

"When did it start?"

I frowned. I couldn't actually remember.

"A few days ago?" I said, picking up Midge's rucksack to hand over.

"Poor you. Don't get dehydrated," she said, taking the rucksack between her thumb and one finger, definitely looking forward to washing her hands. I made myself smile.

"No chance of that," I said. "Nico is looking after me."

"Bye Mummy." Midge had her head against my hip, arms round the tops of my legs. I held her very, very tight for a moment and then sent her off. The car crunched out of the drive. Only then was I happy that she was safely hidden until I could be sure Nico would stay.

The sound of Nico's feet on the gravel gave me a few seconds to compose myself before he appeared in the kitchen. Roo ran ahead of him, not tired out in any way by her walk. Nico seemed surprised to see me still at the window seat, but then smiled, a late addition.

"Midge is quiet?" he asked, scanning the room and then looking in towards the TV room. I waited until his gaze came back to me before I answered.

"She's not here," I said.

"What?" he said.

"She's having a sleepover," I replied. "Because we need to talk."

He froze, frowned. Took his time hanging the dog lead over the back of the chair, before looking at me again.

"What's up?" he said. So he was intending to brazen it out. If he'd said "Yes" or "I agree", or anything that admitted any of the things he'd been doing, things might have turned out differently. If he'd confessed to taking money, or planning to leave, it might have made a difference, although somehow I doubt it. It's what I'm like when I've got a bee in my bonnet.

He came and sat the other end of the window seat. I tucked my feet under to give him room, not wanting us to touch. His eyebrows knitted in confusion.

"I had a message from Matteo," I said.

I saw that hit its mark. Nico's eyes widened until I saw the whites.

"I thought you said you weren't in contact?" he said, mouth tight.

I ignored him, saying instead, "He said that Elena's family are on their way over here to find you."

Nico put a hand to his throat, glanced out the window as though expecting to see them there. The tension in the room increased like a magnetic charge; I could feel the pulse of it from him.

"What on earth is going on, Nico?" I put a hand out towards him but he leaned away.

I looked at him more intently, and my guts plunged.

He wasn't tense, he was scared.

"God, I knew it must have been Matteo," Nico said as he stood, paced a few steps. "Of course."

I shook my head in confusion, not following at all.

"He must have told people in Nerja that he'd seen me. That's what kicked this thing off again."

He was half-talking to himself, circling the table. He stopped, swung towards me. "What *exactly* did he say?"

I couldn't look away from his eyes. "That they were coming to the UK. It could mean trouble. For you and for me," I said, my voice not as strong as I wanted it to be. "He said you know what they are like."

He slammed the table hard and I heard my own gasp.

"Everyone knows what they are like. They're bad news." His voice was loud. "An eye for stolen sunglasses. A scar for a spilt drink. A missing person for a bad deal."

Roo whined and wagged her tail uncertainly. I put a hand on her head to reassure her, and myself, but every nerve in my body was tight as wire.

"So why do they want to see you?" I said, this time making my voice more steady. I needed to know, it was time for the truth. He sat suddenly, rubbed his hands on his head.

"They've never liked me," he said. "Not since the beginning."

Then he was up again, holding on to the back of the chair, indignant. "I had my own business, a tourist attraction. People came from all around for speedboat trips, or snorkelling days, or banana boats." He puffed his chest out, actually banged himself with one fist like a gorilla. "But that wasn't good enough for their sister. Oh, no. To them I was 'boat boy'." He spun to face me, cheeks blazing. "*Boat boy*."

"So they don't like you?" I said, with a shrug as if to say, so what.

"They think I'm *nothing*. They wished their sister married someone else. Someone better."

"What do they want to see you for, then?" I was keeping my voice neutral, not even a hint of judgement in there. I had somehow to use this, to make this work for me. To keep him with me. To stop him taking Midge. Just the thought of her made me ask, "Do they want to see Midge? Is that it? They must miss her."

He shook his head, impatient. "No, they want me. They won't believe that Elena's death was an accident."

Here it came, his full story. I took a breath to steady myself and heard it shudder in and out before he spoke again. He looked at me direct, and his face was almost unrecognisable with pain. "They think I killed her."

He wrung his hands together and then turned them palms-up towards the ceiling as though asking a question. He was waiting, looking for me to shake my head, reject the thought, presume his innocence, but I couldn't. All I could feel was Midge's heaving shoulders as she sobbed. All I could hear in my memory was her trembling voice, '*Daddy has a secret.*' I hid my emotion, made my face softer, reached my feverish hand towards him and, this time, he took it.

"What really happened?" I asked. "Who's telling the truth?"

It was the longest five seconds of my life. Well, actually, that's a lie. But I'll get to that later.

"We both are," he said. He sat suddenly, head bowed. It took me a moment to realise he was crying.

"I didn't mean to," he sobbed. "It was an accident. I loved her."

I hardly dared breathe. Was this going to give me a key to keep them somehow?

"Tell me," I whispered.

"We were out on the boat, the three of us. Elena had been to a family meeting the day before with her brothers. We wanted to borrow the money to buy a second boat." He sniffed, wiped his nose on the back of his hand. I put my own palm on his back, encouraging him on. "They were thinking about it." I rubbed his shoulder soothingly.

"We were way round the bay when she got the text. I knew from her face it was them. I asked her, would they lend it to us?" He lifted his wet face to see me. "She said no. They said to tell Boat Boy it's a no." He shook his head, furious. "*Boat boy.*" He spat again.

I could feel the muscles tense across his spine.

"It was just a split second. I was so angry." His voice was strongly Spanish. "I jammed the throttle on the boat, we jumped forward. I just wanted to move, to go." A strangled noise came from deep inside him and he grasped at my hand.

"She must have lost her balance, hit her head on the side, fallen over the back." His eyes were looking at something else, somewhere far away. "I didn't even know for a few minutes. The sound of the motor, the wind. When I turned round, Magda was crying and pointing and Elena wasn't even there."

I cringed. *Daddy has a secret.*

"I turned the boat around and we sped back, faster than I'd left. But she was dead already. Drowned."

He scrubbed at his face with balled fists, like a kid.

"They tried to take me to court. But she drowned. It was an accident. The judge believed me."

The newspaper cuttings made sense now, the court case reporting allegations of foul play. It was Elena's family that had brought the case to the judge, so it must have been a private prosecution. An alleged murder. I thought back to our conversation about the legal terms.

"Even so, Midge and I had to leave to be safe. We had to go. They made me leave my home, my family—" He glanced at me, caught in his own lie.

"You told me there was nobody there for you any more," I said, but not harshly. I still had to bide my time, make this work. I made it sound like a question, like I was merely interested.

"My mother," he said. "My eighty-year-old mother. I have to leave her all alone, only talk to her on the phone." His voice was tight with emotion. "They threatened to hurt my family as I'd hurt theirs. I couldn't risk it."

The phone call. The postcard. The curly writing that I thought looked European, but actually, now that I thought about it, just looked old and shaky.

"I keep my mother safe by staying away from her, and I keep Magda safe by keeping her away from them. Since I've been here – since being with you – I've felt safe and like I could move on – *with you*. And now, since Matteo has seen us and told people, the brothers are looking for me again." He thumped his own thighs.

"They paid my mamá a 'visit' to see if she knows where I live," he said, making speech marks with his fingers. "They killed her cat last week. She's scared and old and all alone." His eyes brimmed again. The phone call when he was crying. When I could see the love on his face. It was all making sense.

But how to make this work? My mind was racing, spinning off at angles and then sinking into sand. I couldn't think straight, follow a thought from start to finish.

So he'd had a hand in Elena's death. It wasn't the worst thing to hear. But in that case, what was going on with me? Why was he planning on leaving me?

"They can't find me," he whispered, almost to himself, before straightening his back and saying the thing he shouldn't have said. "Midge and I have to leave."

There it was. My worst fear, now out in the open. He was going to leave me on my own, take away everything I'd ever wanted. Instead of finding something to hold him to me, I'd uncovered something that was going to drive him away. I bit my lip to stop a reaction, scrambled through my jagged thoughts before answering.

"But then they win," I said, gently. "Surely we can do something, here, together." I opened my arms, taking in the safety of The Nook, the solitude of the garden. "We could talk to the local police," I said, my thinking coming together. "We could explain the situation – you're being victimised after all."

He blinked in my direction, doubtful.

"You're the innocent party here, Nico," I pressed. "You've been found innocent in a court of law." He lifted his shoulders, liking the sound of it. "We could get you protection, surely. Maybe a new identity?" Maybe I'd gone too far with that, but he didn't seem to think so.

"Everyone knows you're a good person." Even as I said it, I felt the squeeze of his hands, too tight on mine. I heard the family at the home shouting at him, *money-grabbing bastard*. I imagined the look on his face when he jammed the boat throttle, the grip of his fingers on the bar.

No matter. I had to keep him if I wanted Midge. Which I did. With every single fibre of my being.

"Maybe…" he said, and there was a light of something in his eyes, just a glimmer of hope. That I could sort it all out for him. Make it go away.

"Of course," I blustered. "We can do it together."

"You're right," he said, grabbing the lifeline with both hands. "After all, I'm innocent." He stood up with the impetus of it. "I mean, who would ever believe I killed her." And then he used the lifeline I'd thrown him to hang himself with. "Why would I? Everything was tied up with her family, all the money. She didn't have a cent of her own."

The money. It all came back to the money. My bank balance that was being chipped away at. The bank card I'd given him. The withdrawals that were never mentioned.

"She didn't have anything worth killing her for."

They say realisation hits you like a freight train. But it hit me like a dumper truck. The weight of it pouring down on me until I was buried, sucking breath through thick air, pushing me back into that hole I'd spent so long trying to climb out of.

I had the money. I had the house. The security. That's what he wanted. Not me with a scarred face that he'd have to put up with. He'd done well to smile at it on the pillow when he woke for the past six months.

Fuck. What if he was not just planning on leaving me? Judging from what he'd just said about Elena, I was the opposite to her. I had everything worth killing for. His eyes pinned me to the seat.

The clock ticked in the hall. A bead of sweat ran between my shoulder blades and down my spine. A blackbird sang in the garden. In the stillness, it was like an alarm sounding. I was in danger. Matteo had said it himself. "It could mean trouble. For him and for you."

I'd thought he was talking about Elena's family, how they were coming for Nico and I might get caught in the crossfire. Literally. But Matteo had confessed that he couldn't help but suspect Nico of killing Elena, and I had to consider that he might think that I was in danger from my own husband.

Picture-postcard Nico. Look at him, every inch the Spanish lover. Who'd wheedled his way into my life, in double-quick time, to get what he wanted. My house. My money.

Before he and Midge had moved in, he used to bring their toothbrushes round every time they stayed over. His green one and Midge's little purple one with Mickey Mouse ears would nestle next to mine in the pot. It got to the point when I couldn't bear to see my own toothbrush left alone and I told him to leave some stuff, rather than take it home each time. And he hesitated, as if unsure, until I really wanted him to. I was so happy when I saw our three brushes leaning against each other after that day.

Even the marriage proposal, I remembered. The fact that he was talking about moving away made me want him more. It was like a double play; it made me the one making the next step each time. It was never him overstepping the mark and rushing me. It was me. Doing exactly what he wanted me to do.

The same with the bank card. His reticence at taking it, his reluctance to use my money had made me more insistent he should have it. I played right into his hands. He set the trap and I walked myself in. What an idiot.

He was watching me, trying to read my face, realising he'd said the wrong thing but knowing he couldn't take it back. *Nothing worth killing her for.*

A chill crawled over my skin, leaving goosebumps in its wake, but my temperature was soaring. Just how badly did he want what I had? Was he planning on simply cleaning out the bank account before leaving? How far was he prepared to go? My head pounded as I tried to think.

In fact, when had I started feeling ill? What was the last thing I could really remember? It was Nico's face when I told him I wouldn't let him pay Ginny's mortgage. There had been a moment, a split second, an expression he didn't want me to see. The shake in his hands and the underlying anger that he couldn't just make the decision himself. That it wasn't his money to do with as he wanted. His words rang in my ears. *I just don't want it to be something you regret.*

I'd been ill since then, hadn't I? Or from a few days afterwards? Feverish, sick. Sweating till the bedsheets twisted ound my legs.

All through my illness, Nico had been there. Prompting me with little nibbles, offering me sweet treats, all home-made, everything prepared in my very own kitchen.

"Got to keep your strength up," he'd say, holding yet another bowl of broth. "Don't want you to get dehydrated," as another glass appeared beside the bed. I even woke up once to find him supporting my head, holding the glass to my lips.

All those meals, ever since we met, more so since they moved in. Him taking control of the kitchen, making it his domain. Every night a different recipe, cooked from scratch. Always served up on a plate for me. It was at that exact moment that I saw suddenly how far he might be prepared to go to get what he wanted.

It was all the way.

If I were dead, then Nico would have everything.

My blood was pumping so fiercely, I worried he'd hear it rushing through my veins. But at least it *was* still pumping. I was here. Still alive. He hadn't won yet. And there was no way he was going to. If he got rid of me, it left Midge all alone with him. I'd never do that. My husband was a madman. My jaw set firm, my teeth ground against each other.

Nico stood between me and the door.

"Kat?" he said, dragging my focus back to him. Roo turned her head quizzically, one ear cocked in my direction. I opened my mouth to speak, but nothing came out. He took a step closer.

"Stay away!" It came out on a rasp. Roo looked between us, unsure of my tone of voice. Nico looked equally unsure at the change, put his hands up as if surrendering, as if calming an argumentative drunk. I pushed myself up from the bench seat, held the back for support, not taking my eyes off him. He took another tentative step towards me.

"Kat," he said. "You're not well."

"Whose fault is that?"

"Let's get you back to bed," he said. "We can talk to the police later."

I felt then that if I went back to bed I'd never get up again. I laughed and it came out with a string of phlegm, which I wiped off my mouth with the back of my hand. He recoiled at the sight of me.

"Didn't get what you wanted from Elena?" I said. His head snapped backwards as though I'd slapped him. "Thought you'd try with me?"

Roo's tail tucked in between her back legs, black eyes like beads, flicking between us.

"Come on," Nico said, as though talking to Midge. He was dead still, assessing me. "You know that's not true."

A pulse ticked under my eye, like a maggot thrashing its tail.

He moved towards me with his arms out as though to hold me, or catch me. I screamed and Roo, confused by the emotion, and terrified of the vibrations in the air, ran in between us, tail down, ears flat, tripping him. Off balance, he tumbled as I sidestepped just a few inches to his right, and his buffer was gone.

Nico's mouth opened slightly in surprise just before his head hit the side of the bench seat with a dull thud. He was unconscious by the time he hit the floor. It wasn't like the movies, no fan of blood appeared beneath him on the floor, but his face was slack, expressionless. It was hardly dramatic, but it reminded me how death is only a heartbeat away from us all.

Roo whined nervously and licked his face as his eyelids quivered.

I didn't hesitate.

Stepping over his prone body, I staggered out of the door.

I had a head start and I wasn't going to give it away.

I stuffed my feet into trainers and then I was gone. The only thought in my head was to get somewhere safe, so that I could ring the police. Hollow Farm. My sanctuary. Ginny would help.

The Audi sat in the drive and I tried the door. It was locked, unsurprisingly. I glanced back towards The Nook, for a split second considering whether to go back inside to get the keys, but it would mean stepping over Nico again to lift them from the hook. I couldn't risk it. My whole body recoiled at the thought. I could go just as quickly on foot; I knew the countryside around like the back of my hand. Walking dogs for a living meant I knew every short-cut going.

The theory worked but my body didn't. I had hardly been out of bed for days. I lumbered along, legs like jelly, until I reached the first stile. Clambering over, I kept to the footpath that hugged the hedges of the field, around the outside of the ten acres of barley. The breeze was just enough to make it whisper and sway as I ran, although not enough to cool me down, and soon I was dripping. Every ten seconds or so I threw a look back over my shoulder, but the path was empty behind me.

It was the quickest route I knew to get to Hollow Farm. Once I got there, I'd be able to ring the police. I could be safe. And I would make Midge safe too. I wouldn't leave her with him. He was a psychopath. The thought of Midge drove me on.

My foot hit a rut and my ankle went over. I landed hard on the drought-dry earth, the air rushing out with a grunt. Dragging myself back to my feet, not allowing myself to pause, I set off again, a sharp pain shooting through my right foot with every step.

Brown's Copse gave me some shade and I felt less exposed, pushing myself tree to tree. I scanned left to right, hoping to see an afternoon dog walker who could help me. Surely Nico wouldn't try anything with anyone else around. But the copse was empty and quiet, and I made for Fox Corner, the start of a well-known footpath that would take me along to the farmhouse. My breath was roaring, lungs on fire.

When I reached the five-bar gate marking the border of Hollow Farm, I was limping hard. I climbed up, swung my legs over, landed hard the other side and glanced back to where I'd been. And there he was. Nico. Moving towards me in an uneven stumble. But fast, all the same.

By the time I made the courtyard, he was close enough to call, "Kat. Wait, damn you!"

My foot was agony, shooting pain right through me every time I put weight on it. But I didn't give up.

"Don't do this!" he shouted as I lumbered into the porch. "I can explain…"

I ricocheted through the front door and slammed it shut behind me. I searched frantically for the key to lock him out. It wasn't in the door. I swept my hand along the mantelpiece overflowing with papers and unopened envelopes. They scattered to the floor, the metallic clang of the key among them. Falling to my knees, I patted the flagstones until I found it, then turned it in the door. Done. I was safe.

I staggered into the kitchen to find Ginny at the head of her table, a good way through a bottle of whisky. Cleo lay on the floor, head lifted to see who was coming in. When she saw it was me, she thumped her tail on the floor and lay back down. Ginny blinked at me in surprise and then took a large gulp.

"Blimey," she said. "I wasn't expecting you."

"You've got to save me," I said, chest heaving. Momentarily lightheaded, I put my hands on my thighs and my head down while tiny white stars popped and pinged in front of my eyes. When they'd faded, I saw the total chaos of the kitchen properly. The small pile of money on the table, coppers and silvers counted into rows. A pile of paperwork from the bank.

The articles from the paper about the appeal ripped out and pinned to doors, walls. Ginny, swaying lightly in her chair, hair falling out of its bun, old make-up smeared under one eye.

"I need help," I said.

"Funny that. I remember saying the same thing to you a while back," she answered with a sneer. "Shall I launch you an appeal?"

I ignored the dig. There was no time to go back over her problems. I had bigger issues.

"It's Nico," I slurred. "I think he's trying to kill me."

That stopped her, mid-drink. She eyed me over her glass. "What?"

"He killed his first wife," I gabbled, seeing her eyes widen. "And he's planning to kill me too. By Saturday they'll be gone apparently…" My words came out in a rush of air.

"I think maybe you're confused," she said.

"He's poisoning me." I tried to take a step closer to her, but had to keep hold of the tabletop. I had to make her understand, quickly. "He's making me ill."

Talk about the devil and they appear, as my mum used to say. The crunch of gravel outside told me Nico had caught up. He banged on the front door with his fists, shouting our names. I shook my head desperately at Ginny.

"Don't let him in," I pleaded. She looked at the door, then back at me, genuinely confused, definitely drunk.

"He just wants my money," I said over the noise. The banging stopped and we heard his footsteps move away from the porch.

"Don't let him take my baby away," I whispered. "I can't lose her."

"I think you've got it all wrong…" Ginny said with a dismissive shake of her head.

The back door opened behind me with a slam that echoed through the house, and then he was there. I moved to the other side of the kitchen table, putting the wood, and Ginny, between us.

"Kat?" he said, raising his palms in a question.

This fucking innocent act of his was really starting to grate. I ground my teeth, anger taking over.

"I know what you're up to," I spat at him. I held the back of the chair, leaning heavily on it. He took a couple of quiet steps inside the room, eyes on my face, hands out towards me.

"I know everything," I said.

He flicked a quick glance at Ginny. Why was he looking at her? What was he checking for? I witnessed the tiny exchange between them, Nico's raised eyebrow, Ginny's fractional shake of the head. A question and answer that I was no part of. Nico's panting was the only sound in the room. I looked one to the other, realisation widening my eyes. My God. There was something between them. A secret.

Before I could ask, Ginny stood abruptly, pushed the bottle away. She rolled her eyes at Nico and threw her hands in the air, imitating one of his expressions.

"Fucking foreigners," she said. "Should have known it! You can't do anything right."

Nico stepped back as though she'd smacked him. "Ginny, I haven't—" He shook his head at her and put up his hand in a stop sign, but she carried on.

"Why did I ever think you'd be the man for the job?" She barked out a laugh that bounced off the walls.

We all stood, the three points of a triangle, and I suddenly didn't know which way to lean, which side was safe. I gasped for breath, trying to clear the fog that still lingered in the corners of my head. I needed to think, to understand.

"Fuck's sake, all you had to do was slip me the money," Ginny said. I opened my mouth to answer, actually exasperated we were back on that again, especially in the middle of my own crisis, when I realised she wasn't talking to me.

She was looking straight at Nico. It wasn't me she had been expecting to give her money. It was him. And I didn't understand.

"Should have just stuck to the plan." She shrugged then, as though she'd given up on him. He was of no matter. Pointless.

"Plan?" I said and Ginny switched her attention back to me, small eyes hard and rat-like. I realised with a jolt that she didn't like me. Not at all. Her expression was very clear. "You two have a plan?"

"You betcha. Since before you even knew him." She snorted. Her smile was lopsided.

"You knew Nico before?" I said, confused, as I glanced from her to my husband, who was staring crossly at Ginny. "You never said."

A million random thoughts crowded my mind, images of all the times we'd been together – picnics, BBQs, car journeys, bottles of wine. All those times when they'd not told me they already knew each other. Why not? What was going on?

"Where did you meet?" I asked, dreading the answer already.

Nico muttered Ginny's name in warning, but she waved a hand in his direction. She was going to have her say.

"Amazing what you can find on dating apps," she said. I remembered the woman at Coffin Club, the one who thought she'd seen his profile. How he'd denied it. I glanced at him, a sick feeling in my stomach. A flush was starting at his neck, creeping up towards his cheek. So Ginny and Nico had met online. On a dating app. They'd made love before. My stomach turned. And then I grimaced, remembering how Ginny always described her dates. They wouldn't have made love. They would have *fucked*. I felt an overwhelmingly stupid desire to cry.

"If you want it, it's not just cock, you know," she said, leaning in. Her eyes were fox-like. Cunning. Bright.

"And sometimes," she went on with a drunken slur, "if you look *really* hard, and you get *really* lucky" – she leaned towards me, a mischievous look on her face as though telling a story to a small child – "you can find a guy who doesn't want to go home. Ever. A guy who will do anything – *anything* – to stay in this country with his little girl."

Her words plunged to that place where I'd always doubted that someone as good-looking as Nico could want someone that looked like me. The woman with a face that had been zipped up. The weight of Ginny's words pulled my innards down with them and changed something inside me for ever.

When I raised my eyes, the flush had spread up to Nico's ears, his face flooded with guilty blood. So, that's why he married me. To stay here. So that he never had to go home and confront Elena's family again.

"It started that way, Kat," he whispered, "but it's not like that now…"

I was supposed to believe that tiny shake of the head, the earnest look in my direction? A flash of memory, his face, lying on the pillow next to mine, the softest brown of his eyes and his hand on my hair. The weight of his thigh against mine, the heat of his body. How could I misread that? God, how stupid had I been? I had to know.

"Was it all about staying in the country?" My voice cracked. "Or was it that you just wanted the money?"

He looked confused again and shot a glance at Ginny, which made me want to scream. She answered for him.

"I set him up with you," she said and poured herself a shot. "The poor little widow, whining away in her mortgage-free house, with a face only a mother could love." The glass banged back down on the table, empty, and I felt it like she'd hit me with it. Nico looked like a kicked dog, his head dropped to his chest.

"It was a match made in heaven. You want a kid. He has one. He wants a home, you have one." She sounded like a matchmaker ticking off the benefits of a suitor. "It was all going swimmingly. The only thing – *the only fucking thing* – he had to do in exchange was get me some of your money."

My breath caught. All those bank withdrawals from the cash machine, transactions to an account I didn't recognise. Him telling me it was for a surprise – damn sure it was a surprise. What had he said? Can't a man plan a treat for his wife? Well, this was *not* the way I wanted to be treated. Him marrying me for a visa, then stealing my money to give to his pimp, before he got rid of me for good. Something very close to hysteria bubbled in my throat like a giggle and I swallowed it down. It turned to hatred before it hit my stomach.

"Kat," he said again, and I wanted to hit him. "It's not—"

"Don't try wheedling your way out of it now, *Pedro*," Ginny cut in and a wave of dizziness came over me.

I gripped the chair in front of me till my knuckles went white, waiting for the room to stop spinning. When my eyesight cleared, Ginny was peering at me, closer than she had been before, watching my face. I put a hand out to her, desperate to think she would still help me. I didn't care if she wanted some of my money, I just needed help. If I fainted, I might never get up again.

"Can you get me a doctor?" I said, through thick lips. "He's trying to poison me."

Nico's head snapped towards me, an expression of sheer disbelief. "I'd never hurt you, Kat," he said, eyes wide. "I love you. You must know that."

Anyone watching him would think he was telling the truth. Ha!

"What he's feeding me is making me ill."The edges of my vision were blurred.

"I mean it, Kat," he begged. "It might have started like she said, but it's different now. I'd never harm you."

"He's trying to kill me…" I said as firmly as I could to Ginny, ignoring the plea in his voice.

Ginny's laugh was so fierce she shot snot out of her nose. "Him? Kill you? Don't be ridiculous. He might be pretty but he's not bright."

Nico kept his eyes on me this time, shaking his head side to side, bewildered.

"Poisoning me – a family recipe, he says," I managed.

Nico blinked at me, mouth open, and then turned to Ginny with a look of understanding. He pointed an accusatory finger.

"It's not my family recipe, Kat, that you need to be scared of. It's hers. She bought it round for you – said it would help."

I looked at Ginny, and she merely shrugged.

"When he wasn't going to come through with the money, I had to take matters into my own hands," she said once it was clear that I still hadn't fully twigged what she'd done. "After all, there's more than one way to skin a cat. Or should I say a Kat." She cracked out a laugh again, pointing at my scar.

I retched, violently, but nothing came up. My stomach felt shredded. Nico edged towards me, just a step.

"The answer has been in front of your face all this time," Ginny said. She marched to the dresser, stacked with dog food and cardboard recycling. Scattering the surface-level crap, she picked up a small plastic cosmetic pot, exactly the same as the one I had at home. My face cream.

"Ready for a refill? With the secret ingredient?"

Ginny held up a small enamel tin from the dresser, rusted at the top, dented and cracked. I'd seen it before. When we cleared out for the garage sale. For the rats.

I couldn't breathe.

"Such a little goes such a long way. Drugs can be applied topically and it turns out so can poisons. Your skin just drinks it in." She patted her own cheek to taunt me.

I automatically put my hand to my cheek, felt the ridge of the scar. My face tingled, my fingertips burned.

We all looked at each other, like characters in a play, as we all wondered if I had already ingested enough to kill me.

Nico broke the silence.

"What the hell?" he spluttered, and this time he stood straight and angry and I knew in that single second that he hadn't known Ginny's full plan. "You said it was okay, when she wouldn't pay the mortgage and I told you she wouldn't give you the money. You told me not to worry about it." He was enraged.

She considered him, head to one side. "What I actually said, My Little Nicolito, was don't worry your *pretty little head* about it. That *I'd* think of something." By the look on her face as she stared at Nico, she hated him too. "And I did think of something. Maybe your mum knew this saying, Kat — *if you want something doing right, do it yourself.*"

As the colour faded from Nico's face, Ginny nodded towards her toxic jar.

"Well," she drawled as if she was talking to a simpleton, "we asked nicely but the answer was no." She poured herself more drink, slopping it across the table. "It was always a possibility, after the will…"

Nico flinched, pressed his mouth together as he flicked his eyes to mine. He looked ashamed as he understood now that I knew he must have told her about me changing the will. What they didn't realise — either of them obviously — was that this wouldn't make any difference. I faced them both, played my trump card.

"You still won't get any money," I said, "even if I'm dead." My voice was strong for the first time. Both heads swung towards me, Nico broken, Ginny angry. I coughed to keep my throat clear, swallowing bile.

"My will doesn't leave the money to Nico," I said, pulling myself more upright. I had their full attention now. "If anything happens to me, it all goes into trust for Midge until she's twenty-one, with no access before then."

Nico breathed out, long and low.

"I thought that's what we'd both want," I said, directly to him. "Security for Midge. Always."

He closed his eyes and when he opened them again, they were wet. He nodded at me, just once, and the expression on his face looked a lot like love. I'd done the right thing. For our girl.

But Ginny threw something at my head, missing me by a whisker, then banged both fists on the dirty tabletop.

"Selfish, selfish, selfish," she growled. Her face was blotchy like nettle rash she was so livid.

Nico took a protective step towards me, but I backed away. I didn't want either of them near me.

"Always about the children, *baby this, kid that. Midge. Midge. Midge.* What about the animals?" Gobbets of saliva sprayed the air, a wild tendril of hair snaking her neck. "What have they ever done to you? All they ever give you is loyalty. They don't leave you. They don't fuck your best friend. They don't cheat. They don't lie."

As she ranted she spun on her heel and reached for her old handgun on its hook, the one she'd fetched when I ran into the deer.

My heart leapt as she swung its barrel towards me.

"Selfish bitch," she said.

"But we were friends." I sounded weedy, pathetic.

"Friends?" she mimicked viciously. "Ha! Turning up here that morning, killing a perfectly good animal in the process, wanting me to make it all right. Crying about how your money didn't make you happy, how you might have caused the accident that killed your first husband, how you wanted a baby."

I ignored Nico's glance at me.

"Poor little fucking rich girl." I'd never heard words sound so filled with hate. "Boo fucking hoo."

Nico began to edge towards Ginny.

"So I gave you a man and a baby. And what do you do?" Ginny gesticulated with the gun to drive her point home as she wailed, "Nothing! Sweet. Fuck. All."

Nico took another step.

"Fucking selfish and ungrateful," Ginny barked. "No point in you at all really, is there?"

She pointed the gun at my chest.

But it was at precisely this moment that Nico moved between Ginny and me, blocking her from my view as he tried to take the weapon from her.

It was only a split second, a comic grapple, and then the gun went off, the shock echoing longer than the sound.

Ginny's body slumped for a split second, her head resting momentarily on Nico's shoulder like the lover she had once been.

His hands pushed at her in horror and she fell to the floor. Her eyes were open but empty. The wound under her chin was black and mysterious.

351

And then I saw blood blooming behind her head as it seeped into the kitchen floor.

Cleo whined, although I couldn't tell if she were frightened or excited.

As the echo of the gunshot died, all I could hear was Nico's ragged breathing. He sounded like he'd just run a marathon, his lungs at bursting point. We looked at each other blankly. Too much had happened too quickly for us to know how to react.

Then he crouched beside Ginny, picked up her hand and felt for a pulse, although it was glaringly obvious she was dead. He shook his head at me. Nothing.

He backed into a chair at the kitchen table, sank down and put his head in his hands.

My impulse was to go to him but I stayed put.

Everything was different now. Nico was not the man I thought he was.

Cleo nudged Ginny's foot with her nose, then sat beside her like a sentry. Ginny would have loved that, her loyal companion sitting over her corpse. I fought an urge to laugh, biting my lip to keep serious.

Nico muttered to himself in Spanish, just under his breath. I wondered if it was a prayer.

Goats bleated from the barn and for a moment the sound made everything feel normal. Then I thought they sounded mournful, like they were crying.

Nico raised his head, suddenly purposeful. The yellow in his eyes was very bright.

"Have you touched anything?" His glance took in the expanse of the kitchen.

I thought about how I'd arrived. "The front door, the key," I said, "and this," indicating the back of the chair I found myself clutching, not sure I could stand without it.

We looked at each other, and then he picked up a cardigan of Ginny's hanging on the back of the armchair and stood next to me, waiting.

When I didn't react, he gently peeled my white fingers off the wood. The feel of his hands on mine made my eyes burn.

"Okay?" he said.

I nodded and he began his clear-up job, polishing away my fingerprints with the old woollen cloth. When he was happy with the chair he went off to the front door and I heard him do the same to the doorknob, inside and out.

"You were never here, at least today," he said, from the doorway.

A rush of warmth in my chest took me by surprise. He was looking after me, trying to make everything better. Like he really did love me.

"Go home," he told me as he picked up the gun from the floor. Holding it carefully in between thumb and finger, he set about the gun with his cloth, rubbing from muzzle to grip, then placed it again next to Ginny's outstretched hands.

"You'll be all right," he said. "Just go to bed when you get there. Drink nothing but water. Call the doctor tomorrow."

"What about you?" My voice was rough as sand. He chewed his lip, bit it hard.

"My DNA is probably all over her," he said, nodding at Ginny. I could see his mind working as he looked round the dishevelled room, frantically looking for an answer, a solution. There wasn't one. They'd fought. He was probably right that she might have his skin cells under her nails or his fingerprints on her arms, or a tiny fleck of his saliva on her head, or fibres from his clothing on her.

"Even if her fingerprints are on the gun, they will see there was a struggle."

Nico's fingers tap-tapped against his thighs. He looked unsure what else to do.

"I'll have to leave," he declared and I saw the yellow flash against the brown of his eyes.

He came closer and I held my breath, not sure if I wanted him to touch me or not. "I'm sorry," he whispered.

There was a moment then, suspended in time, with Ginny's corpse beside us on the floor, when I could see how regretful he really was. But something inside me had steeled. I felt hard-boiled, brittle on the outside, numb in my middle. So his plan had fallen apart. He'd been shown up for the fake he was. Was he saying sorry for lying to me for months, for marrying me and making vows? Or for making love to me, tucking my hair away, pretending all that time that I meant something? Anything at all? That he wasn't horrified every morning when he woke up and saw my face on the pillow next to his? Or was he just saying sorry that it had all blown up in his face, and now he had to leave when he was on to such a good thing?

I stepped back.

"Yes. You should go," I agreed and I was surprised at the strength in my voice. He should go and leave me and Midge alone. We were better off, and safer, without him.

His eyes held me for a few seconds more, perhaps pleading.

I sniffed and looked away.

And it was then that Nico changed everything.

"Right. I'll go and fetch Midge and we'll be gone."

Maybe he didn't realise what he was saying.

But his words cracked opened an abyss of emptiness within me.

A life without Midge terrified me. Waking up to a house so quiet I'd hear the crows flap in the trees. Car journeys without singing. The back seat empty of a car seat. Days without biscuits and milk. No little hands holding mine; a gap in my lap.

Did Nico not understand that now I was her mum? You can't give something and then just take it back whenever you want. A noise came out of me like a sob, but not because I was upset. It was so much more than that. I was angry, frightened, horrified. Most of all I was desperate. And more than that. I felt mad.

How was it that people just thought they could tell me what was happening with my life? Like you, telling me we'd be fine "just the two of us", when you knew all I wanted was a baby, as though I wouldn't mind at all. Well, look at how that ended up.

There was no way Nico was taking Midge away from me.

Looking at Ginny's body, I suddenly thought that all I had to do was to get to the police and say Nico had killed her. I'd have to do it well and in a way that wouldn't incriminate me in things, and although that wouldn't be easy, I decided that I could manage it. Then the authorities would take Nico away and I'd get to keep Midge. I almost couldn't catch my breath with the sheer simplicity of it.

But first, I just had to get out of there. I glanced round the room, frantically looking for something to help me escape.

"Kat," Nico said, "which friend is Midge with? Where do I pick her up from?"

Cleo scratched the floor next to Ginny's shoulder and I saw my way out.

I shouted as loud and as fierce as I could, making both Nico and the dog physically jump: "Cleo. GET THEM!"

Cleo sprang to attention, hackles up, confused.

I pointed at Nico. "GET THEM!"

The dog barked and it echoed loud in the kitchen. Then Cleo advanced on Nico until he was pressed against the wall, trapped. He held his hands out to calm her as she growled, holding him in place.

Nico could only watch helplessly as I stumbled past him and ran out of the front door.

He called my name as I went but I refused to listen.

The sun was low now, blinding as I raced towards it, heading home over the back ridge. My clothes clung awkwardly, pyjama bottoms flapping, making it harder to run, my ankle almost giving way every time it hit the ground. I wasn't even at the orchard when I heard Cleo's barking shriek to a stop and the front door slam, and knew he was after me.

He called to me, over and over: "Kat, Please. Kat!" as I limped ahead. Perhaps if he'd stopped calling, it would have been different. But with each "Kat" he spoke, I was reminded that my name was no longer – indeed never had been – an endearment to him.

How dare he?

How dare he and Ginny even have thought to use me as they had? Manipulate me, and marry me, all under false pretences?

It wasn't even the money that stung.

It was the fact that neither Ginny nor Nico never really wanted *me*. Nobody ever did. They had just wanted what I had.

Fuckers.

I glanced back at Nico, and my rage crystallised in a pure hate for my weak husband. Fucker. Fucker! Every painful step I took, I loathed him, and how he made me feel, more.

"Kat, wait," Nico pleaded.

Had he really believed he could just change my life for the better and then change it for the worse, just because it suited him? Nobody made those kind of decisions for me. No one. *You* know that.

"Kat…"

I could hear his ragged breath, and snatched another look over my shoulder to see he was quite close to me now. I turned towards the apple trees, feeling like I was running though treacle. All I had to do was get through them and then I would be on the track and I could move faster.

Bees hummed around me as I hobbled away from my husband.

His feet were thudding on the dry ground behind me, fast and steady, not like my lurching. The drone of bees increased as I gritted my teeth and stumbled on.

I got to the clearing, fruit trees surrounding me in a circle. The wooden hives were golden in the late afternoon sun, bees making their way home from the surrounding countryside after a hard day's work. Ginny had told me once that they sometimes travel as far as three miles away and come home tired and irritable, so one should never walk in front of the hive but always approach from the back.

I had no choice here, though. Nico was on my heels.

His fingertips grazed my back and I edged myself forward, just out of reach, and ran at the nearest hive with every last bit of my strength. Hands outstretched, I knocked it straight off its stand, the layers smashing apart as they hit the ground. Honeycomb cracked as confused bees took to the wing to defend their precious nectar, to attack.

They rose in a cloud, their fever-pitch whine incredible; I looked around and the air was alive with them. One caught in my hair, one landed on my arm, but they flew away immediately as if I didn't have what they wanted. I wondered if

Ginny's potion had made me repulsive to them. Oh, the irony if so.

I ducked down and away, to the back of the second hive.

Nico's momentum, however, made him stumble into one of the wooden frames I'd knocked over, kicking it forward and infuriating another army.

As one, they dive-bombed and darted at him, landed on his head, crawled down his collar. Nico windmilled his arms, turned in a circle, panicking. Doing exactly what he shouldn't do.

I grabbed the lid of the second hive and threw it over, screaming with effort and rage as I released the other colony. As I hoped, they were attracted to the predator in front of them, swirling and shouting, all ready to defend to their deaths.

Spent, I crawled to the safety and shade of an apple tree and leaned against its trunk. A few random bees followed me, butting against me in a clear show of aggression, but not stinging. The vast majority were drawn to the threat to the hive as Nico thrashed about, treading on honeycomb, grinding bees into the dirt.

The first stings started.

Nico banged at himself, slapped randomly at his arms and chest. He shouted out for me, wild-eyed, head swinging like a blind animal, and that was the last time I heard him call my name. The air blackened as the swarm came down on him. His knees hit the ground and he managed to crawl a few feet towards me before curling in the foetal position, poor baby. I saw bees crawling on his eyes and in his ears. After that, he just screamed until his tongue was stung so many times it didn't fit into his mouth.

At last he was quiet and all I could hear were the bees.

The next few months were a bit of a blur. Small things got us by. Day by day, time passed. It's amazing how resilient kids are, though. Naturally, Midge took her dad's death really hard and it was up to me to be there for her every minute of every day. The rock she relied on. The mother she deserved.

I was never out of reach. I organised play dates and distractions to keep her busy. We swam and fished for minnows. We caught crickets in our hands and watched them leap free. I reclaimed my kitchen and we baked biscuits, munched them together on the sofa. Funny, though, I've gone right off honey, even though I used to love it slathered on toast.

I devoted the rest of the summer to us, just Midge and me, recovering. Getting used to our new family. Moving on to our own "New Horizon".

Nowadays, she tucks into my side on the sofa. She sleeps in her dad's half of the bed. She looks to me for everything.

We are as we should be.

Still, a week ago she sowed a seed. We were talking as she got out of the bath. I wrapped her in a towel and she sat on my lap on the bathroom floor. I dried her and brushed her hair until it hung long and straight. It reminded me of my mum doing the same with me as we spoke of it just being the two of us.

"How do you feel about that?" I asked, feeling the hollow of uncertainty all of a sudden. Was I enough for her? A proper mummy?

"It's okay," she said, twiddling her hair around her finger, but then after a thoughtful moment, she said the thing I was least expecting. "I'd really like a brother or sister though. All my friends have one."

It made me think. As I tucked her into bed I realised I'd only ever hoped for one child, but maybe I was setting my sights too low. What was stopping me, apart from my single status and a hysterectomy?

I couldn't stop thinking about what Midge had said. I have so much love to give. I am such a good mummy. We could be a whole proper family.

So last Thursday saw me "getting back on the horse", as Ginny would have said. Putting myself out there. Sal came to babysit and I'd put a bottle of wine in the fridge and found a box set for her to watch.

My hand was steady as I sat at the dressing table and ran eyeliner around my eyes. Midge was playing on the bedroom floor behind me, rolling around with Roo, who had finally grown into her ears. With any luck, my daughter would have a sibling to play with before too long. A bubble of excitement made me smile as I added a touch of gloss to my lips.

Midge suddenly appeared next to me on the stool and stared at my face in the mirror. Her eyes had flecks of gold in them.

"I don't want you to go out," she said and her lower lip trembled.

I'd thought this might happen after spending so much time together. She wasn't used to being without me. But it wouldn't be for long. And it was all for the greater good.

"You know I have to," I said and I shot a spritz of perfume on my throat.

"I miss Daddy," Midge said. "I want you to stay home."

I put down the perfume bottle and met her eyes in the glass.

"But you said the other day you'd like a brother or sister?" I reminded her quietly. Head on one side like a little bird, she nodded.

"Then I have to go out," I said. "I have to meet new people."

"Why?" She made her voice more babyish than she really was.

"To find a new baby," I told her.

"Not a new daddy?"

"Well, a new daddy too," I said quickly, turning to her and flicking her cheeks with blusher to distract her. "That's what I meant."

Midge's eyes narrowed and she drew back, just fractionally, but she didn't say anything else.

As I finished putting my face on, I could still feel her watching me.

The bar at The Sovereigns was quiet and the barman was new. I stood at the exact spot where I'd first met Nico, not even a year ago. The place where I'd smelled the lemon of his skin and fallen for his lies. Although to be fair, I hadn't been totally honest myself. Hey ho.

The barman wiped his damp hands on a tea towel tucked into his jeans.

"What can I get you?"

Suddenly nervous, I ordered two drinks, one of which I gulped down in one. He smiled encouragingly as I handed him the empty glass back. "Here for New Horizons?" he asked sympathetically.

I nodded and he thumbed towards the back room. "Through there," he said.

I picked up my untouched drink and headed through the door.

Barely anything had changed. I heard Stephen's braying laughter first and then there he was in his pink trousers, even though summer was well and truly over. Next, I saw Lee, Fiona and a few others I hadn't seen since the funeral.

I was hugged and squeezed and had my hand pumped up and down, everyone welcoming me back and thinking I was the unluckiest person alive. Widowed twice. Little did they know that nowadays I felt truly blessed. I accepted condolences and tried to look mournful but approachable in equal measure. I didn't want to put anyone off talking to me.

There was quite a good turnout. Maybe it was the darker evenings drawing people together again, bringing them out of their homes for a bit of company. There was a sudden burst of laughter and the chat level was high. It echoed in my head. I wasn't used to it.

I found myself a high stool at a round table with Kerry and sat with my back against the wall so that I could see the whole room.

Funny how my entire life I'd longed to belong to clubs, wanted to be a part of something, and I'd finally made it. This, here, this motley bunch was my club. In fact, I'd earned my place here more than anyone else. They all ended up here through no fault of their own.

I'd got here by my own making.

Not once, but twice.

I suppose it just shows what you can do when you set your mind to it.

I sipped my drink and listened to Kerry's updates with one ear, scanning the group. It was mostly faces I recognised, but there were a few newbies. A woman, dressed in head-to-toe beige, and two men.

One of the new men must have been in his sixties. He was extremely well groomed, silver-haired with a small beard. He wore a well-tailored shirt over jeans that would have looked better on a much younger man. A chunky gold family crest shone on his finger. I watched him talk, paying full attention to the other person as he did. He passed drinks. He laughed in the right places. He was perfect – for someone. But not for me.

I looked round for the other man, but he'd disappeared from view. Dammit, had I missed him already? But then there he was, in a corner as he spoke on his phone. Probably in his forties, sandy-haired, big, bear-like in fact. Maybe on the heavier side of fit, but not repulsively so.

I slid off my stool, offering to buy Kerry another drink, which I knew she'd accept, and I padded across the room.

The man was listening so hard to the person on the other end of the line that a crease dug deep between his eyebrows. He stuck his finger in his other ear to hear better.

I slipped past people and edged closer. Suddenly he smiled and laughed and the crease disappeared. He thanked someone and hung up, breathing out in one long sigh.

I stepped into the space nearest him as he slid his phone back on to the tabletop, but in his relief he shoved it too hard and it knocked his keys on to the floor. They landed at my feet. Literally. I almost laughed at the sheer perfection of it.

We both bent down to retrieve them but I snatched them up first. As I stood back up, the keys jangled in my hands long enough for me to see the plastic key ring with its enclosed photograph.

A baby. A boy, judging by the blue T-shirt he wore. Two front teeth and dimples. The roundest, most perfect face. My breathing was loud in my ears. My blood raced.

"Hi," I said with my best normal smile as I pressed the keys back into his hand. "I think these are yours?"

"Thanks," he said with a self-deprecating grin.

As he pocketed the keys I spotted a smear of milk dribble on his shoulder and felt the urge to lean forward and smell it.

"I'm Kat," I said, holding out my hand to shake.

"Rob. Nice to meet you."

Turns out it was Rob's first night away from the baby, Alfie. The babysitter had just confirmed he was sleeping and all was fine. Six months old and never knew his mother, poor little scrap. She died in childbirth. I didn't think that happened in this day and age. But her loss is my gain. Immediately I thought that I wouldn't have to compete with any sentimental memories of the first "Mummy", or put up with stars drawn in the sky in the drawings of our family.

Rob and I drifted to the bar together and ended up staying there. Kerry must have eventually cadged a drink from someone else as I didn't see her again.

By the time the barman called last orders, I knew that Rob loved dogs, had hoped for a bigger family and felt isolated having had to move here for work. He literally didn't know a soul.

I also knew that he had an annoying way of jiggling his leg under the table all the time that sometimes made the glasses shake. And I was pleased to see that he had a touch of eczema on his hands.

He'd tried everything, he told me, to calm it down, but since he and Alfie had moved it was the worst it had ever been.

I lifted his hand, pretending to examine the eczema.

A tremor ran through his fingers, and his eyes held mine, hopeful and needy.

I smiled.

"I've got just the cream for that."

Graveside. October 2016

So, who would have thought it, Sam? You've not been dead two years and I've been married and widowed a second time. Now perhaps you can see why I haven't popped by earlier; I've been pretty busy creating my own little "Coffin Club", as it turned out. But I'm here now, and that's what counts.

Everything worked out for the best, I think. Nico and Ginny probably wouldn't agree, but you can't please everyone all of the time.

The police decided Ginny had shot herself. It looked like an open-and-shut case according to the newspaper reports, which got a lot more coverage than her fundraising appeal did. The articles said that she took her own life after a death on her property from bee stings. Such an unusual event, it made the nationals, TV and everything. Loads of the neighbours piped up and were quoted about how their children had been stung, and the local council gave a formal statement saying they had asked her to remove the hives and she obviously had not complied. No shit Sherlock. There were hundreds of thousands of the poisonous little fuckers back there in the wood. In the end, an extermination team were called in. There were pictures of them in white suits looking like something out of *ET*. They identified the bees as an Asian hybrid strain, bred for honey production levels but spiteful as sin. They set the hives on fire and took cover.

The articles also said that Ginny had died on the day of the farm's foreclosure. I hadn't realised it was actually D-Day, but the newspaper showed pictures of a barbed wire defence she'd put up at the main gate to keep them out. She must have literally been sitting there waiting for the bailiffs to turn up and kick her out when I stumbled in. No wonder she wasn't in the best frame of mind.

I paid for her funeral. It was the least I could do, as her only friend. The newspapers liked that. Just the basic coffin though, no point throwing money away; it was a cremation after all. I made sure they dressed her in camouflage and put her family album of animals in there with her. Not many people turned up, just the dog-food supplier and me. But we sang "All Things Bright and Beautiful". I thought she'd like that – "all creatures great and small". They presented me with the ashes later and I fed them to the goats. Seems they really do eat anything.

Ginny would have been fuming about what happened to the animals at Hollow Farm. I could just imagine her effing and jeffing as they were all crated up and taken off to other sanctuaries. I watched on the TV as they led Cleo out on a lead, tail between her legs. Poor old girl had been found sitting guard over the body two days later. I felt a bit sad, watching that.

Nico's funeral was much more fun. Loads of people turned out for him; seemed he was a pretty popular guy. There were people from New Horizons. Stephen shook my hand and said that "as foreigners went, Nico was a good one." I smiled politely at the time and then later, at the wake, spat in his tea before I passed him his cup.

There was a minibus delivery of residents from the care home, leaning on sticks or walkers, lining the side of the grave. It was like a day trip; they especially liked the sandwiches afterwards. But old Mrs Dennison clutched at my hand and cried proper tears, dabbed her milky eyes with a cotton handkerchief. She said she'd miss him; nobody really listened to her like Nico did.

It wasn't just old people or widows at the service, though, there was a large crowd from school. The mums and dads came in their droves, rocked by the revelation that parents of young kids can actually die, and all of them feeling guilty and thankful that it wasn't them. Jen and Sal have been a great support, they ring and pop round a lot; we're turning into quite the girl gang, which is nice.

I still don't know quite how I feel about Nico. The care home gave him a complete pardon after the Dennison family retracted their claim. Seems they finally believed that he had been acting in their mother's best interests.

And then, the Friday after Nico died, a letter arrived for him. It had three tickets in it. To Venice. Leaving Saturday.

"By Saturday, we'll be gone," I remembered him whispering to Midge.

She'd known all about it, of course. "A surprise for Mummy. Somewhere she's always wanted to go." *A secret.* He'd planned it and booked it, for me. Like he really did love me.

I didn't know any of this at the time, though, not when we were at the hives. Then, I just realised that I wasn't so different from him after all. He had married me because he wanted what I had – security. But I married him because I wanted what he had – Midge. The only difference was, I'd kill for it.

It was pretty horrific sitting there waiting for him to die, but at least he wasn't watching me, not like you did.

It's *your* face I still see in my dreams, that moment of rec-ognition when you realised you were dying and saw me sitting there. When you realised I had my phone in my hand but wasn't going to call for help. I saw your eyes widen, your mouth twitch, blood coming out instead of words. It would have been a lot easier if the crash had killed you outright. But you were pretty smashed up. Worse than a snake in a lawn-mower, as they say in this neck of the woods. Your blood was pumping out so red it looked black; I had to keep moving backwards to avoid sitting in it on the tarmac. Eventually I reached the verge and finally you shut your eyes. I'm still not sure whether they would have had time to save you even if I did call an ambulance, but I guess we'll never know, will we? I just couldn't face a life of "just you and me". No thanks.

Anyhow. There we go, that's me up to date.

Better get on. Midge needs collecting from Sal's. I might take a bottle of wine with me to share over a pizza before Midge and I head home. Probably won't be back to see you again soon, Sam, so I'll say my goodbyes. Life goes on, you know?

Before I go, though, a thank-you from me to you. That's really why I'm here. If you hadn't died, I would never have known New Horizons even existed. I'd never have found Nico and ultimately wouldn't have my Midge. So, truly, from my heart, thank you.

Did I mention Rob is coming round tomorrow? Things are going really well so far and we're going to introduce the children to each other. Keep your fingers crossed for me.

Midge is so excited she can't stand still. Rob's a bit of a slow burner, so it's taking a little longer than I'd like, but that's fine. There's no rush.

I'll get there, I'm sure. Good things come to those who wait.

Acknowledgements

Lots of people played a part in this novel coming to be. Not just while I wrote it, but afterwards, before, in person and in spirit.

I wrote *The Coffin Club* whilst on the Faber Academy 'Write Your Novel' course in 2019. Our course ended in March 2020, three weeks before lockdown and then I had a long pandemic summer in which to re-work and edit the first draft.

Everyone always thanks their agents, but I bet no agent comes close to the lovely Judith Murray at Greene and Heaton who is, quite frankly, the bee's knees. The whole team there, including Sally Oliver and Imogen Morrell, has been helpful, friendly and supportive. Just what a debut author needs.

And everyone thanks their publishers, but mine truly rocks. Jenny Parrott at Oneworld has given amazing advice with brilliant insight and a great sense of humour. Molly, Mark, Laura, Lucy, Margot and Matilda have all helped to bring the book to life, and with Jacqui Lewis for a copy editor, I couldn't wish for a better publishing team.

But it goes back further than that. Thank you to all the writerly people in my life who have been on hand while I moaned, swore or celebrated.

To Suzy Camp with her never-ending cups of tea on our weekly writing mornings. To Ruth Brandt for her teachings at the Tuesday writing group.

To my Faber tribe, who all read bits, or all of, *The Coffin Club* along the way and whose feedback made it better every time. Sabrina Broadbent (tutor extraordinaire), Scott Taylor, Sinead Nolan, Shayna Wilson, Paul Marriner, Stephen Kenefick, Yinka Ayeni, Blanka Hay, Charles Adey, Osman Haneef, Katharine Lewis, Daragh O'Reilly and Ruth Nares. Watch out for their names as you're likely to see them on the spine of a book any day now.

For my other early readers and best of friends, Frances Martin and Annie Reid, and to my mum with her red pen. Thank you all.

Finally, a couple of acknowledgements to those people that I can't tell in person.

To my dad, for the pages I wrote next to your bed. I know you'd be chuffed.

And for my BFF, Kirst, whose death was the only way that I knew that a real-life version of the Coffin Club actually existed. Thanks lovely. Still miss you. X